THE FRONT MAN

In Moscow's infamous Lubyanka gaol there is a prisoner with a very special secret. At a Nuremberg trade conference there is a Russian delegate who is willing to betray that confidence for the price of his ticket to the West. For intelligence agents such as Dan Shears there can be no doubt of the catastrophic implications of that secret becoming known — or of what action they must take to prevent it. But for the extremists of the neo-Nazi powerbase, it is the realisation of their wildest dreams — the bastard son of Adolf Hitler is alive and well, and ready to assume his father's mantle!

MAURICE SELLAR

THE
FRONT MAN

Complete and Unabridged

ULVERSCROFT
Leicester

First published in Great Britain in 1985

First Large Print Edition
published 2002

British Library CIP Data

Sellar, Maurice
  The front man.—Large print ed.—
  Ulverscroft large print series: adventure & suspense
  1. Adventure stories
  2. Large type books
  I. Title
  823.9′14 [F]

  ISBN 0–7089–4632–1

Published by
F. A. Thorpe (Publishing)
Anstey, Leicestershire

Set by Words & Graphics Ltd.
Anstey, Leicestershire
Printed and bound in Great Britain by
T. J. International Ltd., Padstow, Cornwall

This book is printed on acid-free paper

TO ESTHER
WHO STARTED MY JOURNEY AND WHO
STILL HOLDS THE MAP TO WHICH I
CONSTANTLY AND GRATEFULLY REFER,
AND TO THE MEMORY OF MY FATHER,
JONAS.

Acknowledgements

Most grateful thanks are due to the following for all the information and advice they have given to me in the preparation of this book:

Colonel Dr Eugene Lowry, US Air Force; Professor Draper, Sussex University; the Curators of departments at the Wiener Library; the Imperial War Museum; the British Museum; and the Royal Military Police Museum, Chichester.

Invaluable assistance was also given by Israel Rondell, Otto Schmidt and Ilsa Reidel, who are now British based, and whose surnames have been changed at their request.

Continued appreciation, as always, to GIS, PHS, G. and E. Morris, and Doris and Alf Bartlett.

Prologue

On the morning of Saturday, September 19th, 1931, at 09.33 hours, Rudolph Hess stood staring, grim-faced and pensive, at the body of a young girl who lay dead on a sofa. The beige dress that she wore was stained crimson just below her left breast, and blood from the fatal wound had seeped through on to the carpet where it had formed into a dark pool. Tightly clenched in her hand was a Walther Special 6.35 mm, which Hess recognised immediately as being one of the prized possessions from the armoury of Adolph Hitler. The dead girl was Geli Raubel, Hitler's niece and mistress. She was just twenty-three years old.

Hess had been summoned to Geli's bedroom, which was situated on the second floor of Hitler's apartment at 16 Prinz Regentenplatz, Munich, by the distraught housekeeper, Frau Annie Winter. She had stated to Hess that, after repeatedly knocking on Geli's door and receiving no reply, she had tried unsuccessfully to open it. Realising it was locked, she had peeped through the keyhole and saw that the key was still in the lock. At that point, being considerably worried, she had called out to her husband, who was Hitler's manservant, to ask his advice. Herr Winter, equally concerned, proceeded to break the door down. They could see by Geli's stiff posture and waxen face that she had been dead for some time.

After their initial horrified shock, Frau Winter, regaining some presence of mind, decided not to inform the police but to telephone Hess at the Brown House. Frau Winter was aware that of all the higher echelon in the Nazi party, her employer Adolph Hitler trusted Hess the most. It was to him, when they were thrown into prison at Landsberg together in 1924 for their activities in the then outlawed Nazi party, that Hitler dictated the only book he was ever to write about his life — *Mein Kampf*.

Now, with Herr and Frau Winter flanking him as he looked at the once lovely and vivacious girl, he turned to Frau Winter and calmly asked her to tell him everything she knew about the tragedy.

Tearfully, but continually consoled by her husband, she began to reveal to Hess the events leading up to Geli's death. The previous evening, she said, Geli had gone with her friend, Frau Schaub, to the Munich Playhouse to see Maria Bard. Frau Winter was pleased to see her go out and enjoy herself because, ever since she had returned from an unannounced vacation, Geli had seemed tense and depressed. Frau Winter had not heard her return that evening, but in the early hours of the morning she and her husband had been awakened by the sounds of a violent row that was taking place between Hitler and Geli. They listened as furniture was toppled over, and heard a sound with which all the household staff had become only too familiar — the swishing of Hitler's bullhide whip as he relentlessly beat her. Above it all rose the screams of Geli interspersed with Hitler shouting furiously at her.

The row was still going on when Josephine Bauer, the maid, arrived for work, and all three had sat in the kitchen, commenting on how sorry they were that young Geli had to put up with his terrible tantrums, as they were very fond of her. In hushed tones Frau Winter went on to say that some time ago Geli had divulged to Josephine that Hitler had made her do some terrible things in the bedroom. When asked to be more explicit Frau Winter blushed, but, prompted by her husband, she told him that Herr Hitler had often insisted that Geli sit for him in pornographic poses while he sketched her.

When Josephine had asked her why she didn't leave him and his perverted ways, Geli had replied that she loved him and didn't want to lose him, as there were plenty of other girls ready to take her place. She was especially jealous of Eva Braun whom Hitler had been seeing a lot of lately.

At this point Hess stopped Frau Winter from relating any more for the time being. He had to contact his Führer at once. By now, he estimated, he would be somewhere on the road heading for Nuremberg at the commencement of his long party tour.

Hess acted decisively, and ordered the Winters to go to their quarters. He then picked up the telephone in Geli's bedroom and instructed a confidant at the Brown House to send out a despatch rider to intercept the motorcade and to request the Führer to return to his hotel and contact Herr Hess, who was waiting at the Führer's own apartment. It was, Hess added, a matter of the utmost urgency.

Satisfied that this was now in hand, Hess went to the Winters' quarters and asked Frau Winter to continue with her story. Her husband, however, took over as Frau Winter was by now sobbing uncontrollably into her handkerchief. He told Hess that even after breakfast the row could be heard going on in fits and starts, and at one point he had seen Herr Hitler, fully dressed for his journey, come out of Geli's room. He was in a frightful rage. Moments later Geli followed him out and, with tears streaming down her swollen face, blurted out, 'I'm sorry, Alf, but I just couldn't go through with it. It's a sin against the Blessed Holy Mary!'

Winter spoke in a low, tremulous voice as he went on to tell Hess that Herr Hitler had swung round on Geli and hissed, 'Shut up, you little fool!' and had raised a clenched fist as though to strike her. Terrified, Geli had run back into her room but was swiftly followed by Herr Hitler, who was absolutely livid. He slammed the bedroom door behind him, and there followed some further volatile quarrelling. Winter hesitated nervously before clearing his throat and continuing. Although no one could be absolutely sure, they had all heard what sounded like a muffled gun shot. Winter was quick to comment that it could have been a car exhaust back-firing. However, after that sound everything went quiet. Eventually Herr Hitler emerged from Geli's room. His face was ashen and he was visibly shaking. Without a word to anyone he walked, almost in a trance, out of the apartment to join Heinrich Hoffman, the official party photographer, and his new chauffeur, Julius

Schreck, who were by that time waiting for him by his car in the street, ready to leave on the first leg of the Northern Party Tour.

Hess threw Annie Winter a strange look. She hastily turned her head away, not daring to meet his penetrating gaze. Already her account of the story was differing from that of her husband. The big question mark in Hess's mind was why it should have been necessary for Frau Winter to have the door broken down. It was surely most improbable, even in her distressed state, that Geli, with a bullet wound in her chest, could have, or would have, wanted to lock herself up in her room — assuming of course that she was still alive anyway. But Hess did not press this point, being very certain in his own mind that the door had been locked from the outside and the key then removed. It was clear that the Winters, ever loyal servants of the Führer, were formulating a cover story, but had not properly cross checked all the details with each other. It was then that Hess returned to Geli's bedroom alone. There he carefully hunted through all the dead girl's belongings. He meticulously searched her handbags for anything that he felt might be incriminating evidence pocketing theatre tickets, scribbled notes, letters and photographs in the process. Then finally, whilst rummaging through her

6

dressing-table drawer, he found her red leather-bound diary, wrapped in some expensive silk underwear. He sat on the bed and slowly leafed through its pages.

⋆ ⋆ ⋆

As Hitler's motorcade reached the outskirts of the city it was halted dramatically by Schreck who, glancing in his driving mirror, had seen a taxi travelling erratically, trying to overtake the convoy, until it was finally forced into the side of the road by one of the rear guard vehicles. He watched as a badly shaken driver and a young bell-boy from the hotel were dragged out of the taxi and questioned at gunpoint. Eventually Julius Schaub, one of Hitler's bodyguards, limped over to the black Mercedes and informed his Führer that Herr Rudolph Hess had telephoned from 16 Prinz Regentenplatz and suggested that he return home immediately, as there had been a very serious accident. Schreck, on Hitler's instructions, drove back at breakneck speed.

⋆ ⋆ ⋆

Hess stroked his chin thoughtfully. He had read every word of Geli's neat handwriting in the diary. He now knew what he must do.

Taking a box of matches from his pocket and placing the diary in a small rubbish bin, he set light to it. As he watched the flames engulf its pages, he muttered to himself: 'Absolutely no one, not even the Führer, must ever know about the contents of this diary!'

$\star$ $\star$ $\star$

There were two men who adamantly refused to accept the coroner's findings that, on September 18th, 1931, Geli Raubel took her own life with a gun that she had stolen from her uncle. Both men had obtained overwhelming evidence that Geli had been murdered, and both were convinced that it had been the result of a stormy quarrel with her uncle, Adolph Hitler. Furthermore, both men agreed that the quarrel was over an unwanted baby she had given birth to only a week or so before returning to Munich. The first was a highly respected journalist named Gehrlich, who was writing an in-depth series of articles about the case for the socialist newspaper, the *Münchener Post*. The second was the lawyer of Gregor Strasser, Hitler's close friend. His name was Voss — a man who held the belief that the truth was sacred, that no man was above the law, and that no man should be able to escape the consequences of committing murder — even if that man was his Führer, Adolph Hitler.

Both of these men died in mysterious circumstances shortly after the Munich verdict.

1

Dan Shears stirred slowly in his seat. The disembodied voice of the captain crackling through the PA system had intruded into his precious sleep. It was a damned unwelcome intrusion too, Shears thought irritably; he was having a most pleasant dream, in which he was demonstrating the finer points of clay pigeon shooting to film star Jane Fonda, who was making it quite obvious that she had taken a fancy to him. Why he should have had such a fantasy was a mystery to him, as Jane Fonda was far from being his ideal woman, and he'd never been on a skeet shoot in his life. If only the captain hadn't chosen that precise moment to make his announcement, maybe he would have seen how the budding romance could have developed — now he would never know.

As he returned sluggishly to the world of reality, he heard the captain's calm voice continue with the information that they would be landing at Frankfurt am Main in about forty-five minutes; that they were going to hit a little turbulence up ahead; and that passengers should fasten their seat belts in readiness for some bumps. Shears opened his eyes wider and blinked away the last traces of a deep sleep. The visual panel set in the bulkhead facing him lit up, displaying two hands thrusting a seat belt clip into a holding socket. Shears automatically obeyed its silent instruction. He glanced casually around him and observed, in a half-interested fashion, the activities of some of the thirty or so privileged fellow travellers on the first class deck of the 747. A few were reading, a couple were still tuned into their headsets, one or two were prematurely pulling their hand luggage from their lockers, others were engaged in conversation, and the odd ones here and there were quietly drinking. Drink! His gaze dropped to the seat tray in front of him. On it was an unopened miniature bottle of Cutty Sark, a small jug of water, and a transparent plastic tumbler. Straightening himself up, he leaned over eagerly to his favourite brand of refreshment, ordered before he'd fallen asleep, and, unscrewing the cap, he emptied the contents into the tumbler, adding just the merest touch of water. He raised the drink and stared appreciatively at the golden liquid for a second or so, before lowering it to his lips. Ah! . . . That first blissful taste of whisky. Why, Shears wondered, was it so magnificent? Why didn't it taste so good on the second?

And downright unpleasant by the third?

He yawned expansively and ran his hand down the back of his hair, which he instinctively knew — after having curled himself into his usual awkward position — would be sticking up like Jimpey's. Shears always had to twist himself into odd angles. Just over six foot five inches in height, there wasn't a car seat, bed or chair that he did not have to adjust his big frame to fit in some way or another. When he was just a beanpole of a boy he had towered well above his teachers, let alone his classmates, and he had come in for all the usual sarcastic jibes: 'Hey, buddy, I bet it's cold up there.' 'Tell us when the Martians are coming.' 'Shall I climb up and give you some oxygen?' His daddy had always told him to ignore it all. 'You're a Texan, son, and they breed 'em big down there,' he used to say. Dan never bothered to explain to his daddy that the kids in Chicago, where they had gone to live, didn't give a damn about his birthplace — they still called him 'Sticks'. Later, as he filled out and became a fast and powerful football player, with an almost exclusive fan club of adoring high school girls, they called him 'Big Dan' — and he had to admit he liked that a whole lot better. An athletic scholarship to

Bayler Medical School in Houston, where he graduated, an internship at Parkland in Dallas, and a much sought-after residency in psychiatry at Belle Vue, New York, had given him further cause to be grateful to the Almighty for using one of his king-size moulds to make him. Eventually he had returned to Dallas, where over the years he had built up a reasonably successful practice, married the girl his mother liked best and who, his daddy had said, was too darn good for him. Yes, all in all, he had a lot to thank his country for. It had given him a good way of life and he was unashamedly patriotic. In his mind, he would have been perfectly content to spend the rest of his days ambling along in this idyllic manner, and no doubt would have done, had it not been for that extraordinary consultation with a patient which was to change his whole way of life quite dramatically.

Shears let his thoughts drift back in time to that strange meeting. He vividly recalled an appointment with a Mr Mark Vincent. After having carefully studied the notes he had compiled on him, Shears had to admit to himself that he found Vincent's case some-what baffling. He had been sent to him originally by a local MD who had suggested in his letter to Shears that Vincent was suffering from psychomotor retardation. But, after several consultations with Vincent, Shears was beginning to have grave misgivings about his colleague's prognostication. Although Vincent did show many of the outward signs associated with this complaint, Shears was slowly coming to the conclusion that they were nothing more than superficial.

Shears decided to use one of his old tried and tested shock tactics in order to 'persuade' Vincent to open up. As Vincent was happily peeling off his top coat to settle down for the session, Shears told him briskly to put it right back on again, as he was quite obviously wasting both his time and money; whatever it was he had come to see him about had little or nothing to do with depression.

Vincent, a wiry individual in his late thirties, with collegiate-cropped fair hair and fading freckles, grinned broadly, seemed slightly embarrassed, and said how professionally astute Shears had been to spot him as a 'phoney'.

Then, as though he were revealing to him the world's best kept secret, Vincent told him that he was a member of the CIA and, furtively producing an ID card, handed it to him.

Shears was not even aware that the

15

employees of the Central Intelligence Agency even carried ID cards, but he decided to hear Vincent out, at least until the end of his forty-five minute session which he was paying for anyway.

'Well, what can I do for you?' Shears asked, sliding the card back to him across the desk.

'Personally — nothing.' Vincent shook his head and laughed. 'Jeez, I hope not, anyway. You see, I'm what you might call a glorified personnel officer.' Vincent swept a well manicured hand over his brush-top hair. 'My job is to vet people we may consider taking on to our staff one day, and it gets tougher all the time. That's where we believe you may be able to help us, Dr Shears.'

'Me? In what way?'

'Well, we used to recruit many of our number from the Office of Strategic Services, later called the Central Intelligence Group, but with military conscription shelved that source of manpower is no longer available to us. So now we have to cast our nets wider, which leaves the door dangerously open to subversives. You wouldn't believe the lengths some of them will go to get aboard our ship.' He jabbed a finger into the air to emphasise the point. 'Therefore, it has become our practice of late to have the people on our

16

short list screened by our resident psychiatrists at Langley, but as you can imagine, dealing with the problems of a permanent staff that numbers almost 10,000 they are overworked like hell. So we are now enlisting consultant psychiatrists in various areas to conduct this initial screening on our behalf. With your permission I would like to recommend you, Dr Shears, to interview candidates in the Texas area!'

'What you are suggesting is highly specialised work. How d'you know I'd be capable?'

Vincent chuckled as he revealed how thorough his research into Shears' background had been, recounting for him the smallest incidents in his life, some of which even he had forgotten. Shears ran his finger around the inside of his shirt collar — he felt decidedly uneasy.

Vincent continued by discussing procedure. What would happen, he said, should Shears decide to accept the commission, was that a file on a prospective employee would be delivered to him in advance, enabling him to study this information before conducting the interview. He would then be required to complete a confidential report which would include his professional opinion on whether or not the subject would be suitable material for the position envisaged for him.

As Vincent talked, Shears was debating in his own mind if he should admit to being interested in the man's proposal. Eventually, and because by now he was more than somewhat intrigued, he opted to do so.

'Sounds straightforward enough,' he murmured in a non-committal way.

'You see, doctor, being at Langley puts them in a position of tremendous trust. We have to be sure that they have no exploitable weaknesses, or any kookie ideas. In other words, they've gotta be pretty sound up here.' Vincent tapped a forefinger on his right temple. 'Know what I mean?'

Shears glanced at his wristwatch and noted that Vincent had run out of his allotted time. 'Yeah, I believe I get the gist of it.'

Vincent, observing this action, sprang up from the chair. 'I know you're busy. Look, just let me say you'll think about it, eh?'

Shears promised that he would.

Shears had nearly forgotten about the whole incident when a letter arrived, postmarked Langley, N. Virginia. It was a straightforward no-nonsense, almost military type communiqué, and it reiterated in essence all that Vincent had discussed with him. It mentioned fees, which were quite attractive, and suggested that should he consider taking up the appointment, appropriate arrangements for operational briefing would be made.

Exactly two weeks after he had written his acceptance to Langley, Shears was interviewing the first of many 'would-be' employees of the CIA. The time allotted for each individual was one hour, not nearly long enough, he believed, to pass judgement on the widely divergent personalities of the succession of people he saw. It made him increasingly unhappy to think about this. Admittedly, he had been told that all final decisions would be taken at Langley on whether this or that person would be accepted, but he had a sneaking feeling that his reports were greatly influencing their choice. With this in mind, the time he devoted to writing up these reports took longer and longer, and often he'd find himself working far into the night completing them. His wife Shirley, commented on how tired he was looking, and by Christ he felt it. Worse still, he was beginning to neglect his patients, some of whom really needed his help. All too often of late he would just manage to stifle a yawn or pull himself up sharply to stop his thoughts wandering, as patients spoke to him of their problems. At the end of nearly six months he decided that enough was enough.

He tried phoning Vincent several times to

talk it over, but he was answered on each occasion by a girl with the sunny sound of Jamaica still in her voice, who kept telling him that Mr Vincent was not available. In frustration he left a message to be contacted urgently. Two days later Vincent returned his call. Shears explained as pleasantly as he could under the circumstances his reasons for wanting to quit. Vincent listened attentively, grunting his understanding in all the right places. When Shears had finished, Vincent asked him to delay his decision until he'd had a chance to discuss it with his departmental chief, Paul McNabe. Shears agreed.

The following day, with a heavy workload on his plate, Shears went to his office early. The telephone was ringing as he opened the door. It was Vincent.

'I called your home first. Your wife told me you'd left early.'

'Uh huh,' Shears grunted.

'My chief, Paul McNabe, would very much like to meet you, and discuss the situation face to face. Is there any way you can get free to fly to Washington in the next couple of days?'

'Well . . . I guess, er . . . '

'We'll pay all expenses and I'll be at the airport to meet you.'

Shears scanned his diary quickly.

'The only time I have free is in about ten days' time . . . I could make it then.'

'Good, good! Paul will be delighted.'

Shears had told Shirley nothing about his connection with the CIA. What he had said was that he had taken on some extra work on behalf of the Government. So when he mentioned that he would shortly be paying a flying visit to Washington to sort out a few problems she merely said with a bright smile, 'I hear they've got a marvellous Bloomingdales at Tyson's Corner Shopping Centre, darling!' That was one of the advantages of marrying a girl who had fully accepted her role as a doctor's wife — she had learned never to ask too many questions.

'Okay, I get the message,' Shears laughed.

Shirley loved expensive French perfume, and Italian silk scarves. The CIA wouldn't be paying for that little lot though, he reflected sadly.

★   ★   ★

The CIA headquarters in Langley was situated less than two miles from Washington, but if Vincent had not arranged to pick him up and drive him to his destination, Shears doubted whether he would have ever found the place. It was set so far back from the main highway that only those who had prior knowledge of the entry lanes and understood the ambiguous road signs would have been able to reach it.

McNabe, a broad shouldered man with heavy features, unusually large brown eyes and pads of grey at the temples of his otherwise pitch black, crinkly hair, made him feel very welcome. He spoke with just the faintest of lisps — all that remained of what Shears knew was once a severe speech impediment, which must have taken him many determined years to conquer; it gave him an immediate insight into his gutsy character. He asked Shears about his journey, his family, and the weather in Dallas. Then, having dispensed with the aimless small talk, McNabe looked at him hard for a moment or two, lifted his jacket from the back of his chair, slipped it on, straightened his tie and said, 'Let's take a little walk.'

What followed then for Shears was a conducted tour around the main seven-storey building. He was immediately struck by the impression of light and airiness everywhere. The spacious structure with great glass windows, expensive marble balustrades and polished metal fittings covered an area of about two average city blocks. Shears stopped by a massive window and pointed to an ancillary building that was topped by a geodesic dome. 'Looks like a concert hall.'

McNabe turned and followed his gaze. 'You won't find a lot of sweet music coming from there,' he said drily. 'It's mainly used for conferences these days.' He tapped Shears gently on the elbow. 'I want to show you something,' he said confidentially, as he steered him towards an elevator.

'What you are about to witness has been seen by very few outsiders, believe me.' He rummaged through his pocket and produced an electronic key. 'Apart from the odd President, here and there, that is,' he added with a quirky grin. Shears smiled; he was beginning to like this man.

The elevator descended with such swiftness that Shears felt he had left his stomach somewhere up on the seventh floor. There was a speculative silence as they made the journey deep below the ground. Suddenly there was a slight jolt and the doors slid smoothly open. Bright neon ceiling lights greeted them.

'Down here we've got more classified information than all the other intelligence networks put together,' McNabe said proudly.

McNabe's words were no exaggeration. Shears lost count of the number of rooms he was permitted to view, containing documents, films and computer tapes, as they weaved their way through a maze of narrow corridors. Shears looked on fascinated, while men and women went briskly about their business to the accompanying sounds of whirring projectors, humming computers, and all the other audio visual apparatus that helped to make this the world's foremost intelligence organisation.

McNabe was a marvellous raconteur, and he regaled Shears with a string of anecdotes concerning the unorthodox methods they had resorted to in order to obtain some of the information that was now safely housed in this honeycomb of intrigue. Shears could not help but be caught up in the excitement of it all. It rekindled in him memories of his boyhood, when on cold winter evenings he would lie in front of a crackling fire, munching hot buttered toast, while he read the dog-eared, grease-smeared pages of Sax Rohmer, Eric Ambler or Ian Fleming, as they whisked him away to far off places where outrageous villains, double agents, and beautiful spies reigned supreme.

'Well, I guess that's about all I'm allowed to show you down here,' McNabe said finally, hoping that Shears had been suitably impressed — which he was. 'I could use some fresh air. How about you?'

★ ★ ★

An occasional gust of wind was the only blot on an otherwise perfect spring day, as Shears and McNabe took a leisurely stroll round the perimeter of the central building.

'Congress has done you proud,' Shears said, taking in the immense sprawling campus with its acres of forest, plush lawns and gardens.

'Oh, our people budgeted the appropriation very sensibly,' McNabe replied, giving him a heavy wink.

'Must take a lot of maintaining, especially where the security is concerned,' he said, observing the armed guards walking in pairs, with vicious looking dogs at their sides. 'Do you get many trespassers?'

'You kidding?' McNabe exclaimed. 'This whole complex is surrounded by high triple fencing,' he swept his arms around expansively, 'and just below the surface, from that point to this' — he indicated with his finger — 'lies the most advanced sensory grid yet devised. If so much as a ping pong ball fell on to it, at least a dozen guard posts would be alerted at once — so what chance do you think an intruder would have?'

They walked for a while without speaking, then suddenly McNabe stopped in his tracks

25

and turned to Shears.

'Dr Shears, may I say how much I appreciate your having made this trip to see me.'

'I'm enjoying it,' Shears said truthfully.

'I fully understand your predicament. You don't feel you can give the attention you should to your patients, while you're up half the night working for us — right?'

McNabe started to walk again, and Shears fell into step beside him. 'I think that sums it up pretty well,' he answered.

McNabe thrust his hands deep in his trouser pockets.

'Look, I have a suggestion to make which I'd like you to consider. What about packing in the whole shebang in Dallas and joining us up here on a full-time basis?'

Shears was caught slightly off balance by McNabe's forthright proposition, but it was only momentary.

'I don't think I'd be over-keen on the idea.'

'Why?' McNabe inquired with some surprise.

'In all forms of medicine there has to be an element of challenge. The kinda work I've been doing for you is very routine. If I continued much longer it would drive me to drink — or I'd need to see a good psychiatrist myself.'

A ghost of a smile appeared on McNabe's lips.

'Yeah, I can well believe that, but we wouldn't have that sort of job in mind for you here. The people we would want you to see would be mainly top priority cases.'

McNabe's face became taut, as though he were remembering something particularly unpalatable.

'Because, quite frankly, some of these cases I'm referring to, know so much about our set-up that until they're mentally stable again — well, they're just a big fuckin' security risk. Do you get my meaning?'

Shears nodded. 'Yes, I could see how that could be . . . er . . . a problem.'

'A problem? I'll say it is.' McNabe gritted his teeth. 'They're human time bombs. Have to be handled with infinite care. I think you'd find they'd match up to your idea of a challenge all right.'

Although Shears had weighed up several possibilities as to why McNabe should want to meet him, he had never even vaguely entertained the idea that he might be offered a staff post at Langley. He realised he must have been deep in thought as McNabe, mistaking his pensive mood for lack of interest, tried a new approach.

'Look, we know how much you are making

at the moment in Dallas.'

'I bet you do,' Shears retorted a trifle sharply, remembering how well Vincent had done his research.

'$50,000 — give or take a grand, yes?'

Shears made no reply. It was unnecessary — McNabe was spot on.

'We'd up it at once to commence at $80,000 plus expenses, and there's a lot of perks which I won't go into at this stage. We'd assist you and your wife in finding a nice place to live. You've got one kid, haven't you?'

'Yep.'

'And one on the way, I hear?'

Shears felt himself bristle. Christ! Was there anything they didn't know about him?

'Dr Shears — may I call you Dan?' Shears nodded. McNabe continued, really doing a selling job now. 'Your wife would love it here. The social life around Capital City is hard to top. Let's face it, what do you have in Dallas — apart from a lot of cowboys?'

'A darn sight more than that,' Shears answered shirtily. 'I live in North Dallas. We actually eat indoors there, you know, and wear shoes.'

'Okay, okay, a bit of a sweeping statement, I'll agree,' McNabe said with a slightly embarrassed grin. 'But here, not only would you be doing a great service for your country, just think of the sense of achievement you'd derive. You're a good psychiatrist, Dan, very good by all accounts, but you're wasted down there among those farmers. Only kidding,' McNabe smiled. 'Look, . . . er . . . Dan, it's about time I really levelled with you.' He paused for a moment before dropping his bombshell. 'Nearly all those jokers we've been sending to you for interviews were highly trained members of our staff.'

Shears stopped dead. He was absolutely flabbergasted by this revelation. At first he felt numb, then he began to boil. These CIA smart-asses had been using him as mental target practice. McNabe seemed to read his mind; hastily he tried to offer an explanation.

'Dan, every single member of our personnel has been through the most rigorous form of screening themselves. You won't find guys like Blunt, Philby, Maclean and Burgess slipping through our nets like they do at M15. Maybe if British Intelligence took half as much care over the people they select for their service as we do, they wouldn't have wound up such a laughing stock. We had to be absolutely certain about you before I could make you this offer.'

Shears was only half listening. All he could think of was those wearisome reports. 'All those reports I spent so long in writing up

— just a waste of time,' he said quietly.

'No, no, not at all,' McNabe replied forcibly. 'You see, we now know your work is thorough — damn thorough. We know how conscientious you are,' McNabe was almost emotional. 'We just know you're our man.'

Back in his office for some very dry pre-lunch Martinis, McNabe told Shears at length how he saw his future with them. He painted a very rosy picture indeed, and he was still adding plenty of colour to it throughout a splendid lunch and right up to the time he personally saw him off at John Dulles Airport.

Shears had left McNabe with the words that he'd have a good long think about it. What they had both left unsaid was that he would discuss it with his wife, and she would have a good long think about it too.

When Shears had resettled himself in Dallas for a couple of days, he booked a table at the best French restaurant in town, and that night, over a candle-lit dinner, he told Shirley everything. It had often puzzled him that while he could almost always get to the heart of a problem when analysing total strangers, with his nearest and dearest it was another story. He could never be entirely certain which way the scales would tip for his Libran wife, although he could often steer her

30

in approximately the direction he wished her to take; in this instance he just gave her the cold facts, with no trimmings. He wanted this to be, if anything, more her decision than his. After all, it was not easy to ask any woman to pull up her roots and go sailing off into the unknown, however exciting the prospect of discovering new worlds might be. When he had finished speaking, he looked across at her in the flickering glow of a dwindling candle, and she appeared as though she were sixteen again, her eyes sparkling and provocative. It was a chance that was too good to miss, she said. He must take it, and she would help him in every way possible.

She was as good as her word. From organising the sale of their house in Dallas to the purchase of another in the Washington suburbs.

★ ★ ★

It was difficult to believe that it was nearly eight years ago that Shirley had leaned out of the window of their noisy Pontiac waving goodbye to their neighbours. They must have looked a peculiar sight, she bawling her eyes out, he laughing his head off at all the wisecracks being shouted at him: 'Don't come back till those city slickers in

Washington make you President,' or 'See if you can get all them Congressmen certified, Dan,' and so on.

He now had all the trappings of material success. A largish house near Maclean, with a heated swimming pool, three cars and a garage big enough to park them in. His eleven-year-old daughter, Carol, was expert on a horse, and his seven and a half-year-old son, Robert, expert at 'horsing' around. Shirley was an active and enthusiastic member of half a dozen ladies' organisations, covering flower arranging to yoga. And he himself had reduced his golf handicap from twenty to seven, and last year was the mens' singles champion at the exclusive Army and Navy Tennis Club. They were both popular members of the community, and professionally he had gone from strength to strength.

On the face of it everything looked fine. But there were often times, as for instance at the Tennis Club's Annual Dinner and Dance, when he was on the receiving end of those expensive capped-toothed smiles that carried sincerity no further than the orthodontal work on display, that he regretted leaving his beloved Dallas, and the real friends they had had there. He and Shirley both missed the old place a lot, and those dependable, warm-hearted people a hell of a lot more!

Shears stared out of the window as the plane began to taxi towards the terminal. The rain was hurtling against the glass. Agents, he had always been led to believe by all the reading he had covered on the subject, went to exciting and exotic places where the sun blazed down on the neatly cut cotton suits of the enigmatic, devilishly handsome operatives. Just his luck, he thought, that his first assignment abroad had to be to one of the dullest spots in Europe, and on a foul day like this.

2

Willi Prama frowned disconcertedly, as he gazed out of his bedroom window and watched the torrent of rain descend from the heavens, drenching his beautifully stocked, landscaped garden and bouncing off the green billiard table-like surface of his sunken lawn. From early that morning the sky over Nuremberg had darkened and the relentless downpour had shown no sign of easing. Why the hell couldn't it have been dry and sunny, like yesterday, or the last three weeks for that matter, Prama fumed inwardly. It seemed as though it would rain for ever. There was no chance of an outside barbecue now, of course. He had considered the possibility of hiring a marquee, but had decided against it. It wasn't so much the extra expense, although he had to admit that he had been taken aback by the high cost of such a scheme, it was just that the thought of people walking over his well-manicured lawn, trying to balance a plateful of food in one hand and a glass of champagne in the other, struck him as being slightly absurd — reminiscent of clowns in a circus under the big top. And there might, there just might, be others amongst the important guests that he had invited who felt that way too. Herr Prama could not risk even one person feeling awkward or uncomfortable tonight, whatever the setback — and there was no doubt this rain was a setback but, in spite of it, the evening had to be a great success. There was too much at stake for it to be otherwise.

Prama turned his attention from the pointless exercise of studying the continuous deluge and, with a heavy sigh, sat down in a reclining chair. He closed his eyes thoughtfully. Now, if Hannelore were here, she would have known exactly what to do. This rained-off barbecue would have presented few problems for her. He raised his head slowly and looked at the face in the oil painting set in the heavy gilt frame hanging on the wall a few feet from where he sat. That young artist, Waunage, certainly had talent, Prama conceded grudgingly. Arrogant and pricey he may have been, but he had captured that almost elusive, inquisitive expression on Hannelore's face for all time. It was just how he would always remember her. She had been a wonderful hostess — attractive, vivacious, warm, yet incredibly efficient. God, how he missed her! Prama could feel the tears welling up inside him, tears which seemed to come from the very soles of his hand-made shoes. The way she was suddenly snatched away from him after forty years of near blissful marriage was something to which he would never become fully reconciled . . .

He recalled the morning he had come out of the bathroom and had seen Hannelore examining her breasts in front of the dressing-table mirror. He had paused for a few moments to watch her. She still had a lovely body for her age, thickening around the middle maybe, despite her dieting and twice weekly visits to the beautician, but she was remarkably sensuous. Seeing her, as he did then, naked and fondling herself, had aroused him at once. She was so much more magnetic than the empty-headed tarts that he so often amused himself with — having a financial interest in a night club he was never short of a supply of women of that type, but Hannelore had been different, she had brains, beauty, and quality. He had walked over to her and, gently kissing her shoulders, had laughingly suggested that he should take over the task of massaging her breasts. But she had pushed him away, coldly abrupt, and when he had questioned her action she had simply said, with a worried expression on her face, that she could feel a small lump just below her right nipple. Three months later she was dead, snuffed out like a candle, as the cancer spread its murderous tentacles through her body.

*   *   *

Stopping for a moment to regain his breath, after climbing the winding staircase to the second floor, Dietz walked to the large oak door and tapped. Without waiting for an acknowledgement he entered the room.

'Herr Prama,' he said softly, not unaware that his employer had been deep in thought, and, following the direction of his glazed eyes, he knew at once of his preoccupation. He had seen that grey, wistful and slightly stupid expression on Prama's face many times since the death of his wife. Dietz felt it ironic, though perhaps not unnatural, that he should remember only the rarely displayed, pleasant side of Frau Prama's character. She had treated her husband abominably most of the time, and the staff even worse, with her bossy mannerisms and delusions of grandeur. He and his colleagues most assuredly did not grieve at her passing. She had been a bitch of the first magnitude as far as they were concerned, and they were all a damned sight better off without her.

'What is it, Albert?' Prama asked in a

businesslike manner.

'Er . . . the caterers, sir, they wish to know, in view of the weather, er . . . where you would like them to place the main buffet tables?' Dietz queried almost apologetically.

'Well, I'm not sure yet. I've been considering it. You know we may have more than ninety people coming tonight, so we'll need plenty of room for the tables. Any ideas?'

'The main drawing-room would be suitable, sir. It's certainly large enough.'

'No, no. I've already rejected that possibility,' Prama retorted irritably. 'Too bloody formal. No one ever feels comfortable in it, least of all me. Tell the caterers I'll make a decision soon,' Prama concluded, dismissing Dietz with an impatient flick of his hand.

Prama watched Dietz's stooping departure and shook his head sadly as the door closed behind him. Dietz was looking old now. It was hard to believe that this was the same man who came to work for him as a batman just at the outbreak of the war. Then he had been a strapping young lad from the country, with a sprightly gait, cheerful disposition, ruddy complexion and a Schwäbisch accent as strong as fresh cow dung. Never the brightest of individuals, but his loyalty was unquestionable. Even during that horrific period in his life, when he had been indicted for war atrocities, Dietz had made it clear that he was readily available to offer whatever help he could. Atrocities be damned! Prama felt his blood rising. He had acted as any officer in his position would have done, interrogated Jewish scum who were obtaining illegal food rations, food that was vital to sustain the soldiers at the front. Of course he had ordered their executions. They had been guilty, every man Jack of them, and that included the women and their urchin brats.

After the war he had been advised by close friends to change his name and take on a new identity, working for a while in the accounts department at the Volkswagen factory at Wiesbaden. Unfortunately, he had been recognised by one of the secretaries and subsequently arrested by the Americans. For two years he'd rotted in a vile prison, awaiting trial. The trial had been based on a flimsy file of so-called evidence, trumped up by that lunatic Jew in Vienna — whose activities were paid for by trouble-making Zionists — a couple of witnesses he'd never seen in his life before, and a State Attorney General who was quite obviously in league with them. The main accusation seemed to rest on the fact that he had been in the SS. Well, that was no crime. One had to be of a very special calibre to be selected for that elite corps. They chose their recruits very carefully. He had been a qualified accountant before he applied to join, and this was very much in his favour. The SS had a prodigious number of volunteers, of which a good percentage were rejected as unsuitable material. Professional men like himself, however, had been greatly in demand, provided they met all the other requirements — good background, purity of blood, naturally, but in addition to this, an unswerving willingness to serve the cause of the Third Reich. He had justified their faith in him, and at the age of only twenty-three had been a Haupstürmführer with a bright future. Almost certainly he would have been promoted to Standartenführer if the war had gone differently.

Active members of the new movement, ambiguously calling themselves 'The Chain', had seen to it that he had the services of a brilliant defence lawyer, had paid all his court costs and had stood solidly by him, confirming — if confirmation were at all necessary — that the spirit of National Socialism lived on; it was only the body that needed to make a full recovery. The Führer's last momentous words: 'There will rise in the history of Germany the seed of a glorious rebirth of the National Socialist movement' were his constant inspiration. It was his most fervent desire to see that prophecy fulfilled. It was his *raison d'être*. Dedicated men like himself, not just in Germany but throughout the world, were working continuously towards the achievement of that goal.

His trial had lasted three weeks and the case had finally been dismissed for lack of conclusive evidence. The two Jewish witnesses had come apart at the seams, and their statements under cross-examination were shown to be full of contradictions, surmise and hearsay. When he had been completely cleared of all charges, the Kamaraden continued to offer their support and found him a position in a banking house. Here he had rapidly climbed the ladder until he had reached his present elevated position, Director of Overseas Services of the internationally renowned Meyer-Eckhardt Mercantile Credit Bank.

Prama rose from his chair and, through the thick-lensed spectacles he was now forced to wear, caught a glimpse of his reflection in the long wall mirror. The passing years had not treated him too badly, he considered. His figure was now more rounded perhaps, as befitted a man of his standing. His hair, once blond and wavy, was still in plentiful supply, even if the colour had now changed to a dull chrome, but this, he felt, only added to his undoubtedly distinguished appearance. His face, admittedly somewhat fuller than in his youth, had not acquired too many of those time-revealing lines that he had observed on so many of his contemporaries. He broke into a smile, revealing the two gold capped incisors of which he was rather proud. Yes, all in all, he was giving that man with the hour glass and scythe a good run for his money. Of course he took good care of himself, only smoked and drank in moderation, and although he enjoyed most sexual activities, despite a slightly flagging libido, he firmly believed it was the finest exercise ever devised. Then again, he did partake of more conventional ways of keeping fit, such as a brisk workout in the gym every morning, followed by swimming six lengths of the pool. His face suddenly brightened. Of course — the gym! That was where he would hold the buffet. His large, ornate indoor swimming pool with its adjoining gymnasium and combined games room was the showpiece of his fine house. He would get Dietz to send out for a selection of bathing costumes, and those who chose to could take the plunge or enjoy the antics of their fellow guests splashing about. In addition, he would see to it that there were several scantily dressed girls to be ogled at. His highly acclaimed parties were renowned for the number of pretty girls in attendance. That was where his stake in Renate's Night Club paid off so handsomely. Not only did it represent a fair return on the capital deployed, it also gave him the opportunity of selecting the most attractive hostesses who worked there. These girls were always readily available for his friends and, of course, his own enjoyment. He would telephone Anna, his senior and special hostess, and tell her to make the arrangements. Prama was feeling mightily pleased with himself as he pushed the bell to summon Dietz . . .

3

'Jee . . . sus!' Shears hollered out loud as he stepped back from the ice-cold needles of water that descended on him. Quickly he swung the top knob from *Kalt* to *Warm* and gingerly stuck out his palm to feel the temperature. It was still not as hot as he would have liked, but at least it was tolerable. He soaped his body into a thick lather, washing away the weariness of the long journey. He still couldn't quite believe that he was in Nuremberg. In all the years he had been at Langley it had never occurred to him for one moment that he would ever be asked to become personally involved in any CIA fieldwork. The more he thought about it, the more he began to wonder at how easily he had been 'coerced' into taking part in this, his first active assignment. As he watched the sudsy water swirl round his feet, he cast his mind back to an evening just over two short weeks ago.

★　★　★

He was just about to leave his office, when McNabe poked his head around the door.

'Busy?'

'No — come in. Make yourself at home.'

And McNabe did just that. Sucking that pipe of his that was rarely alight, he sprawled himself out on the couch. McNabe's visit was a complete surprise to Shears. He had only seen him at his practice on two other occasions, and they were both to pick him up for lunch. Shears reclined in his chair, and swung his long legs on to his desk.

'Is this a professional or a friendly call?'

McNabe addressed him with half-closed eyes.

'How would you like to go to a party?'

'Sounds a nice idea — when?'

'Sixteen days.'

'Where?'

'Nuremberg.'

'You know, for a moment there, I thought you said Nuremberg.'

'For a moment, you were right.'

'Nuremberg, Germany?'

'There — you're right again.'

Shears made himself more comfortable; he had the feeling that this was going to be a long session, and he wasn't going to commit himself until he knew all the facts.

'So, who's throwing this shindig?'

'A man by the name of Wilhelm Prama, a

wealthy merchant banker with ultra right-wing political aspirations.'

'You mean he's a Fascist?'

'I think the term 'Nazi' would be more accurate in his case.'

'Hmm. So what's it in aid of?'

'On the surface, Prama's house party is being given to introduce some members of a Russian trade delegation from Minsk to the American representatives of Golden Thresher Incorporated.'

'Golden Thresher, Dallas?'

'The same. It's your old home town success story, and you know what hot news they are.'

Shears nodded. He could hardly fail to know. The Agricultural Equipment Manufacturing Combine had recently captured world headlines by announcing that it had developed a prototype remote controlled tractor, that was basically powered by the process of extracting hydrogen from sea-water and converting it into pollution free fuel.

'But under the surface?'

'You're not as dumb as you look, Doc! We believe that this little get together is a front for something more sinister.'

McNabe puffed at his pipe and flicked a reluctant lighter, as he recounted that Prama and his influential buddies were well known

46

to department 'Omega' — a division in the CIA that kept a watchful eye on all activist extremist groups in the United States and Europe. When news of Prama's party filtered through, one of their guys at 'Omega' was checking the guest list as a matter of routine, when the name Nikolai Kotchnov rang a bell in his mind. Further diligent inquiry on his part led to the discovery that Kotchnov was the man referred to by one of the Company's agents in Germany. This agent had received a tip-off, some time ago, from a reliable Soviet contact, that a not particularly important Russian agricultural official named Nikolai Kotchnov was offering what he thought was some very important information by way of a ticket to defect to the West.

McNabe sat up and leaned forward in a confidential manner.

'You know, I can't tell you the number of times we've been approached by would-be defectors who want to hightail it out of Russia on the slimmest of pretexts.' There was a momentary twinkle of humour in his eye. 'Well, they've got plenty of head cases holding top jobs in Russia too — we don't just have an exclusive on 'em at Langley, even if we do seem to have more of 'em.'

'I wonder if they pay their shrinks better than we do here?' Shears chipped in.

McNabe threw him an old-fashioned look, but refused to be drawn off track. 'Sometimes it's worth our while to help, but most of the time we find that the money and effort involved reaps a poor return. The information being offered is usually dated, or we have it already. In Kotchnov's case we decided to pass. After all, we thought, what could an agricultural official know that would be of interest to us?' McNabe grinned. 'Possess a method of producing giant beetroots for borscht?'

Shears pursed his lips pensively. 'But something made you change your mind?'

'That's right,' McNabe replied quickly. 'We found that Prama and his cronies are in the market for buying this information, and are going to help Kotchnov all the way. If what he has to offer is that important to them, it's gotta to be that important to us, too.'

With an exasperated sigh, McNabe reached over and delved into his briefcase. Producing a buff folder, he removed some photographs and handed them to Shears.

'This is the guy, Nikolai Kotchnov.'

Shears studied the photographs of a square-jawed, typically Slavic looking man in his late fifties.

'Any clues as to what it is he's selling?'

'Er . . . no.'

Shears detected a slight hesitancy in McNabe's reply, but didn't pursue it.

'How on earth did Prama set all this up? I mean, you don't just invite a Russian trade delegation to a party in the West, and expect them to turn up like a bunch of teenagers clutching a bottle. I would have thought the KGB would have had something to say about that.'

'Exactly. But it wasn't so difficult for Prama to arrange as it may seem.' McNabe clasped one hand on his knee and leaned back. 'You see, Prama's bank has a sizable stake in the European outlet of Golden Thresher, so that has given him a plausible reason to arrange a little get together for the salesmen from Dallas and potential buyers from the Soviet Union.'

'But, hell, surely the tractor is only in the experimental stage, and it could take at least ten years before it's in full production?' Shears thought for a moment. 'Didn't I read that the kind of dough it'll take to get that baby off the ground is close to the amount NASA spent to put a man on the moon?'

McNabe allowed himself one of his daily ration of smiles.

'You're forgetting one thing, Dan — the by-product. It's the creation of a new source of energy, the breakthrough the world's been waiting for. The Russians are not going to miss out on the chance of getting in on that — right?'

Shears nodded his agreement and stood up.

'Want a drink?'

'Thought you'd never ask.'

Shears looked into a small desk cupboard and frowned.

'It's Bourbon or Bourbon, I'm afraid.'

'I'll take Bourbon — straight.'

McNabe swigged a large slug from his glass and shuddered. 'Boy! Just what the doctor ordered.' He eyed Shears evenly. 'I suppose you must be wondering just where you're gonna fit into all this?'

'Yeah, you could say that the thought had occurred to me.'

'Well, a couple of days back, when we first got wind of what was going on, the Chief had me in his office. Be a good idea, he said, if we could send a 'Company' man along to this banker's party — someone completely unknown to both East and West Intelligence, to act as our eyes and ears. A man who could ask all the right questions and yet not arouse any suspicions; a man who would be capable of giving us a complete run-down on the leading characters, and an immediate on-the-spot reaction to whatever it was he thought was going on.' McNabe paused just long enough to down his drink. 'I suggested you — and he thought that was a great idea.'

'Did he now.' Shears said drily. 'The great white chief himself, eh?' He slid the bottle of Bourbon across the desk towards McNabe, and picked up the photographs of Kotchnov. 'To be quite honest, I can't see what threat a fringe group of Nazi crackpots would be, even if Kotchnov had the secret to . . . '

McNabe held up his hand. 'I'll stop you right there. They are not a fringe group of crackpots, they are highly organised extremists.'

'You're not hinting that this data Kotchnov has might be instrumental in creating a Fourth Reich, are you?' Shears probed scornfully.

McNabe shrugged his shoulders. 'Your guess is as good as mine on that score. What I do have are facts and figures which prove that the possibility of an embryo Fourth Reich is not as ridiculous as it may seem.'

McNabe spent the next half hour expounding his theme, pausing only once to top up his glass. He told Shears that neo-Nazis and Fascist elements had, since the end of World War II, infiltrated virtually every aspect of West German life. There were now uncountable numbers represented in all the major political parties. They held top level positions in commerce and industry — some, like Prama, even operating their own banks, zealously making plans to bring about the reunification of Germany and insidiously piecing together their shattered dream, namely a Europe dominated by an Aryan culture. They were to be encountered right across the board in the Ministry of Justices, from humble attorneys' clerks to high court judges, and as their retirement age loomed up, they were replaced by younger people with the same ideology.

Much of what McNabe had to say was as familiar to Shears as it was to anyone who had the slightest interest in the subject. It had been dealt with at length in the modern history books of most American schools and colleges. Nevertheless, McNabe decided to cover this old ground again in order to provide a back-drop for some uncomfortable new facts he was later to reveal. It was common knowledge, he continued, that the homes of prominent, mostly Jewish, industrialists and businessmen who had been thrown into the gas chambers of concentration camps, had been systematically ransacked, and many priceless art treasures and considerable quantities of jewellery, money and other valuables stolen, the bulk of which, even to this day, had never been recovered. Reels upon reels of film footage had shown, in grisly detail, the irony of how, even after death, millions of unfortunate victims of the holocaust had continued to swell the coffers of their murderers. Few had not heard of the thoroughness of the SS as they extracted gold teeth from endless rows of naked bodies and smelted them down into bars of gold. Who had not seen pictures of the mountains of spectacle frames, shorn hair and clothing, all of which was re-processed, sold and utilised in industry? These sickening spoils alone brought in untold riches to a comparatively select number of the higher echelon of the SS. McNabe revealed that as far back as 1943, when informed sources in Germany knew it was impossible for them to win the war, they had made deals with several sympathetically neutral countries with regard to investing much of their vast fortune. This eventually enabled them to set up and operate various business enterprises and financial empires outside the then crumbling Germany. The organisation of these ship-ments was masterminded by SS General Ernst Kaltenbrunner. Under his direction crates of gold bullion, silver ingots and precious stones were secretly transferred to the bank vaults of countries like Argentina,

Peru and Chile, the largest hoard being deposited in Switzerland.

McNabe rubbed his chin and felt a 6.45 shadow. 'Y'know,' he reflected ruefully, 'it's said that there's not a street you can walk on in Zurich where you're not treading over the melted down teeth of some poor Yid.'

'I should imagine that the interest on that blood money over the years has been pretty sizable,' Shears interjected.

'Yeah. But it wasn't just left to accumulate in the banks. A great deal of it was used to finance some very shrewd and ambitious men at a time when Germany was at the beginning of what is now called the Economic Miracle. Many of these men are today highly successful and powerful industrialists, and they are right behind this new wave of Fascist fervour; some because they're dyed-in-the-wool Nazis and always will be, others because they're shit-scared that their Communist kinsmen across the wall will one day move in and take over. So they've overreacted, just like their predecessors did way back in the early thirties, when they voted Hitler into power.'

Shears frowned. 'You know, I can't understand how the new generation would let what happened before repeat itself. I've met a few young Germans, and if they are typical of today's generation they appear to be pretty well-balanced to me. Those who have opened up about the past seem appalled and ashamed by what their ancestors did in the name of Germany. I can't honestly see them giving house-room to that kind of doctrine again.'

McNabe thrust his head forward like a fighting cock. 'Yeah, maybe that was true even just a short while back, but they can't keep hanging on to a guilty past they had no part in for ever. So, when the hierarchy of this neo-Nazi movement started issuing pamphlets stating that all those death camp stories were trumped up, thousands of young people in Germany were only too ready to believe it. Remember, some of those Fascists know a thing or two about twisting the facts. They have a well-tried blueprint which they inherited from that genius of propaganda, Dr Goebbels.'

Shears made no comment. He was aware that McNabe was well entrenched in his subject, and he spoke with such a burning conviction that he found it difficult to dispute his claims.

'I'll tell you something else, shall I?' McNabe continued. 'In fact, it would be ludicrously funny if it weren't so fuckin' sick. Y'know what they're saying about all those pictures and newsreels we've seen in camps like Treblinka, Belsen, and Auschwitz, to name but three?'

Shears shook his head.

'That they were all faked by Zionist cameramen to discredit the noble ideology of the Third Reich — can you beat that?'

Shears looked at him disbelievingly.

'Well, how in God's name do they explain all those grotesque pyramids of corpses?'

'They say that they were all made of papier-mâché,' McNabe said drily.

'Oh, who'd swallow that bullshit?' Shears felt his blood rising.

'Thousands of kids do, hook, line and sinker. They believe it because they want to believe it. They just can't accept that their sweet old grandads were remotely capable of thinking such dreadful things, let alone committing them.'

Shears pinged the rim of his glass with his thumb and forefinger. He could rarely remember having heard McNabe speak so bitterly.

'You know, it was back in 1977 when it really hit us that these neo-Nazis were getting through to a new generation. That's when three records of the Nuremberg Rally speeches of Adolph Hitler got into the West German charts. We realised then that we might soon be dealing with future terrorists from the right. Up until that time you only looked to the left for trouble, with groups like the Red Brigade, the Baader-Meinhof gang, and the Black September movement. Now, with this latest spate of attacks on Jewish communities, unhappily our worst fears have come true.'

'Have you any idea of the numbers involved in these neo-Nazi movements?'

'Yes, we have a pretty good idea, but as they are growing in numbers and units so rapidly, it's difficult to give bang up-to-date figures. For example, in Germany there are several cells ranging from the National Democratic Party, with a membership at the moment around 25,000, to smaller units like the Viking Youth and the Defensive Sports Club. They are not so big in number, but very militant. You know, it's a disconcerting thought that the German contingent alone have larger numbers now than Hitler did in 1925, only eight years before he came to power. Then, on our own doorstep we have a group which seems to change its name more often than Elizabeth Taylor does husbands. At present it calls itself the 'American National Party'. This, too, is gaining in strength, as are other Fascist and right-wing groups through-out Europe, like Italy's MSI, France's Third

Position, the UK's National Front and League of St George, Denmark's VIK . . .

'Okay, okay. You've made your point,' Shears broke in. 'Just give me the bottom line. How many are there in all, as far as you can ascertain?'

McNabe reached over and placed his empty glass on the desk.

'Well, taking into account all the small cells in different parts of the world who are affiliated to the main body — which calls itself 'The Chain', and excluding groups that are so badly organised that they've been disowned by the guys who call the shots — I'd say around two million.'

If Shears looked a trifle taken aback at that point, it was because he was. It seemed inconceivable to him that a political movement which had, in such very recent history, been condemned and shunned by the whole civilised world, should be able to attract so many followers. He could now see that if this would-be Russian defector, Kotchnov, was a bearer of glad tidings for 'The Chain', it could present all kinds of problems in a world which was going through a very politically unstable phase. But he was filled with doubts about his own ability to be useful in the way that McNabe had outlined earlier.

'Well,' Shears said at last, 'I honestly don't

see how I could be much help to you, Paul.' He grinned. 'I mean, short of gate-crashing that party in Nuremberg, and hypnotising Prama into telling me what dastardly deeds are afoot.'

McNabe remained serious. 'Well, you may be kidding, but oddly enough we do have something of that nature in mind for you.'

'Oh, come on now, I've absolutely no experience in this cloak and dagger stuff at all. It's just not my scene, Paul — you know that.'

'Rubbish,' McNabe butted in, 'we don't have a better man in the company for the job. We . . . ' The jangle of a telephone cut McNabe off short.

Shears threw McNabe a slightly anxious glance.

'Ten to one that's Shirley, wondering where the hell I am.' He picked up the phone and nodded to McNabe as he spoke. 'Hello, honey. Yeah, yeah, I'm with Paul McNabe. Uh huh. Okay. I'll ask.'

He placed his hand over the mouthpiece and spoke to McNabe. 'Got any plans for tonight?'

McNabe thought for a moment and shook his head.

'How'd you like to come to dinner?'

'Delighted,' McNabe replied happily.

'Okay honey, we'll be there in thirty minutes.'

Shears replaced the receiver in its cradle.

McNabe stood up with a mighty effort.

'Right. On the way home, I'll explain the cover we've arranged for you . . .

4

At just about the same time as Prama was preparing to meet his guests, a man was sitting on a bar stool staring into a near empty glass of Scotch. Reaching across to a bowl of peanuts, he glanced at his wristwatch, before grabbing a handful and tossing them to the back of his throat, crunching them noisily, while he impatiently tapped the rim of his glass with his fingertips.

The man, slim, dark and in his late twenties, cursed to himself. The girl should have been here by now. Then a fresh and very worrying thought occurred to him. Suppose she had already called in and left. Due to the unexpected rain, he had been a few minutes late arriving himself, and there were some women, even night club hostesses, who would not be seen dead in a bar unaccompanied. He leaned towards the stony-faced bartender, who was mechanically polishing a glass with a crisp white cloth.

'You haven't seen a blonde girl, rather on the tall side, pop in here within the last half hour by any chance, have you?'

The bartender stopped polishing and

stared at him, then, without altering his facial expression, raised his eyes above the seated man's shoulder towards the direction of the door.

'You mean like that one?' indicating with an inclination of his head the girl just entering. The young man swung round, saw her, and turned back to the bartender with a wide grin: 'Exactly like that!'

He got off the stool and waited for her to recognise him. Anna's green eyes brightened as she saw him. She came over to him, taking off a wet headscarf as she did so.

'I'm sorry to have kept you waiting,' Anna said, lightly planting a kiss on his cheek. 'But in this vile weather you cannot get a taxi for love or money.'

The young man smiled sympathetically. His eyes showed pleasure in seeing her looking so stunning, coupled with the sense of relief that she had turned up at all.

Anna, a few years older than himself, and a good deal more sophisticated, was still rather lovely — surprisingly so, since she worked most of her nights wearing heavy make-up and slept for a large part of the day with her face covered in various beauty creams. The young man gazed fondly at her as he took her hand in his. Without Anna on his arm tonight, he would have had no chance of getting to Herr Prama's party.

'We've still got time for a drink,' he said, displaying an even row of white teeth. 'What will it be?'

'Campari and soda,' Anna purred softly, as she opened her handbag and removed a lipstick holder. The barman, overhearing the order, set about preparing the drink without delay. The slim young man withdrew a wallet from inside his jacket and felt the handle of the gun he carried pressing against his ribs.

There were many ways to kill a man, none quicker than with a bullet, but he'd had strict instructions from Zeigler to use it only if there were no alternative. He was to make every effort to ensure that it looked like an accident. With the exception of one unforgettable blunder, he had managed to make all the 'despatch' jobs he had been associated with appear as though they were accidents. On that one occasion he had been interrupted by a zealous chambermaid entering the bedroom earlier than he had anticipated, just as he was in the process of dumping a victim from an eighteenth storey window. The unfortunate chambermaid was to share the same fate a few seconds later. He could still vividly remember her scream as she hurtled downwards, before breaking like an egg on the pavement below. It reminded him of the sound of those shrieking bombs in the films he'd seen about World War II.

'What kind of a day have you had, darling?' Anna asked, as she pursed her lips to touch them up with the lipstick.

'Boring,' the young man replied, taking some notes from his wallet and depositing them on the bar. He'd only known Anna three weeks. She had been pointed out to him by Zeigler after he had been briefed in Nuremberg.

'Get to know that broad and screw her. She's a hostess at the club Prama part owns. It'll cost us plenty, but you'll need her if you're to get to him. She's like the head hostess — lines up all the hookers for Prama and his buddies. She'll take you into the party if you play your cards right.'

Zeigler was correct, of course. Getting her to bed did cost a bundle, but he turned on all his charm and the girl soon became intrigued with him. He told her he was involved in investments abroad and, surprise, surprise, she mentioned that she knew a rich banker similarly involved. It did not take too long after that to persuade her that he was always on the look-out for contacts of this kind. A bit more wild love-making, and she was ready to effect an introduction and, more important, take him along to the party.

'And what about you?' the young man moved in closer, looking into her eyes.

Anna's legs weakened. She couldn't remember when she had last felt this way about anyone. It wasn't so much his good looks, although he was certainly handsome. It was a compelling inner power that he exuded which seemed to totally mesmerise her.

'Pardon?' she uttered feebly.

'What kind of a day have you had?' the young man said, releasing her from his stare.

'Oh — well — when I did eventually get up, I did a little shopping, then went to the hairdresser's . . . but you wouldn't think so to look at it now, would you?'

'Nonsense. It's beautiful. By the way did you mention to Prama that I would be coming with you to the party tonight?'

'Well, vaguely, yes. He's got loads of girlfriends, but he is rather possessive over me, so I told him you were my cousin and very ambitious,' Anna giggled. She turned her wrist to squint at her Cartier watch. She was as short-sighted as a day-old kitten, but positively refused to wear glasses.

'Darling, we should be going.'

'I've managed to park right outside, and I'm ready when you are,' he said, indicating by a gesture of his hand for the barman to keep the change he so reluctantly offered him. The young man placed a protective arm around Anna and walked with her to the door.

'It should be an interesting evening,' Anna said gaily.

'Yes, it certainly should.' The young man quickly pushed the door open and politely ushered her out into the rain.

5

Unlike the young man who had had to use all manner of inducements with Anna to get an invitation to Herr Prama's party that night, Wolfgang Hollerbach had not so much been invited as instructed to attend. Also unlike the young man, he was not the owner of a gleaming Porsche worthy of admiring glances, but was the possessor of a ten-year-old — and in wet weather cussedly obstinate starting — Volkswagen. Tonight the old jalopy was unyieldingly stubborn and in frustration he had reduced the initially perky battery to a wheeze that sounded like a dying wasp. There was nothing for it, he would have to get a taxi, and, even if he were lucky enough to hail one, a near impossibility on a rainy day in the Altstadt, he would still be late. Miserably tying his raincoat round him, he pulled his hat well down over his eyes and, with head hung low and shoulders hunched like a repentant schoolboy, he squelched off along the Karolinestrasse.

He had not been walking for more than a few minutes when he saw a taxi pull up about twenty metres ahead to allow a passenger to alight. Holding on to his hat he ran, splashing quickly through the puddles, and grabbing the handle of the door, leapt in just as the taxi began to move off.

'St Leonhard,' Hollerbach shouted breathlessly to the back of the driver's head. The driver half-turned to acknowledge the command, and wordlessly touched his cap as he did so.

Hollerbach sat back in his seat and shuddered. What a bloody foul night to go out, he thought, as he placed his hat beside him. Prama would not be too happy either, he considered, as he recalled that tonight's shindig was to be a barbecue. His journalistic mind flashed up a by-line: 'Liquidity no asset at Banker's barbecue!' A faint smile played on his lips, then it slowly faded as he remembered why he was going there in the first place.

He had received an out-of-the-blue invitation to have dinner with Prama at his Club, Renates. Although he had known Prama for more years than he cared to remember, he could not say they were close friends, so it was a little surprising to find Prama being so affably insistent that he wine and dine with him.

When the preliminary enquiries of health, family and friends had been dealt with,

Prama came straight to the point of their meeting, attacking his subject with the same enthusiastic relish he reserved for his second helping of *escargots*. As he prised the garlic-soaked molluscs from their shells, he informed Hollerbach that he was giving a party at the weekend, ostensibly to introduce some American representatives of a Texan farm equipment company to some members of a Soviet Trade Delegation from Minsk. Among the members of the Trade Delegation, Prama went on, was a man who was very anxious to defect to the West. Hollerbach recalled that Prama had eyed him pointedly, stopped chewing for a moment, leaned forward and, exuding a heavy smell of garlic beneath his nose, told him that the Kameraden were going to give this Russian every possible assistance. Prama, noting the puzzled look on Hollerbach's face, laughed and, producing an envelope from the briefcase at his side, handed it to him. He told him to read the contents when he got home and warned him not to speak of it to anyone. After the main course of the meal had been presented with a great flourish by what seemed to Hollerbach every waiter in the entire place, Prama went on to tell him that he might find what was in effect a statement difficult to read, as it had been written many years ago in the dim light of a prison hospital ward, where the man had been held in close custody. Prama concluded by saying that when Hollerbach had thoroughly absorbed the text, they would meet again at the party, when he would explain to him the connection between the statement and the Russian whom they were aiding.

★　★　★

At home that night, comfortably propped up in bed with a glass of milk and two packets of Lords at his elbow, Hollerbach carried out Prama's instructions. He withdrew from the envelope photostatted sheets of tightly handwritten pages. Although the process of photocopying had tended to sharpen the original ink, the actual wording itself was at times very faint and some of the words illegible. This was consistent with Prama's reference to the writer having been a sick man.

Hollerbach, fatigued as he was, became more alert by the second as he studied the pages. He read them not once but three times before he finally switched off his bedside lamp. Even then sleep eluded him for the best part of the night. He could scarcely wait for the morning to arrive in order to visit the reference library and conduct some thorough research into certain questions the statement raised. That had been more than a week ago. Since then he had spent many hours in the library thumbing through yellowed newspapers and making copious notes.

Now, with the assault on his eardrums of frustrated motorists, angrily thumping the horns of their virtually immobile vehicles as the rush hour traffic in the Lorenz district tested their patience to the utmost, he decided to help pass the time by reading the statement yet again. He slid the envelope from inside his breast pocket and asked the driver to flick on the interior light. Smoothing out the pages on his knee, he settled back into his seat. He had almost memorised the entire document, and his lips silently mouthed the words as he read:

'My name is Johannes Bruckner. I was born in Kaiserslautern on May 10th, 1899. I solemnly swear that this statement I make is the truth, the whole truth and nothing but the truth. I deem it my duty, on behalf of the Fatherland which is so dear to me, and the ideology of National Socialism — for which so many of my fellow countrymen have given their lives — to place on record facts that are of the utmost importance in maintaining the continuation of the Party and ensuring the future reestablishment of the Reich.

This statement is written with the knowledge that my days on earth are numbered. But I shall be content to die knowing that stronger and younger members of the Kameraden will act on the information that I alone am now privy to. I am confident that the Party will not only survive, but will become greater and more glorious than ever before. It will inevitably be a long and bitter struggle, but the form which that struggle will take will, I am convinced, be guided and shaped by the disclosures I now make.

On April 4th, 1945, in my official capacity as Senior Administrative Controller to the Deputy Reichsführer, Martin Bormann, I was ordered to join the Reichsführer and his staff in the party bunker beneath the new Chancellory. This was not the complex of eighteen rooms known as the Führerbunker, where the Führer himself was in residence, but a smaller group of rooms that was adjacent to it and linked by a central concrete passageway. Next to our quarters there was yet a third and even smaller bunker which housed SS Brigadeführer Mohnke, the Commandant of the Chancellory and his staff.

My chief had an office in the main Führerbunker and I was often summoned by him to work in a small anteroom, so that I could deal promptly with the ever increasing pile of paperwork and memoranda that passed between him and the Führer. I was also given another important task. This was to read and process all the mail that came to the Chancellory addressed to the Führer personally; even those marked 'Private and Confidential' had first to be censored by me. It had been agreed privately by Dr Goebbels and Herr Bormann that it was in the Führer's best interests that this should be done. It should be understood here why this was considered so necessary, lest the motives be misconstrued in any way. During this period the Führer was acting very irrationally. There were days when he would lose complete control of his temper, and in these demented rages would accuse virtually everyone around him of betrayal. Even my chief and Dr Goebbels were sometimes subjected to these outbursts. But he would quickly calm down, and I once overhead him apologise profusely to Herr Bormann for the unjust charges he had made concerning him.

The Führer, thanks largely to Herr Bormann, and to a lesser extent to Dr Goebbels' constant reassurances, was never in any doubt that he still had the undying support of the entire German people. This, as we now know, was far from true. Literally hundreds of anonymous letters were arriving daily, making the most monstrous allegations. Some said he had made them empty promises, condemned his leadership as a great lie, and blamed him personally for all the suffering they were enduring. How quickly they had forgotten that his entire political life had been devoted to building a greater Germany and restoring its national pride. Through his inspiration and genius he had made Germany — if only briefly — the most magnificent empire the world had witnessed since the great days of Rome. All this abusive filth was immediately destroyed by me. The Führer and his close advisers were under enough stress without having to endure the cowardly criticisms of so many contemptuous traitors. There were, however, many letters from people who still expressed their gratitude, loyalty and continued confidence in him. These I carefully selected, and I would give them to Herr Bormann to pass on to the Führer. My chief told me how much these simple tokens of allegiance from the *deutsches Volk*, whom the Führer referred to as 'the salt of the earth', meant to him. On one occasion, due to a prior commitment of Herr Bormann, I was given the singular honour of handing the day's batch of selected correspondence to the Führer personally, and I could see for myself that although he was tired and drawn, he read every one of these letters avidly, and one could see that the messages of comfort they contained visibly lifted his spirits. He thanked me politely for waiting while he completed reading them. Then, removing his spectacles, he handed the letters back to me. As I reached the door, he addressed me quietly. 'I have heard you are doing a good job down here Bruckner,' he said. 'I, too, have a Bruckner working for me. Any relation?' I replied that he was not. The Führer smiled and said that there must be something about the name that was very dependable. A rare quality in Germany these days. I suppose that was one of the proudest moments of my life.

On April 16th, the day following the Russian assault on the outskirts of Berlin, a letter arrived in the 'Private and Personal' consignment addressed to the Führer. I found this letter so extraordinary that, although my first response was to dismiss it as having been written by a crank, I decided to delay any decision on it until later, when I would examine it again and properly assess its validity. After further study I became increasingly of the opinion that the writer appeared to be not only sincere, but in possession of certain facts that were known only to a very small circle. I decided then that it warranted the immediate personal attention of my chief. With the letter in my hand, I walked into his office. He had just returned from an all morning session in the situations room with the Führer, and one look at his face told me he had probably been tongue-lashed for most of it. He would have been in no mood to discuss what he might then have regarded as trivia, so I felt it prudent to approach him at a time when he would be in a more receptive frame of mind . . .

★   ★   ★

At this point, Hollerbach rummaged through his pockets and finally withdrew a crumpled packet of Lords. Peering into the top he despondently realised that he had only two cigarettes left. Leaning forward, he once more addressed himself to the back of the driver's neck.

'I need some cigarettes. Pull over at a tobacconist's whenever you can, please.'

The driver silently touched his cap again. Not the loquacious type of chap usually encountered among the taxi fraternity, Hollerbach thought as he lit up a cigarette and, settling back in his seat, continued to read . . .

'The following morning Herr Bormann appeared to be more pleasantly disposed, and after covering the day's business with me, I brought up the matter of the letter. Coffee had just arrived and he beckoned me to take a seat while he read it:

Hosena,
7, Hainstrasse.
March 25, 1945.

Dear Herr Hitler,

You must forgive me for writing to you at what must be a time of great crisis in your life, for the whole of Germany's future and that of its people lies in your hands. A heavy task indeed, even for a man as great as you, mein Führer.

It is very difficult to know where to begin, but with the future so uncertain and my health failing, I feel that the secret which I have held for so long must now be passed on to you. What I am about to disclose will, I know, come as a very great surprise to you.

It began one day in March 1931, when I received a phone call from your niece, Geli, asking if she could come to stay with me for a short while. I had been a friend of her mother, Angela Raubel, for many years, and the prospect of seeing this delightful child again pleased me, as I had been living alone since the death of my husband.

She arrived that evening in a very distressed state. After supper she told me the story — you will forgive me, mein Führer, for what I must repeat to you now — she told me how much she loved you, how she had always loved you, and that after she had moved into your apartment at 16 Prinz Regentenplatz in Munich you had become lovers. Of necessity your relationship was a secret one, known only to a few very close friends, but Geli told me that there were often moments when you would speak of your future together, and of the possibility, when it was politically suitable, for you to marry, as there was no woman you had ever loved as much as you loved her. Therefore, when you gave Geli money and the address of a doctor in Vienna who would perform this operation on her, she began to doubt your love and vowed to herself that nothing was going to harm this manifestation of love that she now carried inside her. Being a Catholic myself, I was in full agreement with Geli that she should keep her baby.

We devised a plan between us. Geli should return to Vienna and keep up the pretence of having done as you requested, writing to you regularly, telling you that she had resumed her singing lessons, was visiting the theatre, and generally enjoying herself.

She was to return to me three weeks before her confinement. Being a qualified midwife, I had no fears regarding the birth, and on the 24th August, at 17.10, I delivered to Geli a beautiful baby boy weighing three and a half kilos.

Geli was delighted and also very relieved, as she was beginning to fear that maybe you were right in thinking that any child born to you both would be either mentally retarded or physically deformed in some way, due to the closeness of your blood, and that this would be just the sort of scandal your enemies would seize upon to denounce your proclamations of a pure Aryan race.

The days following the birth were ones of great anxiety for Geli. On the one hand, she wanted so desperately to tell you of her proud moment of motherhood and to witness the joy she prayed you would feel when she presented you with your baby son. On the other hand, she was torn by intense feelings of guilt at the way she had deceived and disobeyed you. In the end it was decided that she should return to Munich alone as soon as possible. Geli had explained to me that although you had, on many occasions, discussed the possibility of marriage with her, there was no likelihood of this happening for some considerable time. I must add that she understood only too well that the love and admiration felt for you by the entire German nation could only be marred by such a marriage during that crucial time in your political ascent. But Geli felt that there would come a time when it would be right and appropriate for you to be joined, not just in the eyes of God, but for all the world to see. Until then, I was to bring up the child as my own. Geli would provide for his upkeep and education from the generous allowance that you made her, and would come and visit me and the baby whenever possible.

Before Geli left to return to you, she took the baby into Dresden and had a tattoo artist prick into his tender skin — in true SS manner — under the left armpit, the initials 'AGU'. These stood for Adolf, Geli, Unehelich — lovechild.

The next day she departed. That was September 17th, 1931. On September

18th, as we all know, she died tragically.

When I read about it in the papers I was stunned and brokenhearted. I will never believe the coroner's verdict of suicide, mein Führer, as I knew that girl as well as if she were my own daughter, and I know — I just know — that she did not kill herself.

For weeks afterwards I lived in constant fear. Every knock at the door brought terror into my heart, for I was sure that someone would come to take the baby away. I even thought of moving, but where could I go? I had a little money, but not enough to cover all the expenses involved. In any case I knew that the police, if they set their minds to it, would have found us wherever we went. The weeks turned to months, the months to years, and when no one came I slowly began to realise that Geli could not have told you in the short reunion you had with her, and that the secret we had shared was now known to me alone.

Your son, mein Führer, is now fourteen years old, and bears a marked resemblance to you as a young man. He has a strong will, but can also be kind and considerate. He is very artistic, and has a keen interest in the countryside.

81

I am a religious woman and feel in my heart that the Almighty may have used me for a special purpose in his great plan for the future of our people. Perhaps it is His hand that has guided me to write all this down to you at long last.

I pray that this young man, your son, will be a new inspiration to you, symbolising the youth and spirit of tomorrow's Germany. Even now, mein Führer, with disaster at our very door, I know that you, and you alone, can save us. May God, in His infinite wisdom and mercy, give you the strength to do so.

I remain your obedient and devoted servant,

Ilse Wolters.

When Herr Bormann had finished reading the letter, he looked up at me and asked me what I thought. I said it seemed so preposterous it could conceivably be true. Saying that he was of the same opinion, he told me to leave the letter with him while he considered what action was to be taken. Later that day I heard Herr Bormann and Dr Goebbels arguing furiously in the latter's office. From the snatches of heated conversation that I overheard, it seemed that Herr Bormann was pressing that the Führer be advised most strongly to leave the bunker and continue the fight from his stronghold at Berchtesgaden. There at least, he said, he would be out of the main firing line. Herr Bormann believed even then that some kind of peace settlement would be agreed with the Allies. 'Where there's life, there's hope,' I heard him state. But Goebbels was totally nihilistic. His whole demeanour was that of a man who had accepted inevitable defeat. He said that the Führer, himself, and his entire family had decided to remain to the bitter end, with a planned suicide in the last moments if the much hoped for reinforcements did not arrive. He would not recommend any proposal where there was the slightest risk of the Führer being captured alive. If that dreadful thing were to happen, he said, the Führer would be subjected to ridicule, mockery and persecuted openly in a public trial. It would be a pitiful epitaph to the once omnipotent Third Reich legend, which he himself had been so instrumental in creating. A journey anywhere out of the protected bunker would run that risk, and he would not condone Bormann's plan for that reason.

Herr Bormann stormed out of Goebbels' office, and swept past me, tight-lipped with anger, muttering loudly some very disparaging remarks about 'that stupid, stubborn little cripple.'

The following morning my chief called me into his office and told me he had made a decision regarding the declarations in the letter. He said that, despite Dr Goebbels' opposition, he was still optimistic that he would be able to persuade the Führer to leave the bunker and carry on the campaign in Berchtesgaden. My orders were to go to Hosena and thoroughly interrogate the woman Wolters, and if I were satisfied that she had been telling the truth and was not merely possessed of a vivid imagination, then I was to take her and the boy to Berchtesgaden Obersalzburg, where Herr Bormann then fully expected to be. My chief placed an arm around my shoulder and in a confidential manner, never displayed to me before, explained that my mission was of paramount importance. He believed that if the battle for Germany were lost, a Reich established in exile was not beyond the bounds of possibility, and that he had already sounded out certain sympathetic governments abroad with a view to achieving this. Although it was very unlikely that the Führer would be allowed to head such a proposed new Reich, the fact that he had a proven heir could be a vital factor in such a scheme. For this young man would be a symbol of a future revival of National Socialism to millions of patriots, a 'pretender to the throne' as it were. He also briefed me on a contingency plan if it should not be possible to reach Obersaltzberg, due to an intensification of the enemy advance. This was a specially prepared, detailed route that would take us through Austria, Italy and eventually into Berne, Switzerland. Here a Jesuit priest would take us under his wing until further instructions came directly from Herr Bormann. He also gave me letters of authorisation, travel permits, Italian and Swiss currency, and a list of names and addresses of contacts at various points en route who would assist us in every possible way. This list was to be committed to memory and destroyed. When the time was right, Herr Bormann said, we would be sent to join him — in a country he chose not to reveal to me at that time but where our safety would be assured. Then, reminding me to be certain to obtain the boy's birth certificate and other identification papers that could substantiate Frau Wolters' claim, he handed me her original letter, saying that if it all proved to be an idiotic hoax I should act as I felt fit, and punish whoever was responsible for wasting our time. Whatever the outcome, I was to follow his instructions implicitly, as 'I will always be able to use a good man like you,' he said. Finally he made me swear an oath of secrecy unto death, wished me luck, shook my hand warmly, and told me to pack in readiness for my journey that very night.

I set off from the bunker at about 22.00 hours on the 18th April. It had been arranged that an army vehicle would be available for me to collect outside the Chancellory. By travelling at night it was hoped that I would be shielded by darkness for most of the way, but when I emerged from the bunker I was staggered by the bright illumination of the whole area. The constant shelling of the Russian guns seemed to set the sky alight. I found my vehicle — a Kübelwagen — easily enough, but the journey along the Friedrichstrasse was hazardous, to say the least. There was barely a building standing intact, and mountains of rubble from crumbling edifices would suddenly loom up in a great cloud of dust in front of me, often making the road completely impassable. When this occurred, I would use my Geheimsicherheitsdienst letter of authorisation, signed by the Deputy Reichsführer, to enlist the aid of some of the Hitler Jugend who were patrolling the streets in their hordes, shooting at anyone who looked remotely like a looter. They were willing enough helpers, but it was still a long and laborious business, and all the time the sound of the Russian guns was becoming increasingly louder.

It was almost daybreak before I was out of Berlin and on the road to Hosena. Already the homeless had taken to the streets in that slow pathetic march that was to become such a familiar sight to me on my journey. Many times I was forced to drive at a pace little more than a crawl, and a distance that I would normally have covered in less than four hours took me the best part of two days. At one stage of this tedious drive I became so tired that I just pulled off the road and fell asleep behind the wheel.

At precisely 09.35 hours on the 20th April I drove into Hosena. Although it would not be true to say the war had by-passed this village, it was almost tranquil in comparison with other places I had seen. Only the odd demolished house here and there disturbed the aura of a peaceful country scene.

After some preliminary enquiries, I eventually located No. 7, Hainstrasse. It was a pretty little cottage, and it was plain to see that the front garden had once been lovingly cared for. Amidst the unruly shrubbery crocus and daffodil were still vying for attention, colourfully reminding the onlooker that spring had arrived, and that however destructive war is, it will never stop Nature's seasonal roll call.

I knocked loudly at the door, and after waiting for some time without receiving a response, I walked to the rear and saw a frail, elderly woman with grey hair removing some washing from a line. I asked her directly if she were Frau Ilse Wolters. She hesitated nervously for a moment before admitting that she was. Producing her letter, I explained that I had been sent from the Führer's headquarters to ask her some questions.

Relaxing a little, she invited me into her home and brewed up some rather foul-tasting *ersatz* coffee. I asked her where the boy was, and she told me that he was out fishing, 'a pastime he is devoted to'. I observed that although her eyes were bright and alert, she was quite clearly unwell. As she answered my questions, her voice trembled and her whole body shook continuously. But she reaffirmed in very positive terms that every word she had written was true. I explained that when I had fully checked everything in accordance with my instructions, and if I was fully satisfied with my findings, my orders were to take her and the boy to Berchtesgaden. She appeared to be agitated at this prospect, and when I sympathetically asked if she was worried that her health might not stand up to the long journey, she shook her head, and said that it was her cat that was giving her cause for concern — she did not want to leave it behind. I am afraid that such a frivolous remark about her bloody cat, after all I had been through, and with what I still had on my plate to accomplish, was too much for me and I lost my temper. I shouted at the stupid woman, telling her that she had better get her priorities right, and if the thought of leaving the cat behind was all that was on her mind, I could soon solve that little problem by putting a bullet through its brain. Suddenly her cheeks became ashen, her cup fell to the floor with a crash, and she clutched her chest, groaning. I realised at once that she was having a heart attack. I quickly loosened her clothing and tried to assist her. As I was making her more comfortable the front door opened, and in stepped a youth aged about fourteen or fifteen. He was wearing gumboots and was dressed in rather shabby clothing. His face and hands were mud splattered, and across a shoulder was slung a canvas bag and fishing rod. He took one look at me, leaning over the semi-conscious woman, let out a yell, and rushed at me. He repeatedly hit me about the head with the heavy wooden handle of his fishing rod, and I had the devil of a job restraining him. The shock of the boy's reaction seemed to revive the woman temporarily, because she made a sufficient recovery to pacify him and explain that I was helping, not harming, her. Then, between painful gasps for breath, she told him why I was there, and that he was to co-operate with me in every way. The youth was absolutely stunned. He sat down slowly, staring blankly at the wall in front of him, scarcely moving a muscle.

The woman's breathing became more laboured, and I could see that she was failing fast. I urgently demanded the whereabouts of the vital birth certificate, and she pointed weakly upstairs.

In the drawer of her dressing table I found an old chocolate box which contained the birth certificate, a bundle of letters from the Führer to Geli Raubel, and some photographs of them, posing happily together.

The certificate registered the date of birth as August 24th, 1931, and named the infant as Alois; father Adolfus Schicklgrüber, soldier; mother Angelica, student.

I could scarcely believe my eyes, for I knew that Schicklgrüber had been the old family name of the Führer. I was so engrossed by this document that it was sometime before I heard the youth sobbing. When I returned to the sitting room he was kneeling on the floor, with his head on the woman's lap. I could see that she was dead.

The youth turned towards me with tears streaming down his face. It was the first time I'd had the opportunity of studying his features properly. The resemblance between him and the pictures I had seen of the Führer as a young man was quite uncanny. This boy was a little stockier all round, perhaps, but otherwise the similarity was startling. The intense, deepset blue eyes, the straight unruly hair, the high cheekbones, but above all, despite the country air, that same pallid grey complexion. Although I had yet to check the tattoo marks under his arm, to my mind there was no doubt that this boy was indeed none other than the son of Adolf Hitler.

I covered the woman's body with a sheet, and comforted the youth as much as I could by telling him that I would notify the proper authorities to ensure that his guardian had a burial worthy of a true patriot. But he was inconsolable, and wailed like a baby, until eventually I had forcibly to command him to pull himself together and behave like a man. Then I told him to get cleaned up, change his clothes, and pack a small travelling bag in preparation for our journey to Berchtesgaden.

He seemed to me at the time to be a most

obstreperous individual; even allowing for the fact that he had just been through a traumatic experience, this did not really excuse the surly attitude he had towards me. I was conscious that he sensed that I now regarded him as a rather special person, but this served only, if anything, to make him even more belligerent. His mood was such that I felt it unwise to mention that, if we were unable to get to Berchtesgaden, we might have to trek hundreds of kilometres further, to Switzerland. As it was, it took the utmost persuasion on my part to get him to co-operate in any way at all, and it seemed an interminable time before he was ready.

The dramatic events that had taken place inside the cottage were, however, nothing compared to what we were to encounter outside. It was as though an evil sorcerer had waved his magic wand and transformed the sleepy village into a mass of human misery. For the ever increasing number of dazed and bewildered refugees had grown from a steady trickle into a huge surging tidal wave, and were flooding through Hosena as they retreated from the burning cities. Everything on wheels was being used to transport whatever pitiful belongings these reluctant nomads had managed to salvage. There were prams, carts, bicycles, wheelbarrows; tens of thousands filed at funereal pace through the narrow streets and away into the distance, making our progress at times almost impossible. All this had occurred in just the few days since I had left the bunker in Berlin. That bunker — it seemed so far away from me now. There its occupants were living in a rarified world of blissful ignorance, planning military tactics like overgrown schoolboys with armies that no longer existed, totally unaware of the true situation that prevailed outside.'

★　★　★

Hollerbach raised his head. Although the taxi had been forced by the endless stream of traffic to travel with all the urgency of a bottled snail, this time it was the driver who had deliberately brought the taxi to a halt. Glancing through the rain-splashed window, a blazing neon sign informed him that Albert Praeger was a purveyor of fine quality cigars, tobacco and cigarettes.

Now, Hollerbach thought, if this taxi driver was determined to conduct all communication by mime — damn him — so would he. So, indicating wordlessly to the driver with his hands, Hollerbach informed him that he would be in and out of the shop as soon as possible. Then, dropping his head like an angry bull, he charged out into a near solid wall of cascading water.

Returning to the taxi some moments later, a good deal wetter but with three packets of Lords tucked safely inside his pocket, he grandly waved the driver on.

Taking the last remaining cigarette from the old packet, Hollerbach lit up and exhaled a long thin swirl of smoke. With a satisfied smirk, he crumpled the packet into a tight ball and furtively pushed it into a space at the back of the seat. Then he resumed his reading of Bruckner's statement:

'At last I found a narrow country lane that seemed to be virtually uncluttered, and although the road surface by its very character was uneven, it was at least consistent, and I managed to make much better progress. I drove for several kilometres along this route, and in all this time the youth had not uttered a single word, although I had done my utmost to be communicative, talking of topics from scholastics and sport to our present grave military situation. But it was like talking to a brick wall — he was totally unresponsive. Then, suddenly out of the blue, he broke his silence to ask politely if I could stop while he relieved himself behind some bushes. I gladly agreed, thinking that at least he was possessed of some good manners. I decided to use this unscheduled break to pinpoint our position and study the route. The sound of a startled bird taking flight made me look up. To my great astonishment I saw the youth racing across the meadow with the speed of a hare. He had too much of a start for me to catch him on foot, so I took a chance and swung the Kübelwagen in the direction that he had taken, and doggedly pursued him. I ploughed through soggy marshland and moon-pitted fields, until finally I saw the youth drop from sheer exhaustion. Pulling up close by him, I jumped out and quickly removed the belt from my jacket. Angrily I told him that I was strapping his wrist to mine to prevent him from running away again. He was far too tired to protest, as I marched him back to the vehicle. Restarting the motor, I found to my despair that the back wheels had become deeply entrenched in the mud, and despite all my efforts to get the vehicle on to firmer ground it would not budge, the wheels just spinning uselessly around. I concluded that there was no alternative but to continue on foot. Collecting my attaché case containing all the documents, and a small bag of food which I had found by rummaging through Ilse Wolters' almost empty pantry, we left the remainder of our luggage behind and resignedly set off.

After walking some distance the youth began to falter in his step. He, like myself, was becoming very weary, so I asked him if he would like to take a rest and he nodded his head gratefully. We sat down on a fallen tree. Delving into the food bag I produced two of the most appetising items; a hunk of black bread and a rock-hard piece of goat's cheese.

While we were almost breaking our teeth on this Spartan meal, a lone Russian Stormavik suddenly appeared from out of the clouds. Spotting us, the pilot immediately dived into an attack. Hastily tugging the startled youth by our manacled wrists, I rolled over backwards behind the log, pulling him with me, and shouted at him to keep his head down as tracer bullets kicked up dirt in all directions. The pilot seemed hell-bent on our destruction, and kept on returning to renew the attack. After what seemed an eternity, the Stormavik eventually soared away. We got up, and while we were brushing the mud and foliage from our clothing, the youth turned to me and complained that the strap had cut into his wrist, causing it to bleed. As I was loosening it a little, he addressed me with these words:

'Please, Oberführer Bruckner, do not take

me to meet my father.'

It was a plea straight from the heart, and I felt very sorry for him, because he was obviously desperately unhappy. The youth went on to say that he could never accept Adolf Hitler as his father, and although he might be the world's most feared and powerful ruler, he could never have any love for him and he could see no purpose whatever in their meeting. I explained that there was nothing I could do; I was a soldier and had to obey my orders. I tried to cheer him up by saying how lucky he was to be the son of such a great man, and that destiny would surely have a meaningful role for him, too, to play one day. But he was not impressed, and once more fell into a morose silence.

Now and again we would meet up with small bands of refugees, and of course the odd exchanges of conversation would inevitably include the conditions of various places in the area.

Although most of the town and village signs had been removed in order to confuse the enemy, I had calculated that we were now approximately two kilometres south-east of Königsbruck. I knew it was imperative that we try to reach Dresden that night. Here I hoped to make my first contact, a butcher by the name of Franz Erlmann. I would require his aid in obtaining transport, as it was quite obvious to me now that we would never reach our destination without it. I will never forget that agonisingly harassing walk. It was as though we were a pair of lost souls in hell, ever looking over our shoulders towards the sound of Russian tank tracks squealing in the distance, and we were constantly being made aware of their ominous presence by the heavy artillery fire, the crackle of machine guns, and the drone of bombers overhead.

As our journey continued, I realised that I had been over-ambitious in my goal, and with the youth now stumbling at every other step, I slowly became resigned to the fact that we would have to rest. We eventually found an old barn still standing near a bombed-out farmhouse. My intention was to take a short nap, but when I awoke it was already daybreak. I hastily shook the slumbering youth at my side, and as we were preparing to leave I heard the sound of a small vehicle pulling into the yard, followed quickly by another. I stood rooted to the spot as the barn door burst open and in rushed about eight Russian soldiers carrying machine guns. I thought they would have us shot instantly, and I am sure they would have, but a sudden series of clipped commands sent four of them scurrying off to search the rest of the barn, while the others stood with guns at the ready like a pack of trained dogs. The man with all the mouth moved further into the barn and, although his uniform was thickly covered in dust, I could just make out that he held the rank of corporal. He was a grim looking son-of-a-bitch, and by his battle weary appearance had seen a lot of action. I instinctively raised my hands slowly above my head; the youth had no alternative but to follow my action and his trembling hand began to shake against mine. The corporal stood looking at us with a puzzled expression, and it was then that I realised what an odd combination we must have made — a dishevelled, high-ranking German officer with a young civilian boy bound crudely to his wrist. It was this spectacle, I was sure, that was keeping us from death.

Satisfied that we were alone, the soldiers began to relax a little, but inside my guts were in a turmoil, wondering what these murderous bastards would decide to do with us. The corporal had us thoroughly searched and anything of value was distributed. During all this time I had been quietly trying to move hay with my foot over the half-hidden attaché case, but this movement soon caught the attention of one of the soldiers. The corporal picked the case up from the floor and forced the lock open with a commando knife. He flicked disinterestedly through the documents, until his eyes fell upon the photographs of the Führer and Geli. He started chortling, and the place became like a cheap cabaret as he passed them on to his men with a heavy wink. As the photos went from hand to hand accompanied by crude gestures and raucous laughter, the boy began to cry. I think it was more out of fear than anything else, but whatever the reason it had the most stultifying effect on the Russians. The merriment faded and they began to shuffle uneasily; perhaps the boy presented such a pathetic, frightened picture that it ignited a spark of pity in them. One of the men whispered something in the corporal's ear, he nodded in agreement and started sorting through the papers again, then he snapped out a brisk order and the boy and I were bundled out into the yard and on to the back of a Bantam field car.

We were driven to a town which I recognised as Radeburg. The Bantam stopped near the town centre at a large house that was being used as a temporary HQ by the 1st Ukranian Army. Once inside the building, we were untied and marched off in opposite directions. I was taken to a small room on the ground floor that was serving to store broken office equipment, and there I was left for many hours. I must have paced the floor for God knows how long awaiting the expected interrogation, inventing in my mind story after story concerning my involvement with the youth, and rejecting each one in turn as being implausible. I was still wrestling with the problem when a huge soldier entered with a mug of tea, some salted herring and bread. He stood in the door frame, almost filling it, as he silently watched me wolf the food down. I had just finished eating when the door opened again and in strode an officer of about my own age. The officer was waving a letter in his hand, and I could see immediately that it was the one from Ilse Wolters. He leaned against the wall and folded his arms; smiling pleasantly he addressed me in fluent German. He said that it appeared they were now host to a very important young guest, and he wanted to know what my connection with the young man was, and in particular, where I was taking him and to whom? I told him, with as much conviction as I could muster, that the youth was my nephew and that I was taking him to my wife in Dresden, as his mother had been killed in an air raid. When asked why we were handcuffed together, I explained that with so many refugees on the road I was afraid that we might lose one another. He looked at me disbelievingly and switched his line of questioning to ask about the contents in the attaché case. I played dumb, saying that I knew nothing about it, that it must have been in the barn before I got there. He scoffed and said: 'Very well, Oberführer Bruckner, but if you value your own life and the boy's I advise you to think again. I will be back in half an hour, by which time I hope you will have come to your senses.' With that he and the guard left. I mentally prepared myself for some rough treatment; I knew all about their brutal methods of interrogation and I did not relish the idea.

I walked to the window and surveyed the war-ravaged town. I had known Radeburg in more halcyon days and recollected cycling there when I was a lad. It held fond memories for me. While I was reminiscing a staff car pulled up. A few minutes later I saw the youth, flanked by two Russian officers, walking towards it. He appeared to be quite happy, and was chewing what looked like a bar of chocolate as he was ushered courteously into the car and driven away. I felt absolutely desolate. The fact that I had failed abysmally in my mission had not really sunk in until that moment. I was filled with bitterness and shame and would have taken my own life had I had the means to do so. Sitting down on a buckled filing cabinet, I slowly started to collect my thoughts. Uppermost in my mind was the key question; where were they taking the boy? I had the feeling that the Russians, having put two and two together had ascertained who he was, did not intend to harm him physically. I must have sat pensively for God knows how long, mulling over the various ways in which he could be of use to those Bolshevik bastards, until my attention was alerted to the sound of engines throbbing above. Looking out of the window I saw the sky darken as hundreds of bombers flew overhead. They were so low I could see at once that they were American Flying Fortresses, and I offered up a silent prayer for the poor Berliners. Then, unaccountably, they began to unload sticks of bombs on us. Absolute pandemonium broke loose, and I heard the clatter of soldiers' heavy boots running this way and that, as NCOs screamed out orders.

An ear-splitting explosion threw me across the room. I must have struck my head on something, for I lost consciousness for what could only have been a matter of seconds because, when I came to, the trickle of blood running down my forehead from a slight gash above my right eye was still warm. That aside, I was miraculously unhurt, although my hair was covered in fragments of plaster and my uniform was in tatters. As the dust and smoke cleared, I saw that the outside wall of my room had been completely blasted away. I was seized with excitement — it was a God-sent opportunity, and in the ensuing chaos I made my escape.

My conscience would not permit me to try to reach Berchtesgaden now, although I felt that fate had ordained that I should survive, and that one day the reason for this would become abundantly clear.

My immediate plan was to get picked up by the Americans, who were advancing in the west. It was essential that I get rid of my SS uniform and take on the identity of a Wehrmacht soldier. Sadly, the task of selecting an appropriate uniform was not difficult, as every ditch seemed to be strewn with our fallen comrades. I eventually turned over a body about my size and from that moment became Obergefreiter Hans Klausener of the 6th Panzer Division.

I managed to fall in with a group of limping, bloodied stragglers who accepted me without question as one of their number, and we surrendered to the Americans near Reisa on the 20th April. We were herded with about two or three hundred other prisoners, into a field, and later we were all marched to Leipzig. Here, the 1st US Battalion had converted an old army barracks into a POW camp. This was where I first became ill, and eventually found it necessary to see the American camp doctor — a Jew — who, while examining me, discovered my SS blood group tattoo. Soon after this I was interrogated by a de-nazification panel, and within days I was taken by Military Police escort to Dachau concentration camp. A place which once housed the vermin of the human race is now being used to imprison high-ranking members of the SS. Like most of my Kameraden here, I am waiting to appear before a war crimes tribunal.

I was sharing a cell with SS Sturmbannführer Ernst Schact before my condition deteriorated and they finally moved me to this filthy infirmary, where I am now completing this statement.

Schact and I would often talk long into the night about our feelings and objectives. He is young and strong, and will overcome his present ordeal, of that I feel certain. He is still passionately loyal to the cause, and it is to him that I shall finally entrust this statement.

Never forget that we, the Kameraden, are united by unbreakable bonds. So take heart and rekindle your courage, for all that I have so painstakingly written on these scraps of paper is unquestionably true. I have, with my own eyes, seen conclusive evidence offering proof beyond doubt that the youth, whom I had all too briefly in my care, is the rightful heir of Adolf Hitler.

I am thoroughly convinced that he still lives. I have thought of many reasons why the Russians should want to keep him alive. What, for example, could be more damning to our cause than to have the son of the Führer condemn all that his father stood for? By brainwashing this boy into embracing their evil doctrine, the Communists could achieve a victory that would make all their fleeting military conquests pale into insignificance. We must not allow this to happen. The boy must be found. Obtain his release at all costs, by whatever means are available. Make him aware that his destiny is to continue his father's great work in the furtherance of National Socialism.

The future of Germany depends on you, my Aryan brothers. We are the white light that will forever blaze a path to truth and glory. We are the sworn and avowed enemies of Marxism and International Zionism. We are the descendants of the mighty Teutonic Knights. Let us remember the words of the

Führer — 'The strongest are the best, and the best will survive.' This is nature's law. We are the strongest, we, the German people.

The Führer is dead. Long live the Führer. Long live the Reich.

Signed this 19th day of October, 1946.
SS Oberführer Johannes Bruckner.'

Hollerbach slowly replaced the statement in the envelope and, using it like a drumstick, tapped his knee thoughtfully. Yes, it was a fascinating document all right, but why had Prama shown it to him? He couldn't help wondering how he was to fit into all this, for he knew the banker well enough to know that he hadn't taken him to lunch just for the pleasure of his company. Still, he consoled himself with the thought that he would obviously get some, if not all, the answers at the party tonight — if ever he got there, that was.

The traffic had started to inch forward again, but at the present rate, he calculated, it would still take him the best part of an hour to reach Prama's home. So Hollerbach did what he always did when he felt totally thwarted and was powerless to control the circumstances — he closed his eyes and fell asleep . . .

6

Shears was feeling greatly fortified by the shower. This, combined with a couple of shots of Jack Daniels, had given him a sense of pleasurable anticipation and he felt like a child about to go on a picnic. Although the assignment was uppermost in his mind, there was nothing in the rule book that said he couldn't enjoy himself.

The telephone on his bedside table jangled, momentarily cutting through his thoughts. He picked it up.

'I bet you look beautiful!' the gruff voice at the other end said mockingly.

'Doug?' Shears queried.

'George,' came the reply.

'What can I do for you, George?'

'Listen, how long you gonna be, buddy?'

Shears glanced at his wristwatch. 'Oh, I guess about twenty minutes — okay?'

'Okay. We'll meet you downstairs in the Peacock Bar, 'n set you up a Jack Daniels, all right?'

'What are you into now, George — telepathy?' Shears said, looking at the glass in his hand.

'Pardon?'

'See you there in twenty minutes.' Shears replaced the receiver with an amused smile on his face. 'Nice guys,' he murmured under his breath as he tossed his bathrobe on the bed and began to get dressed. He'd first met the likeable duo of Douglas and George when he was introduced to them as a Mr Daniel Andrews . . .

*   *   *

'Daniel Andrews?' Shears raised an astonished eyebrow at McNabe.

'Yep, your cover name for this assignment. Here's your passport made out in that name,' McNabe said in a businesslike manner, tossing a bulky package across the desk at him. 'Also in there is your air ticket, first class, baggage labels, hotel arrangements etc. I've also included a string of notes on a memo covering all the points we've discussed. Learn it and burn it, as we 'pros' say.' He went on to tell Shears that he would shortly be returning to Dallas to take a crash course on the agricultural equipment manufactured by the giant Golden Thresher plant that was based there. The president of GT, or God's Town, as it was referred to by the many hundreds of local inhabitants it gave employment to, had been briefed only to the extent that an FBI agent would be joining them undercover to investigate certain aspects of industrial espionage. To everyone else at the company he was just a new addition to the sales force.

'You'd better learn fast, boy, you've got about ten days to cram in a six months' course before you fly to Nuremberg — but I've every confidence in you.'

'Thanks.' Shears said glumly. Then suddenly he began to perk up. The visit to Dallas, however brief, would give him a heaven-sent opportunity to look up old friends he'd not seen in years. McNabe, as he did so often, seemed to read his thoughts. Shears had always felt he would have made a great psychiatrist.

'And no trips down memory lane for you, old pal — understand?' McNabe glared at him. 'Nobody at GT knows you're a local boy who's made bad.'

McNabe saw the look of disappointment that must have registered on his face.

'Look, if anyone recognises you, it could blow everything. So stay in the rented apartment we've taken for you near head office, and maintain a low profile at all times — you hear?'

'I hear you, Boss!'

★ ★ ★

The president of GT, a benign but tough-looking cookie, had introduced him to Douglas and George as the third and privileged member of the team to represent the company in Nuremberg.

'He'll ask all the questions,' the president said. 'You ask him nothing — but teach him all you can.'

Douglas and George had set about their task with vigour, and he was plied with pamphlets and literature expounding the unparalleled virtues and quality of the equipment manufactured by the company. These he boned up on at night; confined to barracks, as it were, he had little else to do. Douglas and George also gave him some tips on sales pitch technique and general company policy in regard to overseas business. He'd grown to like the two men, and when the course was completed he told them, with some truth, that he'd really enjoyed it. The arrangements were for Douglas and George to arrive at Nuremberg two days earlier than him, while he reported back to Langley for a final briefing from McNabe. This would also allow him a little time with Shirley and the kids. All had been smooth sailing until he got that wretched phone call.

He had packed in readiness for his flight to Germany, and early that evening Shirley had seductively suggested that she had a more interesting way of inducing sleep than watching TV! A couple of hours later the phone bell, sounding in his deep repose like a four-minute warning system, crashed into his consciousness.

Shirley reached drowsily over and picked up the receiver. 'What did you say?' She listened in silence for a moment before letting rip. 'For God's sake, he has a plane to catch in the morning. Isn't there another doctor on call?'

'What is it, honey?' Shears mumbled with his eyes still only half open.

Shirley covered the mouthpiece with her hand. 'It seems that one of the guards at the Company has gone berserk, shooting the place up.'

Shears sprang awake immediately, and almost snatched the telephone from Shirley. It was Rawlings at the other end, sergeant-at-arms in charge of the main guardroom. Shears listened while he explained the situation. As he spoke, Shears held the receiver between his ear and his shoulder and awkwardly started to get dressed.

'I'll be there in ten minutes. Just keep everyone away. Whatever you do, don't force him to panic any more than he has already — okay?'

For the rest of that night, almost until departure time, Shears had nearly talked himself hoarse. A young soldier on picket duty at HQ had suddenly run amok, firing an automatic rifle at all and sundry and creating general terror and chaos among those still working late in the building. Luckily few people were there at the time, mostly cleaning staff and security officers. Only one woman had been injured and not too seriously at that. When Shears arrived, the young soldier had locked himself in a mens' toilet and was hysterically threatening to blow his brains out. Shears went into an adjacent toilet and sympathetically started to talk to him. For many hours there had virtually been no response from him, then slowly he began to communicate and Shears knew he was at last getting through. He finally convinced the desperate youth, for he was little more than that, that no woman was worth committing suicide for, and the kid eventually slid his gun under the partition and gave himself up.

Shirley had met up with him in the departure lounge at Dulles airport with his valise, and for the best part of the plane journey he'd managed to catch up on at least some of his lost night's sleep.

7

Shears ambled into the Peacock Bar, so called, he guessed, because of the stuffed bird of that species perched prominently at the entrance, and the interior decor, which was a Teutonic attempt at High Arabian. The place was crowded, and the sounds of a German pop group emanating from a juke box were just about rising above the competition of a dozen different audible conversations held in an assortment of languages. As he was making his way closer to the bar, he heard a reedy American voice shouting through the clamour.

'Over here, Dan.' Shears swung round and at a shadowy corner table he could just make out Douglas and George. Doug was beckoning him over. They were both wearing dark blue lounge suits and friendly white smiles. Squeezing himself towards the seat that had evidently been defensively reserved for him, judging by the two briefcases and a rolled umbrella that rested upon it, Shears waited while they removed the items, before planting himself firmly down. Lined up in front of him were three large glasses of Bourbon. Spotting his look of surprise, George raised his glass.

'We're into the third round — saw no reason why you shouldn't catch up.'

'Very good,' Shears said pleasantly, if a trifle hesitantly. He knew full well that there was no way he'd be drinking that lot. He had to be very alert tonight and that meant staying sober.

After some 'chat' about his flight over to Frankfurt, Shears told them about his hair-raising car journey from the airport to their hotel in Nuremberg.

'I think the guy must have been a wheels man for a hold-up gang, and it was my luck to have him on his day off,' he said, wincing at the memory.

'Well, you just wait and see the chauffeur we've got tonight,' Doug chortled. 'He's a dead ringer for Erich von Stroheim — no kidding!'

And by Christ he wasn't, Shears thought, when he was finally confronted by the man with his immaculate grey uniform and his hairless bull-neck thrusting its way upwards into a tight fitting peaked cap. All that was missing were the leather riding boots — and, of course, Gloria Swanson. But at least he was a good driver.

Douglas and George were in great form, swapping gags like a couple of night club comics, and although they were travelling through teeming rain, Shears enjoyed every minute of the half hour it took to reach their destination.

As the limousine glided noiselessly up the broad, winding driveway, Shears peered out of the window and casually observed some of the guests who were arriving just ahead of them. Glistening car doors were opening, and in the muted light that shone from the porch they looked to Shears like the fins of prowling sharks. Simultaneously women in colourful evening dresses began stepping out, some lifting coats, scarves and even handbags over their coiffeured hair-dos, in a vain attempt to shield them from the wind-blown rain. In complete contrast, their male escorts sauntered behind, almost leisurely, as if to show that the elements held no threat for them.

'What's the hold-up here?' George light-heartedly asked the chauffeur. Shears noted that even his voice was not unlike that of Erich von Stroheim, as he replied that he could get the car no nearer to the entrance for the moment.

'I think, perhaps, it would be better for you to get out here, gentlemen,' he said, and as if to emphasise his point, he turned off the engine and sprang from behind the wheel to open the door for Shears and his companions.

'I understand some refreshments are being given to the chauffeurs in the servants' annexe, and I will be there, or back in the car, should you need me.' He gave the smallest hint of a bow.

'Okay. Very good,' said George, obviously enjoying this unaccustomed treatment.

Four curved marble steps led to the open front door and the inviting warmth of a high, oak panelled hallway. Shears had just taken a pace or two inside when he was suddenly encircled by flunkies wearing black trousers, red waistcoats and wing-collared shirts with stiff white bow ties. One removed his topcoat, while another handed him a numbered plastic disc, before they moved on to Douglas and George to repeat the process. Hovering in the foreground just ahead of them, Shears picked out an impeccably dressed man in his early sixties. Even if Shears had not seen a photograph of him, he would have known at once that this silver-haired, portly figure, smiling at all those arriving, was none other than mine host, Wilhelm Prama. There was a presence about him that even Shears could sense from where he stood. His whole demeanour was one of a man used to giving orders and being obeyed without question.

Power seemed simply to exude from him. He turned, and for a split second his eyes met those of Shears. Despite the thick lenses of his gold-framed spectacles, those hard blue eyes almost made Shears' blood run cold; they reflected an indefinable malevolence. Then Prama's gaze darted to Douglas and George as he came towards them, flabby hand extended.

'I am Wilhelm Prama,' he announced genially, shaking hands with each in turn. 'I have the honour to be your host this evening. I am delighted to meet you — delighted.'

After the formal introductions had been effected, Prama snapped his fingers at a nearby waiter who was expertly balancing a tray full of bubbling champagne glasses on one hand. Prama reached over and handed a tulip-shaped glass, first to Shears, then to his two colleagues, telling them as he did so that it was his own favourite vintage, Bollinger '74. Clearing his throat, he began a short welcoming address. He said how privileged he felt that the Americans had travelled such a long distance to be present at their special celebration. A faint patter of applause came from around the room as Prama concluded his speech. The loudest clapping, Shears noted, came from a small gathering of men, all of whom seemed to be wearing thick, ill-fitting suits. In the middle of this group, looking a few years older and quite a bit fatter than the photographs he had been shown of him, was Nikolai Kotchnov.

* * *

Waves of laughter, the clinking of glasses and a buzz of animated conversation, often completely drowning the pianist's frozen-smiled efforts to provide sophisticated background music, provided happy confirmation for Prama that the party was going well. The catering company staff were superbly professional, circulating among the guests constantly, with a seemingly endless variety of tasty titbits ranging from caviare and frogs' legs to more substantial savouries like hot suckling pig, roast pheasant, and just about every type of traditional German sausage. The champagne flowed like a sparkling spring, and corks popped with the frequency of cartridges being fired by a bunch of gun-happy novices at a duck shoot, explosively punctuating the convivial hubbub. Prama strutted around like the prize turkey cock, mingling with each group for an exact and precise amount of time. A stopwatch could have been used on him, and the period he allocated for each one of these little cliques would have varied by no more than a few seconds.

Wolfgang Hollerbach entered the hall, vigorously shaking his sodden trilby and shedding what was, when dry, a light fawn raincoat, now darkened by the quantity of water it had absorbed. Prama, who had been anxiously awaiting his arrival, watched as Dietz removed the dripping garment. Politely disengaging himself from a talkative industrialist and his gay companion, Prama put down his glass on a nearby table and with a broad smile walked over to greet him.

'I was wondering if you'd manage to make it,' he said as he shook his hand warmly. Hollerbach regarded Prama sombrely as he released his grip.

'That makes two of us.' With a wry grin, he inclined his head in the direction of the front door. 'Tell me, have you ever seen a June day like it?'

'No,' Prama agreed, the smile still on his face. 'But mostly everyone is here and they all seem to be having a good time — so to hell with the weather, eh?'

'To hell with the weather,' Hollerbach echoed loudly. 'Where's my drink?'

Prama signalled to a waiter who was skillfully manoeuvering his large tray of drinks between furniture and clusters of people. Recognising the host, he immediately spun on his heel and came over. Hollerbach glanced at the tray of champagne, proudly displayed before him, and disdainfully turned up his nose.

'Haven't you got anything stronger?' he scowled at Prama. 'I can't stand this stuff — okay for women, maybe.'

'Bring a bottle of schnapps and some glasses,' Prama ordered briskly, 'and ask one of the waitresses to bring some hot food — chicken, sausages, something like that. We'll be in the upstairs drawing room.'

Without waiting for the waiter to acknowledge the command, Prama placed his arm around Hollerbach's shoulder and guided him towards the stairs. A group of people who were mingling there made a respectful pathway for them. Prama nodded courteously before leading his friend up the wide staircase to the first floor.

* * *

Shears, having partaken liberally of the succulent fare forever being thrust beneath his nostrils by a succession of uniformed waiters, had decided to switch drinks. When Bollinger '74 was flowing like a tap with a faulty washer, Jack Daniels somehow seemed

121

to lose all its magic. Already he had established a comfortable rapport with the Russians, and had had plenty of opportunity to slide some oblique questions to Kotchnov. Shears considered him to be a most amiable and relaxed individual who didn't appear — outwardly at least — to be at all edgy or nervous over his impending defection.

Kotchnov raised his glass of champagne and proposed a toast.

'Here's to our friendly co-operation, to our good business relations and to the success of the T19 tractor.'

'I'll drink to that,' Douglas guffawed, and clinked his glass against Kotchnov's.

'Tell me,' asked Maganovitch, a member of the trade delegation who seemed hell-bent on aiming his questions directly at the man who knew least about the product, 'do you anticipate many teething problems? For example, the extraction of the hydrogen to supply the energy?'

'Well . . . ' Shears hesitated.

'Absolutely none, sir,' said George, hastily taking over from Shears. 'We have virtually perfected the fusion process and have successfully extracted the reacting plasma gas. All the trials we have conducted on the T19 have gone without any serious hitches, and you know what?' The Russians listened with an air of wondrous expectation on their faces. 'It has made every other standard type of tractor seem as out of date as a horse-drawn plough.'

The Russians nodded sagaciously.

Shears felt that he'd better justify his presence by divulging the one piece of knowledge he had fully memorised about the T19.

'What is so impressive, aside from the new fuel aspect, is the silicon chip remote control panel,' he said smugly, almost as though it had been his own invention.

'We have had that on our standard models for over two years,' a burly Russian delegate boomed in a baritone voice, deflating Shears at once.

'Ah, but perhaps not quite in the . . . er . . . way that, er . . . we have installed it,' Shears responded, lamely trying to pick up the brick he had dropped.

'Well, one thing's for sure,' George said cockily, 'you ain't managed to run 'em on water yet!' He winked, and that seemed to do the trick. Everyone in the group laughed loudly.

The shop talk between the Golden Thresher team and the Russian delegates continued, with the conversation inevitably turning to which country had made the greatest contribution towards modern technology — the 'anything you can do, we can do better' adage. It was at this juncture that Shears disengaged his mind from what was becoming a dreary dichotomy, and began to focus his thoughts with microscopic sharpness on the other guests at this oddly mixed gathering. Like an enthusiastic lepidopterist with a collection of rare butterflies, he started to mentally pin them to cards and label them. Not unnaturally his attention was first drawn to the female of the species. As he eyed the many beautiful women, he was able to pick out with consummate ease the hookers who mingled amongst them. To the layman they were not distinguishable by the way they looked, although it could be argued that some were over made-up or under-dressed, or both. It was more the manner in which they behaved towards their male escorts, hanging on to their every word and greatly over-acting with animated responses — massage the male ego and loosen the wallet, was the stock-in-trade of these high class whores, and they all appeared experts at it. Shears found it most entertaining watching these ladies at work, but decided it was about time he got down to the real business of his mission — to observe and study the men who were there, and in particular the ageing emissaries of the 'master race'. Although the years had sculptured and formed each man differently, collectively they shared a definable presence, and Shears found no difficulty in picking them out either. True there was a certain uniformity that was mirrored in the well-cut suits they wore, but he was conscious of the fact that it went far deeper, and was a lot more sinister than that. They had all retained that same arrogance, that air of superiority, masked by a thin veneer of charm and a clipped politeness, which stopped just short of operetta heel-clicking.

Hovering in the shadow of this old guard were a number of young men. They were the very epitomy of the tall, fair, blue-eyed Aryan race, as depicted in the hysterical rantings of Hitler. The irony of Hitler's mad dream, of Germany being governed by these Nordic god-types, had always puzzled Shears, for the gang of thugs who sycophantically surrounded him didn't remotely resemble the image he so fanatically tried to project. There was Goebbels, the crippled dwarf; Goering, the grossly obese drug addict; the mild-mannered, bespectacled Himmler; and the squat, short, bull-necked Bormann; and reigning supreme over this court of assorted misfits the mighty Führer himself, with his Chaplinesque moustache, and pallid, pudgy features, over which hung a hank of slicked down, brown hair, and who stood at just five feet, eight and a half inches. A motley bunch, if ever there was one, thought Shears. Yet the power they had wielded had been terrifying, as their roaring ocean of steel raced across and crushed most of Europe for nearly five horrendous years.

Watching them as he did now, Shears had the spine-crawling sensation that these men, the youthful and the avuncular, still reflected that brand of iron-fisted fanaticism that had been so solidly drummed into their very being. McNabe's words came flooding back to him, and he knew that the old bear was right. If these people, and thousands of others like them, were not checked, and decisively so, at this stage, they could once again emerge as that near invincible, conquering army of evil extremists who once so nearly ruled the world.

A shiver ran through Shears, and he was overwhelmingly gripped by a feeling that Nazism had never died — it had merely been hibernating.

8

Hollerbach was aware that Prama had been fidgeting anxiously, and was now running his finger around the rim of his glass, while he waited for him to finish eating. Barely suppressing a burp, he placed his plate, with the remains of a heartily consumed meal, on the table in front of him.

'Excellent,' Hollerbach said, nodding towards the discarded plate. He eyed Prama steadily for a moment, before withdrawing an envelope from his inside jacket pocket. 'Fascinating. I've read it many times,' he said, handing it over to Prama.

'Well?'

'I decided to do some research on the subject matter,' Hollerbach began rummaging through his pockets, until he produced a small notebook, 'and I came up with some rather interesting information.'

'Oh, yes?'

'Naturally I've read and heard a lot of rumours about it before, but nevertheless I believe, in view of your obvious interest, that this is worth listening to if you can bear with me for a while.'

'Of course.'

'Well, there are many people who have claimed to be, or at least know of people who have professed to be, Hitler's offspring.'

Prama smiled enigmatically. It was an expression totally missed by Hollerbach, who by this time had his chin tucked well into his chest and his eyes lowered over the notebook he was busily thumbing through.

'A lot of these claimants, of course, are lacking in credibility and some are quite obviously off their rocker, but others . . . well, for example, here's a United Press report published in the New York Times dated 11th June, 1945: 'Supreme Headquarters said today that it had no comment to make on an unconfirmed report issued in London that Allied officials in Germany were hunting two children, a boy aged seven and a girl of five, said to be the offspring of Adolf Hitler and Eva Braun.' Hollerbach raised a pair of fat caterpillar eyebrows anticipating a comment from Prama, but none was forthcoming, and he quickly referred back to his notes.

'Well, this communiqué sparked off a great deal of activity, and stories about these children were rife throughout Europe. It was widely believed by observers of the time that

Hitler's son was born to Eva in a San Remo hotel in Italy during the night of January 1st, 1938.'

Hollerbach paused for a moment and lit up a cigarette. 'The proprietor, who incidently is still alive, says he clearly remembers the occasion and I quote: 'There was a good deal of drinking and celebrating among Hitler's entourage that evening. Although I wasn't informed as to who the father of the child was, I assumed it must have been someone very important as I was warned to forget the whole incident.' In fact, the birth might well have remained a closely guarded secret, but in January 1939 a top official at the Reich Chancellory was arrested and summarily executed for indiscreetly proposing a toast to the Führer's firstborn on the infant's first birthday.'

Prama nodded thoughtfully and placed an ashtray in front of Hollerbach.

'There is a final follow-up to that report,' Hollerbach said, glancing again at his notebook. 'In 1945 a French Intelligence source stated that the children were flown to a German naval base in Norway and from there they were evacuated by U-boat to an unknown destination.'

Hollerbach lifted his glass of schnapps and drained it, still expecting a remark from

Prama, but the banker maintained his air of gracious silence.

'Now there is another account totally contradicting that one,' Hollerbach continued. 'It stated that the boy — no reference to a girl this time — was given to Eva's sister, Gretl. Soon afterwards Gretl married one of our Kameraden, Gruppenführer Hermann Fegelein. Now it seemed that whilst the Führer had no doubts that Gretl could keep the secret, he was equally positive that Fegelein, whom he didn't like at all, could not. The opportunity to take care of that situation occurred during the last days of the war when Fegelein left the bunker without the Führer's permission. He was tracked down, brought back to the bunker and shot. Many believed that the execution order by the Führer personally was to protect the secret of his son.' He slid Prama a sideways glance to ensure that he still had his undivided attention, before continuing enthusiastically.

'There are other claims that warrant closer scrutiny, like the one made by Gisela Heuser. Her mother, if you remember, was Tilly Fleischer, the Olympic javelin gold medallist in 1936, and it was common knowledge at the time that she had a bit of a thing going with the Führer. Anyway, Gisela wrote a series of articles about the relationship in the Italian magazine *Oggi*. In it she stated that certain classified Reichssicherheitshauptamt papers, now allegedly in the American Documents Center at Alexandria, Virginia, present positive proof that she is the daughter of Adolf Hitler. I know that the fact that she is a woman might not particularly arouse your interest, but it does add weight to the belief that the Führer, far from being impotent, sired at least one, if not more, children.'

'Quite,' Prama said a little sharply.

Noticing the banker's change of mood, Hollerbach flicked quickly through the notebook. 'I've just one more.' He looked up at Prama. 'It's worth listening to, believe me.'

'Very well,' smiled Prama, patronisingly.

'This is quite a recent claim, made in October 1977, and, for me at any rate, it's the most convincing. Mainly because Dr Werner Masser, the historian and biographer, gave the story his backing. It was made by a Frenchman called Jean Marie Loret who was born in March 1918 in the village of Seboncourt. His mother was a French girl called Charlotte Eudoxie Alida Lobjoie, who was born in 1898. Hitler, it is said, met her while he was stationed at the village of Wavrin during the First World War. She had an affair with the Führer, who was then a corporal, had a child, and later married the man who, Loret believed, was his real father. It was only in 1948, three years before she died, that Loret's mother told him that he was the illegitimate son of Adolf Hitler. Dr Masser stated that he has masses of evidence to support Loret's claims, including blood tests that could prove that he was Hitler's son.'

'Could prove?' Prama repeated the words pointedly.

'Well, yes. In the cases I've mentioned, and in the dozens of others that I haven't, they are all based on circumstantial evidence. There is no positive proof about any of them.'

Prama was grinning broadly.

'Have I said something funny?' Hollerbach looked almost piqued, as he forcibly stubbed out what remained of his cigarette.

'Would it surprise you to learn that most of those stories you have so painstakingly researched have been fuelled and fired by us? If you had come to me first, I could have saved you a lot of legwork and quite a bit of eye strain. I know what it's like using those microfilm machines.'

Hollerbach inhaled deeply on a freshly lit cigarette. 'Fuelled and fired by us? Who the hell is us?'

'The inner council of the Chain,' Prama

breathed dramatically.

'For God's sake, why?'

Prama walked to a chesterfield and sat down. Facing Hollerbach over the massive onyx coffee table, he clasped his hands together like a preacher about to lead his congregation in prayer.

'It's imperative that everyone, and in particular the Russians, believe that our organisation is merely grasping at straws. You see, while these absurd tales continue to circulate, the Russians will remain blissfully unaware that we do not have the real facts.' Hollerbach cocked his head to one side, like a puzzled spaniel. Leaning forward, Prama dropped his voice to little more than a whisper.

'The Führer did have a child, only one, a boy. He was captured by the Russians in 1945.' The two strips of fur on Hollerbach's eyebrows shot up again.

'You're not referring to the one in Bruckner's so-called statement are you?' he asked, somewhat scornfully.

'I am.'

'Look, Willi, I don't wish to pour cold water on the authenticity of that document, but . . . well . . . in my view that evidence is no more conclusive than all the others I've mentioned — unless of course Bruckner is still alive?'

Prama shook his head. 'No, I am afraid he died shortly after completing that statement in Dachau infirmary. Stomach cancer, I believe.'

'Mmm — pity.'

'Well, at least he didn't have to suffer the humiliation of standing trial to justify what he did as a serving soldier under orders. Unlike so many of us who had to go through that grotesque farce.' Prama spat out the words bitterly.

Hollerbach stared at Prama thoughtfully, while he crushed his cigarette into the crystal ashtray.

'Well, you've obviously got something else to go on, apart from that photostatted document.'

Prama cleared his throat and smiled.

'Haven't you forgotten Bruckner's cell mate who smuggled it out?'

'Er . . . this Ernst Schact, you mean?'

'I do.'

Hollerbach's eyes lit up. 'Yes, I had given him some thought — he could have faked the whole thing!'

'For what reason?'

'Money, of course. Would have made a good news story if he'd sold it,' Hollerbach laughed. 'Might have paid a few thousand marks for it myself.'

'But he didn't sell it, did he?' Prama said coldly. 'But to save you any more wild speculation, I'll tell you exactly what he did with it. When he was finally released he took it straight to the headquarters of the Chain, which at that time, if you recall, was in Munich.'

'Well, there you are then, as I said, the man was after money. He knew the Chain was bound to reward him handsomely for conveying information like that.' Hollerbach shook his head. 'No — the whole thing smells highly suspicious to me.'

He paused just long enough to light another cigarette before adding sarcastically, 'I don't suppose this Schact is still around to retell his tale?'

Prama flipped open the lid of a silver cigar box on the table and selected a Monte Cristo. Hollerbach watched him as he expertly clipped off the tip with his gold cutter.

'Yes, this . . . er . . . Schact is still around — very much so,' he said quietly.

'Huh! I'll tell you what, Willi,' Hollerbach smiled. 'If I had the chance to question him, I bet I could blow a few holes in his story.'

'Go ahead,' Prama challenged, leaning back and puffing luxuriously on his cigar.

Hollerbach regarded him suspiciously.

'When?'

'Why not now — you're looking at him.'

Had Hollerbach's cigarette not been glued to his lower lip it would have fallen from his mouth as his jaw dropped in amazement.

'You're . . . Sch . . . Schact?' he stammered.

'I am,' Prama asserted. 'And I can tell you that every word in that statement is true. I got to know Bruckner very well in the time we were together. So you see, Wolf, it was my duty and privilege to deliver the information. There was no question of any gain. True, the principals behind the new movement did help me find a job, but I was treated no differently than any other loyal Kamerad who needed their help, then or now for that matter.'

'Was the evidence in the statement ever followed up?' Hollerbach asked with greatly renewed interest.

'By God, was it!' Prama said fiercely. 'Exhaustive enquiries were conducted through our many and increasing number of contacts in East Germany and the Soviet Union, and the Chain let it be known that any clue as to his whereabouts would be handsomely rewarded. But absolutely no trace of the boy could be found. After all, one fourteen-year-old looks very much like another.'

'Did it ever occur to you that they might have killed him?'

'Yes — but it would have been far more advantageous for them to keep him alive. An ace card up their sleeve, you might say.'

'What the blazes for?'

'Oh, come on now, Wolf,' Prama began to show his impatience. 'Amongst our number we had some pretty brilliant scientists, and the Russians were well aware of the great advances we had made in aerospace engineering. We knew they were anxious to get their hands on the formulae for certain chemical weaponry we had been experimenting with, and we could have done a deal with them on an exchange basis.'

'I see, yes, stupid of me,' Hollerbach mumbled sheepishly. A half inch of ash dropped from the end of his cigarette, and tumbled messily down the front of his lapel.

'But to this day we have never been approached.' Prama moved the ashtray pointedly in front of him.

'Perhaps the boy was killed during the fighting or a bombing raid?'

'Yes, we had also considered those possibilities. In fact, it wasn't until the Russians released their first batch of prisoners that we received positive proof of the boy's survival. A member reported to the Chain that while he was at the camp he heard that the Russians were holding a very important prisoner, and rumour had it that the prisoner had been very closely connected to the Führer. He assumed that he must have been a high-ranking officer. One day, while coming off a working party, however, he was surprised to see some guards from the special compound playing football with a young boy. Later, he was even more surprised to learn that the boy was the VIP prisoner referred to. He had managed to get a look at him, and from his description it fitted that of our boy exactly.'

Hollerbach let out a low whistle.

'That was well over thirty-five years ago. Since then the Chain has methodically followed up every snippet of information and rumour that has filtered through. He had been identified in such and such province, working as an architect; he had become a dentist in an obscure Russian village. The rumours were always different and some were highly inventive.' Prama let out a roar of laughter. 'Like the report we received that he had become an acrobat and was now a clown with the Moscow State Circus!'

Prama topped up their glasses and lounged back into the embracing leather of the chesterfield.

'As you know, Wolf, over the years our organisation has progressed from strength to strength, but what we lack, and have lacked since the death of the Führer, is a new charismatic leader. We conduct ourselves virtually by committee these days, and it's not a satisfactory arrangement. I'm telling you now because I believe this could all change.' Prama paused for effect. 'It looks as if our dogged persistence has finally paid off — we are sure that we have traced the Führer's son at last.'

For more than fifteen minutes Hollerbach sat in almost immovable silence, as Prama recounted the story that led up to this discovery.

⋆　⋆　⋆

A trusted and loyal member of the Chain had, for many years, been serving as a translator at the West German Embassy in Moscow. During most of that time he had been passing back bits of information, mainly concerned with the latest techniques and developments being made by Russian scientists in the field of electronics and industry — nothing of great military importance, but nevertheless of considerable commercial value to the Chain. The translator's contacts were well spread out and came from a variety of sources. The Chain always paid generously for what they received, and this ensured that there was a constant flow of fresh information. One of the translator's regular informants was an agricultural official named Nikolai Kotchnov, an expert on the production of grain. The grain yield had always held a place of special importance in the Soviet Union as they needed to produce a minimum of 260 million tons a year. Kotchnov had so improved the output of grain in his area, that in 1979 he had been awarded a state prize for outstanding achievement. This had given him many concessions not usually granted to those working in other forms of agronomics, and he had been allowed to travel freely throughout the USSR giving lectures to rural farming communities on the latest methods of cultivation. He had progressed steadily to the top of the pecking order, and at one time had even been considered as a candidate for the Supreme Soviet, narrowly losing the vote to an older, and more politically motivated, colleague. He had also been granted special dispensation to attend various study courses in the West, and was a frequent visitor to Northern Scandinavia, where the soil and weather conditions closely resembled those to be found in his own province.

In time he began to acquire an insatiable appetite for the Western way of life. It represented to him all the things that were unattainable and unavailable in Russia, and he loved most of them from good food to bad women. With the state only providing the minimum of expenses, he soon got into debt. The translator heard on the grapevine about Kotchnov's high life, and past experience had taught him that someone in his position might — if he were not already on the take — be open to a few suggestions as to how he might improve his sagging bank balance. A 'chance' meeting was arranged, and very soon a friendship was struck. The translator's suggestions came like manna from heaven to Kotchnov, especially as all that he was required to find out initially was little more than could be gleaned from reading the pages of *Pravda*. But once the Chain had him hooked on the easy money, they began to apply pressure through the translator to get Kotchnov to take bolder risks. Soon he was obtaining highly sought-after information about the latest experiments that Russian botanists were conducting in their laboratories. This data was put to immediate use by the considerable number of the Kameraden who had chosen a career in farming, particularly those who had built their ranches on the wild and hostile plains of South America.

This arrangement between Kotchnov and the translator continued amicably until just a few months ago, when Kotchnov turned up at their prearranged venue in a state of near panic. It appeared that the KGB had raided the department where he worked, and had confiscated all the books pending an investigation into suspected fraud. That same day, two men who held responsible posts in the administrative section asked to speak to Kotchnov privately. He knew them only as working colleagues and he wasn't particularly fond of either of them. Their names were Vladimir Sokol and Garnik Tremski, and it was Tremski who elected to act as their spokesman. He said that for some time now they had become very suspicious of Kotchnov's extravagances, his expensive suits, his visits to fine restaurants, his many girlfriends. Although they knew he was well paid by Soviet standards, the salary he received would certainly not have been enough to maintain such a high life style. Tremski said that in view of this he had decided to carry out a little private detective work on Kotchnov, and had often tailed him to various venues where he had observed his activities. He added that on several occasions he had seen him meet up with a man he later identified as being one of the personnel at the West German Embassy.

He had even taken photographs of them talking furtively to each other. As Tremski so menacingly put it, he and Sokol might well end up mining salt in Siberia, but Kotchnov would just as assuredly be placed against a wall and shot. Then, quietly and sinisterly, he outlined his proposition.

Apparently, unbeknown to Kotchnov, Tremski and Sokol had been double invoicing certain items of agricultural equipment that had been supplied to some of the black African nations and pocketing a substantial sum in foreign currency, negotiable bonds and cheques. They now, as a matter of great urgency, needed to enlist his aid before they were arrested and charged with serious crimes against the state. Tremski threatened that if Kotchnov did not help them, he would feel obliged to pass the dossier he had compiled on him over to the appropriate authorities. Kotchnov could not be sure whether the devious Tremski was bluffing or not, but felt he was in no position to call it. Then Tremski dropped his bombshell. He said that Vladimir Sokol's real name was Alois Hitler, and that he was the illegitimate son and heir of Adolf Hitler, who, at the age of fourteen, had been captured by the Russians near the town of Radeburg, whilst being taken to meet his father for the first time. Kotchnov's immediate reaction to this statement was that Tremski had cracked under the strain. But Tremski stressed most convincingly that irrefutable documentary evidence to support this claim was being held at the Central State Military Archives in Moscow. It was essential, he said, for Kotchnov to obtain that file on Sokol and see that his contact at the West German Embassy placed it in the hands of Nazi sympathisers. He was supremely confident that once these pro-Nazis, some of whom held powerful positions in West Germany, were convinced of Sokol's true identity, they would move heaven and earth to organise an escape plan for him. Tremski hinted that due to the nature of their close friendship, Sokol would not consider going alone, and that arrangements should be made for both of them to defect together.

Sokol was noticeably reticent about the value Tremski had placed on his birthright. For most of his life he had kept the secret of his parentage to himself, and he was beginning to rue the night when, while in his cups, he had confessed everything to Tremski about his past. Tremski, being the opportunist that he was, had seized on the idea of using Sokol's background as a means of escape, now that the KGB were breathing heavily down their necks. He had persuaded Sokol that their only salvation, and indeed only chance of remaining free together, was to get his amazing story heard in the right quarters. Kotchnov promised that he would do everything that he possibly could to help them, and he meant it, too. A frightened man moves fast, and Kotchnov moved like one possessed. Within hours of leaving Tremski and Sokol, he had met up with the translator and related the whole incident to him. The translator could barely conceal his excitement, and asked Kotchnov to repeat what Tremski had told him again, while he took notes, constantly questioning him as he went along. When he was satisfied that Kotchnov had remembered every detail, he emphasised how correct Tremski had been in his thinking, and that the key to any future move now lay in Kotchnov's ability to acquire these vital documents. Kotchnov was totally unprepared for this kind of response, and explained the difficulties and risks that would be involved. The translator insisted that no expense or effort should be spared on Kotchnov's behalf in obtaining them. He added that if all went well, Kotchnov would be most substantially rewarded for his endeavours and the opportunity to defect to the West himself would always be available if he should, at any time, feel it was necessary to make a hasty exit.

Kotchnov needed no further prompting, and using his not inconsiderable influence he gained admission to the top secret wing of the CSMA situated in Baumanskaya, Moscow. Here he bribed an acquaintance, who was working in a position of some authority, and was allowed unobtrusively to peruse classified wartime papers filed away in the maze of cavernous vaults that lay beneath the ground. It took several days of exhaustive research before he finally unearthed the original birth certificate along with some NKVD inter-departmental memos on the subject, and some correspondence in German which he did not understand. When he was fully satisfied that this was all of the prized evidence he had been instructed to procure, he placed them in several pockets of his suit, and, with his heart pounding in his ears, he brazenly strolled out of the building.

★   ★   ★

Prama scratched an adhering fragment of tobacco leaf from his tongue with a glossy, manicured fingernail. The effort of talking non-stop for such a sustained period of time had caused small droplets of sweat to appear beneath his nose and in the folds of skin above his collar. He dabbed them away with a snowy white handkerchief.

'Nikolai Kotchnov is one of my honoured guests this evening,' he said, with a glint of satisfaction in his eye. 'You will meet him later on, after we have completed our transaction.'

Hollerbach shifted uneasily in his chair. He sensed that Prama was at last coming to the point of his involvement in the affair, and for some reason he was not at all happy about the prospect.

'By transaction, I assume you mean that you will be purchasing the documents Kotchnov has acquired — correct?'

'Correct,' Prama replied.

'May I ask how much he is to receive for them?'

'One million marks.'

'Fucking hell!' Hollerbach gasped. 'That's a lot of money.'

Prama's eyes rolled upwards as he tutted his impatience. 'Not when you consider the vital importance these documents hold for us. The absolute proof that Hitler did have a son; and that he is still alive. Haven't you been able to grasp the significance of that yet?'

'Yes, of course!' Hollerbach said a trifle sharply. He was beginning to get annoyed by the way Prama was talking down to him, and decided to be more forthright in his own attitude.

'All right, Willi, stop beating about the bush. What is it you need me for?'

Prama smiled patronisingly. 'We would want you to go to Moscow and run a check on Vladimir Sokol. We would want to know before we lifted a finger if he is indeed the same person referred to in the statement.'

'Me? To Moscow?' Hollerbach exclaimed weakly. 'Why me?'

'Why you?' Prama could barely control his anger. 'Because you are an investigative journalist. Because you speak fluent Russian. Because you work for a highly respected newspaper. Because you can get to most places in the Soviet Union without arousing too much suspicion. Because you are a member of the Kameraden, and because you took an oath of allegiance that bound you for life. Let me remind you how that went.' Prama thrust his chin out proudly. 'I swear to thee, Adolf Hitler, loyalty and bravery. I vow to thee, and the superiors of your choosing, obedience unto death. So help me God.'

Hollerbach shook his head sadly. 'That was a long time ago. I was no more than a kid then, and the world's changed a hell of a lot since those days of glory.'

Prama was finding it extremely difficult to keep his temper, but keep it he did.

'So the world's changed a lot since then, has it?' he said acidly. 'International Zionism and Communism are more powerful than ever before. It's still the Jews who control commerce and industry in the free world, and those Bolshevik bastards at the Kremlin won't appease their voracious appetites until their missiles, tanks and guns are sited on every square inch of our land, and they turn us all into Marxist puppets. What, my complacent friend, has changed?' Prama's voice was choked with emotion. 'I say this to you, Wolf, only a force as powerful as a reborn and reunified Germany, a great and glorious Fourth Reich, honouring the concept and ideology of the Führer, can save the world from the evil that threatens to engulf it.'

Hollerbach was silent for a small eternity. He had already resigned himself to the fact that he would have to comply with Prama's wishes. He suspected what had happened to those of the Kameraden who had not bent to the will of the Inner Council, and had been regarded as traitors — there had been more than a few unsolved murder cases of former SS men who had been found dead in mysterious circumstances. True, in some instances, they had quite obviously been the victims of fanatical Zionist terrorist groups seeking revenge, but that only accounted for some of them. His theory for a long time had been that those who had fallen foul of the Inner Council by not honouring their lifetime obligations in one way or another, had been summarily dispatched as a warning to others not to stray from the Chain's single-minded resolve. But it was not so much his fear of an act of reprisal that had given him second thoughts, although he had to admit it did unnerve him. It was Prama reciting the oath of allegiance of the SS Brotherhood, with its powerful mystical ring and echoes of the ancient Teutonic knights, that had stirred within his breast memories of his youth, and poignantly brought back to him a time when he had been burning with a sense of purpose. For too many years now he had been comfortably content to churn out newspaper articles that were just a permutation of everything he had written before. It was about time, he thought, that he did something really positive with his life again.

'You are quite right, Willi, in everything you say. But I do have one major question which has puzzled me throughout, and I would like it answered.'

'Well?' Prama said testily.

'If this Vladimir Sokol is really who he claims to be, why have the Russians kept it a secret, and why haven't they capitalised on it? I mean, thirty-five years is a hell of a long time to do nothing.'

Prama let out a long sigh.

'Yes, I know, and we have discussed that point many times among ourselves. To be quite blunt, we are not sure. The most rational explanation we came up with was fear.'

Hollerbach screwed his face into a frown.

'You see, Wolf, you would have to take into account the political situation that existed in Russia at the time of the boy's capture. Stalin ruled with a rod of iron, and those around him lived in daily fear of their lives.'

Prama drew on his cigar and, finding it extinguished, he tossed it disgustedly into the open fireplace.

'Now, let us assume that the Russians' original idea for holding on to the boy was to use him when he was older as a propaganda tool. To have him publicly denounce all that his father had stood for. That would have been so much in keeping with their character.'

'Precisely. So why didn't they?'

'Well, our theory is that the Russian officers dealing with the boy weren't really

151

convinced enough.'

'In spite of all the documentary evidence they had, eh?'

'You yourself were very sceptical,' Prama snapped sarcastically. 'Remember, they didn't have Bruckner. He had escaped before they could extract any information from him. Ilse Wolters was dead. All they had to go on were papers and photographs which could have been forged by the Americans.'

'Why should they have thought that the Yanks would go to such lengths?'

'Can't you see what idiots the Russians would look if they'd banged the drum about this most celebrated convert to Communism, only to find the whole damn thing a hoax?'

'Yes, I see,' Hollerbach scratched the scalp beneath his thinning hair.

'Thus we came to the conclusion that no one was prepared to risk the wrath of Stalin by sticking their neck out and openly declaring that the boy was the son of Hitler, just in case the whole episode blew up in their faces,' Prama smiled. 'And, as with all things, in time the impetus waned, and from what we can piece together, after the war the boy was fostered out to a family who worked on the land, and grew up as a model Soviet citizen.'

'Mmm. A fascinating theory.'

'Just that. And no doubt we shan't learn the truth until . . . ' The door suddenly burst open, freezing Prama in mid sentence, and making Hollerbach, who had his back to it, almost leap from his chair. He turned to see half a dozen laughing people very nearly falling over themselves as they tumbled into the room.

'So this is where you've been hiding yourself.'

Anna, who was leading the group, addressed Prama petulantly. 'We've been looking all over for you. Naughty ol' Willi — are you bored with us?'

Prama, tense as he had been a split second earlier, unwound like a broken watch spring.

'Yes, bad show if the host skips off,' said one chap jauntily.

'Wasn't something we said, was it?' added another with a hiccup. A girl giggled and shushed him to be quiet.

Prama, who had regained his composure, simply oozed charm. 'What must you be thinking of me?' He glided over to Anna, took her hand in his and kissed it.

'Oh, do forgive me, my children,' he said, throwing his arms out as if to encompass them all. 'It was just that Wolf here,' he turned and acknowledged Hollerbach, 'is a very old friend whom I've not seen for years.

153

We were just trying to catch up on all our news.'

Anna flashed a smile at Hollerbach, who got up at once and bowed his head slightly in her direction.

'I thought only women gossiped,' Anna pouted teasingly, as she snuggled closely to Prama and spoke to him softly. 'Willi, I would like to introduce you to my cousin. He's been simply longing to meet you.'

Prama turned to follow Anna's gaze and faced a bleary-eyed, slim young man, whose arm was tightly interlinked with an attractive brunette from his club, called Margrette. Prama was not sure if this was a gesture of affection or whether he was holding on to the girl for support, as he looked very much the worse for drink. There was something else about his eyes that he observed as well — they seemed as cold and menacing as a snake's.

'How d'ye do, sir.' The young man detached himself from Margrette and came forward to greet him, almost knocking over a table displaying a vase of flowers in the process. He quickly steadied it — a little too quickly perhaps for one apparently so intoxicated — and shakily extended his hand.

'I've been looking forward very much to meeting you,' he slurred.

Prama gripped his limp palm. 'Yes, Anna . . . er . . . has said some rather complimentary things about you,' he said pleasantly. Prama did vaguely recall Anna speaking of her cousin as a potential financial whiz-kid who might be useful to him in his business. 'We'll have a little chat later, yes?'

Then, directing his attention to the group again, he shooed them towards the door like a harassed mother with a bunch of unruly kids beneath her feet.

'Now off you go, all of you. Dance, eat, drink, swim, go and enjoy yourselves. You don't need me for that,' Prama laughed. 'I will join you very soon, I promise.'

'All right, but don't be too long,' Anna, the last to leave the room, murmured sulkily.

'Go on with you.' Prama scolded, affectionately slapping her backside. She let out a startled little squeal as he laughingly closed the door behind her.

'Sorry about that,' he said, with the smile vanishing from his face.

'Well, maybe you should be mixing more with your guests, Willi. After all . . . '

'Damn the guests,' Prama erupted. 'We haven't got much time, and it's important that I finish what I have to say. Your life may depend on it, so I want you to listen carefully . . .'

He walked over to a Victorian burr-walnut davenport and opened a drawer, taking from it a large manila envelope.

'In here,' he said, punctuating each word, 'you will find a detailed itinerary which starts when you board a Tupelov 144, flight number 828, leaving Frankfurt am Main Airport for Moscow at 17.50 hours tomorrow.'

'Tomorrow?' Hollerbach spluttered, hardly believing his ears.

'For official purposes you will be covering an assignment on behalf of your newspaper *Deutsche Nationale Zeitung*.'

'I . . . I couldn't do that without first having the clearance from my editor.'

'That has already been taken care of.'

'Oh,' said Hollerbach, a little peeved at the way he was already being manipulated. 'Er, might I enquire as to what this official assignment is?'

'Certainly,' Prama beamed magnanimously. 'You are writing a series on great soldiers of the twentieth century. You will be researching and interviewing people who fought with the first subject in your series — Marshal Zhukov. A nice touch of irony, don't you think, since it was his men who first entered the Führerbunker in 1945. Now I would like you to study the contents of the envelope quickly, and ask me questions on anything you are not absolutely sure about. Then I shall take you downstairs and introduce you to Kotchnov.'

★   ★   ★

The pianist, having fought a futile battle in trying to communicate the lyrical subtleties of Gershwin, Porter and Hart to an audience who, he was now convinced, were a crowd of musical morons, was more than relieved when his allotted session drew to a close and a disc jockey took over to pollute the atmosphere with what he regarded as 'mindless, monotonous mush'.

As the sound pulsated through the quadrophonic system, and the guests began to gyrate to the beat that hammered out, Anna and the slim young man took to the floor. He moved loosely and rhythmically opposite her, in a none too subtle fuck. But his mind, like that of Shears, was concentrating on more important matters. He had sighted and identified his target some time ago, and had scarcely taken his eyes off him since. So preoccupied had he become that it compelled Anna to comment.

'You seem so far away, *Liebling*.'

'Er . . . oh, I was just wondering if I'd managed to make the right impression on

Herr Prama, I suppose,' he said quickly. 'You must admit he does seem rather formidable.'

Anna laughed. Moving in very close to him, she slipped her hands behind his buttocks and held him firmly to her. She enjoyed the experience of feeling the young man's penis becoming erect and hard as she swayed slowly from side to side.

'Listen,' she said, with a mischievous twinkle in her eye, 'when this party thins out, Willi puts on a rather special form of entertainment for a few of his intimate friends. He has a very interesting collection of naughty video tapes, and you can just imagine all the fun and games that go on when those films are being shown.' She giggled coyly. 'Believe me, when you've seen Willi prancing around in the nude with the cheeks of his bum wobbling like a blancmange, he'll never hold any fears for you again.'

Poor, stupid bitch, he thought contemptuously. The last thing on his mind right now was an orgy with a lot of drunken old fools and a bunch of hard-headed whores. But he managed to muster a keen response as he nibbled her earlobe and manoeuvered her around to a position which gave him a more advantageous view of his target.

His mind had been clicking like a

computer, programming and erasing several permutations on ways in which to snare his target alone. But he still had not arrived at a solution that would allow him to act without arousing suspicion. Then, all at once, an incident occurred that was to galvanise him into quick-thinking action. It began when a well-oiled guest, whose raucous voice had been heard bellowing above all the others in the swimming pool area, had surprised everyone, and not least his unsuspecting partner, by gathering her up in his arms and charging with her like a wounded elephant to the side of the pool. Barely controlling his mirth, he went through the motions of tossing her in. In his befuddled brain it was all a great joke, intending only to scare her, and this he certainly did, as her kicking, screeching protests bore out. But as he turned away from the pool, he lost his balance on the wet tiles, and both he and the hapless girl toppled in with a mighty plonk. This brought an immediate group of spectators to the poolside, and soon they were laughing loudly at the plight of the drunken sot and his furious girlfriend. One onlooker gallantly offered his hand in assistance, and found himself pulled in for his trouble. And suddenly the mood became infectious. Girls ran shrieking and shouting from their male pursuers, who had no intention of being left out of this great new sport. Those who were unfortunate enough not to escape were cornered, captured and, struggling in useless resistance, they too were hurled into the pool, each loud splash being accompanied by ever noisier cheers from the increasing number of onlookers who had come to watch the fun.

Soon the water was alive with fully clothed people, for the most part women, bobbing about on the choppy surface with their hair, which had taken the best part of a day to prepare, now hanging limply over their faces, while mascara ran down their cheeks like fine black ribbons. In minutes the dance area had been virtually cleared, and almost everyone in the gymnasium complex was either milling around the pool looking down on it, or, if less fortunate, thrashing about in it.

★   ★   ★

The Russian and American contingents were still locked in earnest conversation but, clearly amused by this impromptu entertainment, they too drifted to the poolside to get a closer view.

The slim young man watched with the concentrated intensity of a kestrel about to dive on his unsuspecting prey, when he saw his target whisper briefly to the man at his side, break away, and head purposefully towards the mens' room. Before the observer could make his move, he first had to disengage himself from Anna, who was clinging on to his arm as tightly as a tourniquet, and giggling like a schoolgirl at the antics of several of her girlfriends in the water. He toyed with the idea of sweeping her in to join them, but rejected it as he felt he might need her later on to establish an alibi. Taking her to one side, he laughingly warned her to be careful not to get pushed in, while he went to freshen their drinks. Within seconds he was just a few paces behind his target.

Kotchnov shook his head with mirth as he pushed the toilet door open. He was still delighting in the knowledge that these capitalist fellows could behave so irresponsibly — so childishly. He was looking forward immensely to the new life of freedom, anonymity, and prosperity that would follow after he had conducted his little business transaction that evening. He was still chuckling as he turned to close the door behind him. The toe of a highly polished black shoe barred the way. Startled, Kotchnov looked up and found himself staring into the grim, set features of the slim young man.

Instinctively he sensed danger, and tried desperately to shut the young man out. Simultaneously he attempted to shout for assistance. He accomplished neither. With the speed of an arrow in flight, the young man's hand shot out to Kotchnov's neck. Fingers as tough as steel gripped it, and expertly dug into his carotid artery. The faint, gurgling cry stifled in Kotchnov's throat was totally inaudible, obliterated by the sound of the flushing toilet. For a brief moment Kotchnov's bulging eyes glared accusingly at his assassin, then the light behind them faded and an empty blankness came into them. As his limp body started to slide slowly down the wall, the slim young man caught it awkwardly and propped it into a sitting position on the lavatory pan. Hastily, he systematically went through the pockets. He found a wallet with a wad of notes in Russian and German currency, a Communist Party card, and a couple of signed photographs from attractive girls, a shoe repair ticket and some scraps of paper with scribbled messages on them; keys, a lighter, a pack of cigarettes, a comb, some loose change, but little else of significance. He felt himself beginning to panic. He could have sworn that Kotchnov had not passed the papers over yet. In fact, he had observed him reassuringly tapping his breast pocket a few times during the evening — always a dead giveaway that. He had lost count of the number of times he had seen that nervous reaction before. Someone trying to conceal something, subconsciously checking it was still in place, and unintentionally pin-pointing it.

'It's just got to be here,' he murmured under his breath, and thrust his hand inside Kotchnov's breast pocket again . . . nothing! As he took his hand away in disgust, his fingers brushed upwards against the dead man's shirt — then he felt it. He flicked Kotchnov's necktie over one shoulder, grabbed the bottom of his shirt and tore it open, scattering the buttons as he did so. There it was all right — an official looking, brown envelope taped to his chest. Feverishly he tugged at the package. It made a sickening, ripping noise as he wrenched the tape away from the body, some of the matted hair and skin still firmly adhering to the sides. He slit the envelope open with his forefinger, took a deep breath and carefully withdrew the contents. Scanning the documents he allowed himself a fleeting smile of satisfaction before tucking them safely into his pocket. The slim young man, observing Kotchnov's position, decided that with one or two touches this would be as good a place as any in which to leave him. Unbuckling the dead man's belt and unzipping his trousers, he yanked them down to his ankles, then tidied up the dishevelled shirt and jacket.

'Now then, comrade, to all intents and purposes it looks as though you are having a shit — even if you do look a little constipated perhaps . . . but . . . ' He smiled to himself as he turned to the sink. Beneath the gold-plated dolphin-mouthed taps he methodically washed his hands, paying particular attention to the one which had throttled the life out of Kotchnov. Drying them on a thick towel, he eyed himself approvingly in the large oval mirror, made a slight adjustment to his tie, smoothed down his hair and, without giving Kotchnov a second glance, made his exit. He had just managed to close the door behind him when he was confronted by a largish man with his head down, who was just commencing to unzip his flies.

'It's occupied,' the slim young man informed him pleasantly.

'God! I'll have to go upstairs then — I'm dying for a piss.'

'Yes, I think he was too,' he nodded his head in the direction of the door. 'Dying for something anyway,' he muttered to himself, as he coolly walked away.

'Ah, there you are, *mein Schatz!*' Anna

shouted excitedly above the din as he came to her side.

He feigned pleasure at seeing her.

'Where have you been?' She linked her arm through his again.

'Couldn't get near the damn bar to top up, so I went upstairs and got rid of some instead.'

'Oooh, I bet you really tried to get a sneak preview of those blue movies,' she teased.

He grinned. 'My needs were earthy functional — not earthy erotic!'

Anna squeezed his arm affectionately. 'I'm getting bored watching these overgrown undergraduates. Come on, let's dance.'

The slim young man watched her as, with an exaggerated wiggle of her bottom, she undulated towards the middle of the dance floor. Several other guests, who had also tired of the antics in the swimming pool, were already displaying their skills. As the beat pounded and the coloured lights bordering the DJ's turntable flashed in sequence like a gaudy Broadway theatre sign, Anna picked up the tempo and began to dance. Every muscle in her loose-limbed body seemed to move in metronomic precision to the rhythm. She was a natural — a choreographer's dream, and she knew it. She was aware that in a matter of moments all eyes would be on her, as she gave a totally uninhibited solo performance. The slim young man knew it too. When Anna got going she was almost in a trance, and wouldn't even notice if he were there with her or not. Come to think of it, he thought derisively, the myopic little bitch wouldn't see him if he were leaping about a mere three feet in front of her. So now would be as good a time as any to part company. Speed was of the essence and he had to move very quickly before the Russian's body was discovered. But he had one more task to complete before he got the hell out of there.

Picking up a half-empty glass of champagne branded with a crimson crescent of lipstick, the slim young man once again adopted the characteristics of the well inebriated fellow. He tottered purposefully across the room, until he was adjacent to a man earnestly engaged in conversation. At this point, he clumsily tripped and splashed what remained of his drink down the man's sleeve.

'I'm so sorry, sir,' he slurred, looking up at the man who stood a good six inches taller than himself. 'I should have looked where I was going.' He took out his top pocket handkerchief and started to dab the damp sleeve.

'That's quite okay, don't worry,' Shears

said, withdrawing his arm. 'No real damage done — apart from wasting some good champagne,' he added good-humouredly. The slim young man tottered again, and as Shears steadied him, he became conscious that something was being pushed into his pocket. He was about to find out what it was when the drunk, affecting a huge fixed grin, hissed between clenched teeth, 'Get it to McNabe.'

Before the look of astonishment on Shears' face had faded, the slim young man had slid into the shadows and was gone from sight. Shears' mind was racing now — what the hell was going on? What was in his pocket? How did that guy know about McNabe — or that he was working for him? One thing was for sure, he wasn't just going to stand there without knowing what had been stuffed into his pocket.

He turned amiably to Doug. 'Say, this sleeve of mine is kinda sticky — think I'll pop along to the john and get some water on it.'

'Yeah. Cold water — that's the thing for taking out stains,' Doug agreed.

'Vinegar. That's what you need, fella,' said George, trying to be helpful.

'That's for putting on French fries, you schmuck.'

'No, really. It's great for getting stains out,

my wife swears by it. I had a pair of white . . . '

Shears couldn't help smiling as he left them to it. He walked swiftly towards the toilet, but was careful not to appear unnerved in case he was being watched. As he approached, he saw a small cluster of people standing anxiously around an elderly man. They appeared to be in an agitated state, and kept pointing back towards the toilet door. Shears couldn't quite make out the phrase they kept repeating, but it sounded like '*Tot . . . mausetot.*'

9

Shears, unshaven and suffering miserably from jet lag, stormed into McNabe's office. McNabe, who was glancing through his morning mail, looked up at him nervily, half expecting trouble.

'You lousy bastard,' Shears blurted out. He could scarcely believe the rage that he felt. 'You set me up, didn't you? You shit house.'

McNabe did not answer the accusation. Experience had taught him that in a situation like this, it was wiser to keep his mouth shut.

'Go along, observe, that's all you have to do,' Shears mimicked McNabe's voice. 'What you didn't say, what you carefully avoided saying in fact, was that I was to be your unwitting messenger boy. At least when you work for Western Union you get tips! You know what I could'a got if someone had seen that guy slip me these?' He tossed the brown package angrily on to his desk.

'I could'a got a one-way ticket to oblivion, like that poor bastard Kotchnov.' Shears slumped down into a chair and took a few deep breaths to calm himself. Then, looking McNabe straight in the eye, he spoke in a low, clipped voice. 'You had better have a very sound reason for not levelling with me, Paul.'

McNabe nodded, but still maintained his silence. He picked up the package and shuffled the contents out into his hand. Shears watched him thoughtfully, as he looked casually at the dog-eared, sepia snapshots, and then ran his eyes over the bundle of pages, shaking his head, sighing, and tutting irritably from time to time as he did so. Eventually he paused, and met Shears' steady gaze.

'Dan, I know you must be feeling pretty sore about this caper, but remember, it's standard procedure for us to let our agents know only so much. It's a protection for them and for us.'

Shears stared at him dubiously.

'Look,' McNabe growled in justification, 'if we had come clean with you, not only would you have been a high security risk, you might have been so jumpy you could'a fucked up everything!'

'You're wrong there,' Shears said caustically. 'If you had come clean with me — I wouldn't have gone.'

To cover his smile McNabe coughed, and began to scrutinise the documents. Shears was about to continue his verbal assault, but saw that McNabe's eyes were glued to the faded birth certificate, which he studied with the thoroughness of an expert.

'How good is your German?'

'Good enough to understand what that is all about,' Shears replied with emphasis.

McNabe held it up to the light, searching, Shears imagined, for tell-tale signs that might indicate a forgery.

'How genuine is that?' Shears asked.

'It's for real.' McNabe said with authority. 'Frightening, isn't it?'

Shears frowned. He failed to see how a birth certificate and a letter purporting to be from the child's guardian, merely proving that Hitler did have a son who had probably lived to be fourteen or fifteen, could possibly be termed 'frightening' — and in no uncertain terms he said so.

But McNabe was no longer listening. He was busily patting his pockets searching for something. He had just opened the top drawer of his desk, when it suddenly dawned on him.

'Oh, Jeez! I keep forgetting — I've given up smoking,' he said sheepishly to Shears. 'Clearly, you don't read Russian?'

Shears shook his head. 'It wasn't mandatory at Bayler.'

'Obviously.' McNabe said drily. 'Well, if you did, you would have known by these early NKVD memos and from the much later notation of the GRU and KGB that Hitler's son lived to be a lot older than fifteen. In fact, according to one little KGB snippet here . . . ' McNabe quickly rummaged through the papers and extracted the one he was referring to, ' . . . Hitler's son, known as Vladimir Sokol, is in his mid-fifties and is very much alive. Now, can you understand the implication and importance of all this evidence?'

'Holy shit! I'm beginning to,' Shears said at last. 'So what's your next move?'

'What's *our* next move, y'mean, don't you?' McNabe said deliberately.

As fatigued as he was, Shears was receiving McNabe's message loud and clear. 'Oh, no! I've played my part in this little drama. I've delivered the package, Merry Christmas, and that's me out, pal.'

McNabe folded the documents carefully and replaced them in the envelope.

'I'm afraid it's not gonna be quite as simple as that, Dan. Those guys are going to be in hot pursuit of this package. How long do y'think it's gonna take 'em to find out you don't work for Golden Thresher Inc.? A mere process of elimination through their extensive network will pin you down in next to no time. Sorry, Dan, whether you like it or not, you're in this now, right up to your stubbly chin.'

'Oh, you're just beautiful, y'know that.' Shears' eyes blazed. He felt defeated, deflated, and damned exhausted. 'So what happens now, then?' he inquired submissively.

'Three things. First, we put a round-the-clock surveillance on your house, until things cool off. Just in case you get some unwelcome callers.'

'Oh, Christ! That's just great, man. Do you know I don't even own a gun.'

'Well, we can soon remedy that. But knowing the way you feel about me right now, maybe it's a good thing that you don't,' McNabe retorted with a grim smile. 'Two. I'm gonna take this little packaged time bomb right to the top — and I mean to the top.'

'And?'

McNabe looked at him oddly.

'Y'said three things,' Shears mumbled.

'Oh, yeah. Three you go home and get a good long sleep.'

Shears rose wearily from the chair, and wordlessly took his leave. He had no sooner closed the door behind him than McNabe picked up his internal phone and pushed two buttons in the hand-piece.

'He's just left my office. Don't let him out of your sight, night or day.'

He replaced the receiver and eagerly put his hand into his pocket, only to remember, with a silent curse, that his pipe was no longer there.

10

Chief Inspector Hostler and his Nuremberg murder squad were proceeding with their enquiries in their well practised and meticulous manner. Results would come in time, he was sure of that. A tip-off here, a chance remark there. Someone was bound to talk, they nearly always did. He therefore bitterly resented the pressure that was being loaded on to him concerning this case from the Ministry of Justice Offices. He quite understood that the unfortunate homicide of a Soviet official on Federal Republican soil was rather embarrassing to them, and he was aware of the assurances that had been made to Russian Security authorities that they would do everything in their power to bring the case to a satisfactory conclusion. So why not let him get on with the job for which his track record had proved beyond question that he was most ably qualified. Why should he have to put up with a lot of faceless civil servants ringing him up at all hours of the day to check on his progress? What annoyed him perhaps more than anything was the fact that, since he was only two years away from his retirement, he had to placate the silly sods. It would have been foolish to risk his hard-earned pension now.

So it was a less than good-humoured Franz Hostler who heaved his bulky frame out of his official Opel car and waddled up the steps that led to the large, imposing house. He glanced up at the superb stone frieze depicting a medieval battle scene, set into the wall above the massive oak door with its heavy brass fitments. It was a most impressive entrance. His old friend, Willi Prama, had certainly done well for himself, very well indeed, he murmured under his breath. Not that he could truthfully call Prama a friend — more what one might call a long standing acquaintance. Still, that wasn't going to make life any easier for him one way or the other. There were a lot more questions to be answered by Prama. And, although he knew that Prama would not particularly relish the idea, ask them he must. Hostler sighed audibly as he pushed the bell.

Prama got up from behind his desk, as Dietz ushered him in to his study.

'Good of you to see me at such short notice,' Hostler said, shaking Prama's out-stretched hand.

'Not at all, not at all. Nasty business, eh?' Prama grunted.

'Yes, very.' he concurred with feeling. They sat down in two high-backed leather chairs facing each other.

'Well, now,' Hostler continued. 'Thank you for the guest list. We've interviewed most of them, although a few had left before the murder took place of course.'

'Yes,' Prama said non-committally.

'But we shall have to see even those in due course.'

'You're ... er ... quite sure now that it was murder? Not a heart attack or anything of that kind?'

'Quite sure. The post mortem revealed that he'd been asphyxiated. A thumb and forefinger job.' Hostler demonstrated on his own throat. 'He was done away with all right, and professionally so, too.'

Prama regarded the fat policeman with the dome-like bald head, neat grey moustache peppered with flecks of its original ginger hair, as a plodder. But he was aware that his dogged determination and attention to the minutest detail had often rewarded him with unparalleled success. He was greatly admired by his own colleagues and had a fine reputation in his chosen field. Prama would have to be very careful in his handling of Hostler, if he were to keep certain facts he had learned on the night of the murder to himself. From the moment a distraught guest had informed him of Kotchnov's death he had left no stone unturned. Before ringing the police, he and Hollerbach had scrupulously searched the dead Russian and the surrounding area for the documents. Finding none, the motive for the murder had become obvious to them. Further diligent probing by Prama of two guests who were in the vicinity of the urinal at the time had given him a fairly strong lead as to whom the killer might be. Both had independently described the slim young man, who had that night escorted Anna. It was this information that Prama was keeping very much to himself. For, if the slim young man had committed the crime and stolen the documents, for whom was he working? Who else knew about their planned transaction? These questions were extremely worrying to Prama and the higher echelon in the Chain. It was vital that Prama should have time to reflect and conduct a personal investigation without Hostler and his men cramping his style. With this uppermost in his mind, Prama sat for almost an hour as he went through the motions of being a co-operative citizen and, without revealing a thing, cleverly evaded every leading question Hostler threw at him. Eventually, when he felt his own patience wearing, Prama looked pointedly at his watch.

Hostler observed the action, and stood up to take his leave.

'Well, let's hope we can get a breakthrough soon, eh? You know, some people expect miracles at once — if they don't happen right away . . . ' Hostler shook his head sadly and left the rest of the sentence unfinished.

Prama opened his study door. As Hostler was about to leave, he stopped suddenly in his tracks and looked straight into Prama's eyes. 'We're rather anxious to question a young man known as Heinz Middler.'

Prama looked puzzled.

'He was the escort of one of your guests on the night of the party, one Anna Weise.'

'Ah, yes. Her cousin, I believe,' Prama said, as casually as he could, but was quite taken aback.

Hostler kept his gaze steady. 'Really? When we spoke to her she didn't even know who we were talking about, until we showed her some mug shots we had of him. Didn't know his address or his real name.'

Prama felt himself slowly seething and dug his toes into his shoes. 'He has a criminal record, then?'

'Let us just say he is known to us,' Hostler smiled secretively. 'Of course, I don't suppose you have any idea of where we might locate him?'

'No,' Prama replied truthfully.

'No, of course not,' Hostler said, proffering his hand. 'However, if you should hear of anything . . . '

'Naturally, I'll contact you at once,' Prama lied.

Hostler smiled again. 'I'll see myself out.'

Prama waited until he heard the inspector's car drive off over the gravel path, before picking up the telephone.

'Yes?' Anna answered in an affected husky voice.

'I want to see you right away,' Prama said in a no-nonsense manner.

'Oh, Willi darling, I'd love to — but I have a hairdressing appointment in ten minutes. But I could . . . '

'Then cancel it,' Prama snapped and replaced the receiver.

11

Anna's apartment was situated in the fashionable Steinbulstrasse. The fourteen-storey block had only been completed the previous year, and Anna had moved into her one-bedroomed suite soon afterwards. It was pricey by anyone's standard, but Anna had persuaded Prama to loan her the money. A loan to Anna meant a gift as far as he was concerned but, like property, Prama had considered Anna a good investment. That is why the thought of her deceiving him over the identity of the slim young man made him burn with anger. Cousin be damned! Prama's knuckles whitened as he tightly gripped the steering wheel. The more he thought about it, the more he realised that for Anna to have gone to such devious lengths, her feelings for the young man must have meant a hell of a lot more than just a one-night stand, and he didn't like that one bit. More to the point, her crass stupidity had been the cause of his present predicament, and he liked that even less. But Willi Prama hadn't got to the top by letting a setback of this sort throw him off balance. He'd always managed to turn a disadvantage into an advantage, and he was determined that this situation would be dealt with in the same tenacious manner in which he dealt with all his problems.

Prama let himself in with his own key, and cast his eyes quickly around the apartment. It was always spotlessly clean. The scatter cushions, cuddly soft toys and the pretty potted plants summed up Anna's personality at a glance. Very feminine, but not much in the cerebral region — there wasn't a good book to be seen anywhere. Anna appeared from the bedroom. She was stunning, dressed to the nines from the tip of her Gucci shoes to the top of her immaculately coiffeured hair. The little bitch had lied about going to the hairdresser's, that was for sure. She was obviously off on some romantic assignment, and he had a damn good idea who the lucky chap might be. Anna kissed him lightly on the cheek and ushered him to the sofa. As she walked, two long gold and turquoise earrings swung from her delicate shell-like ears — pierced ears which seemed almost too fragile to support them. She sat down opposite him a little nervously. Prama sensed there was likely to be a bit of a cat-and-mouse game about to be played, and he was determined that this little mouse would finish up very firmly beneath his paw! With a contrived movement Anna crossed her legs slowly and provocatively, allowing him to see just enough to titillate him. Prama checked his thoughts, no young lady, that isn't going to work at all this time. Anna saw from the look on his face that her feminine wiles were useless in his present mood and changed her tactics almost at once.

'Can I get you a drink, Willi?'

Prama shook his head. 'I believe you had a visit from the police this morning?'

'Eh, yes . . . ' she stammered. 'I feel very ashamed about telling you that little white lie.'

'About going to the hairdresser's you mean?' Prama intended to let her squirm.

Anna blushed visibly. 'Er . . . no . . . I mean the other night at the party, when I introduced you to . . . er . . . my escort. He wasn't really my cousin, you see.'

Prama feigned surprise. 'You don't say!'

Anna's confidence grew slightly. 'He was just a regular client I met at the Club, and . . . well . . . he was attracted to me and spent a lot of money. He was so nice and he told me how interested he was in banking, and I thought you might find him useful. You've always told me how difficult it is to find good, reliable people.'

Prama stared at her meaningfully. 'Yes, it still is.' He patted the seat next to him. 'Come here, Anna. I don't like you sitting as though I were interviewing you.'

Anna giggled in her childlike way, and eagerly snuggled up against him, slipping her hand between his thighs. Prama placed his arm around her almost at once, but was careful not to spoil her hair as his fingers slowly traced a pattern up and down the side of her neck. Anna sighed. She was beginning to relax now.

'How becoming these earrings are,' he whispered, as he started to play with the one that dangled near his fingertips.

'You bought them for my birthday two years ago, *Liebling*,' Anna responded brightly.

'So I did,' Prama stated. He pulled gently on the earring.

'It always gives me pleasure to buy you lovely things, and in return I expect your appreciation . . . '

'Oh, do be careful, Willi,' Anna winced.

' . . . and your loyalty,' Prama said, ignoring her. 'Do I have that, too?'

'You know you have,' Anna said quickly, as she tried casually to brush his hand away. Prama simply tightened his grip.

'Then perhaps you would like to tell me more about this chap, Heinz Middler.'

Prama felt her stiffen and her breathing became deeper.

'Where does he live?'

'I've no idea,' Anna replied, wide-eyed.

Prama was tugging on the earring with a little more emphasis.

'Do you know, I had this odd sensation when I came here that you might be going out to meet him?'

Anna laughed feebly. 'Goodness. What gave you that idea? I haven't seen hide nor hair of him since the party.' She was becoming frightened, as if she could sense that something unpleasant was about to happen.

'I think you do know where Middler is, Anna,' Prama said with a voice as cold as steel.

'I . . . really . . . don't, Willi — honestly.' Anna struggled to free herself, but Prama merely held on to the earring and Anna's face contorted with pain. 'Please, Willi, you're hurting me,' she cried.

'You've hurt me, too, Anna. You've hurt me with your stupidity and lies. I'll give you one more chance to make amends for that.'

'But, Willi, I don't know . . . ' A penetrating scream of pain echoed round the apartment as Prama tugged fiercely at the earring. The gold wire cut through Anna's earlobe like a piece of soft cheese. Blood spurted all over her exposed white shoulder, and oozed down her pink dress in dark crimson streaks. She sprang up at once, still screaming and holding a hand to her ear. She rushed to look at herself in the nearby mirror. Prama unclenched his fist, and tossed the earring on to the table, before moving towards her. He grabbed Anna round the waist. Blood was still flowing freely from her earlobe.

'Now then,' he said menacingly. 'If you don't want a repeat performance with the other ear, I suggest you do exactly as I tell you . . . '

12

The engine of Prama's black Mercedes purred like a contented panther as it glided up the hilly, winding back streets. He was taking this circuitous route south-east of the town centre for two reasons. First, he was anxious to avoid the heavy congestion of traffic that was now building to its peak in the heart of the city. At this time in the afternoon, he mused, it was always bad — but with the start of the annual Organ Festival it would be impossible. It struck him as very odd that one of the major tourist attractions in Nuremberg in late June was a bloody organ festival. His second reason was far less practical, and was rather in the nature of a pilgrimage. It was one which he often made when he was conducting business on behalf of the Kameraden that contained an element of risk, and he had allowed himself plenty of time to get there before driving to his ultimate destination later that afternoon. He smiled to himself as he recalled the scene in Anna's apartment. Before he had left her in a state of sobbing hysteria — such sweet revenge — he had not only elicited from her the whereabouts of Heinz Middler; but had made her make that vital telephone call.

'Heinz?'

'Who is it?'

'Anna.'

'You should have been here by now.'

'Er . . . yes . . . I, er . . . Willi Prama has found out.'

'Found out what?'

'That you are not my cousin.'

'Oh, is that all?'

'No. He says you might have some information that he'd dearly like to know about.'

A quiet chuckle. 'I bet he would.'

'Listen — he wants to meet you.'

A murmur of interest. 'Does he now.'

'He also mentioned that if you had what it was he wanted, or could confirm certain matters — oh, I really don't know what he means . . . '

'I do . . . '

' . . . then he'd be prepared to pay for that information quite handsomely.'

'How handsomely?'

A pause, while Anna watched Prama mouth a figure.

'Er . . . 50,000 marks.'

'Anna?'

'Yes?'

'I'll talk to him personally, if you don't mind. I know he's there listening.'

A stammer of protest. 'Of course he's no . . . '

An interruption from Prama. 'It's all right, Anna. You're quite right, Middler, what can I do for you?'

'Isn't it more of what I can do for you?'

'That depends on whether you have what I want.'

'I'm afraid that I no longer possess what it is you're after.'

Prama became a little excited. 'Then who does?'

'Now, that I can't tell you.'

'But you did see the documents?'

'Oh yes — and I have a very good memory.'

'Then can we meet?'

'When we've agreed the terms.'

Prama sucked his bottom lip. '75,000 marks in cash?'

'The price is 100,000 marks, and by this afternoon. Can you get it?'

Prama forced a laugh. 'My business is banking — remember?'

In a quiet, deliberate tone, Middler arranged the rendezvous for 16.30 that afternoon. In the Hauptbahnhof Parkplatz, bay no. 185. The money was to be in old bills and carried in a plastic shopping bag. He warned Prama to come alone, unarmed, and to make sure he wasn't followed. This secretive intrigue amused Prama slightly, but being in no position to do otherwise, he readily agreed.

★   ★   ★

Prama glanced at the digital clock set into the polished mahogany wood in the dashboard. It read 14.53, and there, looming up in front of him, was the familiar landmark he knew and loved so well, standing now like the sombre ruins of an ancient Roman temple. Just after the war the US Airforce had used the area as an air base. When they had finally vacated it, there had been many developers who had tried to take it over. Their plans had ranged from the erection of a hypermarket and shopping precinct, to a West German Disneyland. In every case he, and other like-minded influential citizens, had applied pressure on the local government and every single scheme had been vetoed. To this day, the site of so many happy and glorious rallies was still barren and desolate. All that remained of the once magnificent Zeppelin-eweise was a shell-cratered dais and a handful of pitted bricks which stood atop those long, wide steps. He turned off the engine, applied the handbrake and got out. There was still, in that vast windswept, overgrown area, a tremendous, almost touchable, feeling of power. It was difficult to comprehend, but these bits of rubble symbolised to Prama, just as assuredly as the ancient Greek or Roman columns did for latter-day historians, the embodiment and achievement of a mighty and omnipotent empire. He walked the few yards to the steps and felt the hard concrete underfoot, now almost concealed by the moss and wild grass that threatened to completely envelop it. He sat down on the lowest of the five steps, a solitary figure in that great expanse. Slowly he allowed the memories of his past times there to come drifting back.

He had attended his first meeting on the Party Day of Unity in 1934. He was then just a fresh-faced boy, so proud of his new Hitler Jugend uniform that he was fit to burst. He was too young at the time to understand what all the speakers were talking about, but he did remember, with crystal clarity, the goose-bumps that were raised on his skin when he listened in awe, with 30,000 other youngsters like himself, to the spellbinding oratory of the Führer. There were nearly 500,000 adults in attendance as well, in that huge stadium

— party members, soldiers of the SA, and spectators alike — all crammed like sardines, listening to the bands and watching the flags and banners being held aloft. Then at 18.30, he recalled the time well, the Führer took the stand and the hush that descended on that massive audience was truly electrifying. It was a moment which he would never forget. The Führer spoke with a burning passion. He told them that the German nation had a God-given mission. He listed the virtues required for Party leaders — loyalty, obedience, discipline, a spirit of sacrifice and comradeship — principles by which Prama had lived ever since. With the exception of 1937, when his mother had forbidden him to go for fear of spreading the scarlet fever he had contracted, he had attended every rally until the outbreak of war in 1939. That year he had been honoured by being allowed to bear a Party standard. It had been heavy for his skinny frame — damned heavy — but he had carried it with pride and didn't feel his aching muscles till long after the ceremony.

Prama stood up, the ghostly faces of the past still in his mind, the sounds of the marching still in his ears, and the echoes of that triumphant spirit of a Germany that was, all around him.

Grim-featured and resolute, he walked

slowly towards his car. He caught a reflection of himself in the window and adjusted the expensive Homburg that perched awkwardly on his head. He climbed into his seat, glanced quickly at the plastic shopping bag that contained the banknotes, and purposefully drove off.

★　★　★

Disjointed and random thoughts still spun through Prama's mind. Perhaps he was being sent on a wild goose chase? For as well as being a murderer, and a ruthless one at that, Middler was also a very devious young man. Yes, he would have to keep his wits about him. Prama checked the time on his watch with that of the digital clock. He was still five minutes ahead of schedule. He slowed down and drove leisurely towards Königstrasse and the nearby multi-storey car park where he was to meet Middler. As he approached the rendezvous, Prama wiped away the images that had kept him company on the journey like a schoolmaster clearing the chalky ramblings on a blackboard. Now, only one thought remained, and he intended to keep it that way until his task was completed. An electronic buzz informed him that his ticket had been ejected by the dispensing machine.

He pressed the electric window button, waited for it to roll smoothly down, reached out and plucked at the ticket. Immediately the gate rose and he drove through, eyeing the numbers of the parking bays to his left and right as he did so.

As Prama negotiated the bend that took him up on to the third level, he saw a man standing at the far end. Prama stopped the car and steeled himself. He glanced quickly at the bay numbers; yes, this would be the right floor, but from his position at that moment he could not be quite sure whether it was Middler or not. He watched intently as the man stepped out of the shadows and beckoned him onwards. Prama eased the car forward cautiously until he recognised the man. It was Middler, dressed casually in a fawn suede jacket, open neck shirt with dark green trousers, and the bastard looked even more handsome and youthful than he remembered him at the party. Following his directions, Prama swung his car into bay number 185, switched off his engine and waited for Middler to make his next move. He didn't have to wait long. Middler came from behind the pillar and stood at the offside of the car. Holding a gun at Prama, he silently motioned him to step out.

Prama obeyed, making sure he left the shopping bag behind.

'You said come unarmed.'

'I said you were to come unarmed. I didn't say anything about me,' Middler nodded towards his pistol. 'This is merely to ensure that you have stuck to our bargain. Please be so good as to place your hands against the car and spread your legs apart.'

Prama did as he was told, and Middler speedily and expertly frisked his clothing.

'Okay,' Middler said. 'Now get out the money and no funny business.'

Prama opened the door of his Mercedes and reached to withdraw the shopping bag from the seat. He was aware that Middler had the gun trained on the back of his neck. He picked up the bag slowly. 'Look, how do I know you're not just going to use that thing?'

Middler grinned sardonically. 'You don't. Open the bag please.'

Once again Prama meekly did as he was told. Middler glanced inside, seemed satisfied, and relieved him of the money. 'We will conduct our business in my car. It's over there.' He pointed his gun towards a gleaming white Porsche. 'Right. Let's go — after you.'

You can never trust these unpredictable maniac Nazis, Middler thought, as he fell into step a couple of paces behind Prama.

Reaching his car, he ushered Prama into the front passenger seat then, sliding himself behind the wheel, he checked the money and with an almost nonchalant air he tossed the bag on to the back seat. Prama sent up a silent prayer as he then watched Middler undo his jacket and place his pistol in a shoulder holster. With careful deliberation, Prama removed his hat and placed it on his knees.

'All right. Let's talk. Who do you work for?'

'Anyone who pays well enough,' Middler replied.

'So — who paid you to kill Kotchnov?'

'I've already told you that question is out of bounds.'

'Mmm — I could make an intelligent guess. The Mossad?'

'Look, we made a deal. I was to tell you only about the documents.'

'Yes, yes, of course,' Prama said quickly. 'Now, I want you to think carefully about the questions I'm going to ask you. And for this kind of money the answers had better be right.'

Middler had not boasted about having a good memory for nothing. It was part of his job — note every detail and imprint it firmly on the brain. He could see that Prama was impressed by his almost total recall. He answered every question without a moment's hesitation until he considered the subject totally exhausted. Prama eyed him steadily. 'I don't suppose you would reconsider telling me to whom you passed the documents? Naturally I would make it worth . . . '

Middler cut in, showing his irritation. 'Look, this matter is at an end. I've told you all I'm prepared to reveal.'

'I'm sorry to hear that,' Prama said pensively. But Middler was no longer listening. He switched on the ignition, indicating that there was nothing further to discuss. He leaned slightly towards Prama to release the handbrake. It was a movement he was never to complete. Prama's hand had slid under the Homburg on his knees, found the trigger of the Saur pistol that had been taped inside the crown, and squeezed off a single round. The 9mm parebellum bullet entered Middler's face just below his right eye. His head rocketed back, and in the split second it took to reach the restraint above his seat, he was quite dead. A crimson ribbon of warm blood seeped slowly out of the hole in his cheek and trickled into his half-open mouth, while his eyes froze in a final expression of surprise and horror.

The first thing Prama did when he was satisfied that Middler was dead was to reach for the plastic bag on the rear seat, then he calmly went through Middler's pockets. He withdrew a wallet and sifted through the contents. A slim address book caught his attention. Thumbing through the pages, he turned one back quickly as he spotted a name that was vaguely familiar to him. It was listed under tennis coach, but Prama knew differently. 'Zeigler . . . Erich Zeigler. So the CIA are in on this are they?' he muttered under his breath. 'Well, well, well! Then the hunt is on in earnest.'

13

President Samuel B. Jones stood up briskly from behind his desk to shake hands with each man as they filed in to greet him. As they resolutely took their seats, he observed that it was the room that their eyes focused on, not him. He did not regard this as any slight to his authority. Indeed, he had noticed that the Oval Office had always seemed to have this hypnotic effect on first-time visitors. He recalled his own feelings when first being shown into this room so many years ago. He knew it was not so much the regal trappings, for apart from the display of the five flags representing the armed services, sprouting their colourful battle streamers and surmounted by gold eagles, there was little else to proclaim that this was one of the most important offices in the world. It was, he considered, an awareness of all the great leaders of the past who had somehow left something of themselves there. The ghosts of giants like Lincoln, Roosevelt and Kennedy seemed to linger and watch his every move; and in thinking about these men, President Jones was constantly reminded of the awesome responsibility he held. He thought of the card President Truman once had affixed to his desk in this room which read: 'The buck stops here'. He fully concurred with that sentiment, and believed with all his heart that it was in this Head of State room, not the Senate nor the House of Representatives, nor the Pentagon, but in this room alone, that all the really historic decisions were made. That was why, without consultation with any but the very closest of his colleagues, he had convened, under a veil of the utmost secrecy, an urgent meeting with the chiefs of three of the world's major intelligence networks.

Seated opposite him, to his right, was Sir Leslie Payne, head of Britain's MI6. Facing him was his own Harvard friend, Arnold Wilmot, Director of the CIA, and next to Wilmot, that leather-faced legend of so many desert campaigns, Brigadier General Yekotiel Rabin, Controller of the Israeli Mossad. Sitting behind these men was Amos Barnett, the President of National Security Affairs, a mouthy and sardonic New Yorker whom President Jones disliked intensely, but for whom he nevertheless held a grudging respect. To Barnett's right was Tim Coogan, boss of the shadowy CIA Omega Division, and at his side his Langley aide, Paul

McNabe. The President cleared his throat, and with just a hint of emotion in that soft southern drawl of his, now so familiar to Western ears, explained why he had summoned them together with so little warning. Raising a file stamped 'Top Secret — Highly Classified' from his desk, he turned his head slowly to take every man briefly into his gaze.

'Gentlemen, in this file, copies of which you all received on your arrival at the White House this morning, and which I trust you have all thoroughly absorbed' — he gave them that boyish grin, the one that had destroyed his only other serious rival in the electoral race for the world's top job — 'you will have read some very disturbing new facts. These facts indicate that a powerful right-wing organisation is planning to bring out of Russia a man who, according to documentary evidence now in our possession,' he replaced the file with deliberation on his desk, 'is the son of Adolf Hitler.'

Barnett gave an embarrassed little cough, whilst the others just threw a few odd glances at each other, all of which the President keenly observed.

'Okay, okay, I can just imagine what you're thinking,' the President said impatiently, 'but just you hear me out.'

They sat in total silence while the President

covered the events leading up to the discovery of the documents. Then, taking out another file from his drawer, he leaned forward.

'Now the latest information we have here reveals that Hitler's heir, now called Vladimir Sokol, has been imprisoned in Moscow's Lubyanka Jail — not for any apparent political misdemeanour, but for fraud, can you believe?' He placed the file on the desk and clasped his fingers tightly together as he addressed them.

'We are convinced that this group of neo-Nazis, who have both the financial resources and the single-minded purposefulness to organise his escape, intend to do just that. Then possibly in a blaze of publicity to elect him as their Führer. Now if this is allowed to happen it would, at a stroke, instantly unite all the dozens of right-wing groups operating in the Western hemisphere into a single cohesive and dangerous force.' The President took a sip from a glass of water at his elbow. 'The way these neo-Nazis present their case these days is to play down the racist element, but play up their avowed intention of destroying all forms of Communism. They will claim that their policy is the only real solution to Soviet domination. And let me say right here and now, gentlemen, an awful lot of support would come their way.'

The President went on to say that, although Hitler's heir was unlikely to pose any great threat with regard to his potential leadership qualities — because from the information they had on him he was a weakling and could barely remember a word of the German language anyway — it was how the Chain would make use of him that would present the real problem. With the technology we have today, they could stage satellite-linked rallies in Nazi sympathising countries such as Chile, Brazil and even Spain. In terms of numbers and support, these would make the old Nuremberg gatherings look like a private house party. What also greatly concerned him was the very strong possibility that the Russians might be behind the whole business.

The President stood up and walked slowly round his desk, watching his small audience react to his last supposition. He thrust his hands deep into his trouser pockets and sat on the corner of the desk.

'Let us just assume,' he said, 'that this man, Sokol, is successfully removed from the USSR and is then given the full treatment as leader of the new National Socialist Party, or whatever it decides to call itself. Remember, there is nothing illegal in democratic West Germany in the promotion of any political party, provided it is not of a paramilitary nature. As this new party grew in confidence, as it gained more and more support, so it would become more and more militant.' The President's eyes searched the faces of the group to see that he had their full attention. 'All right,' he continued, 'now we all know that it has long been the dream of every nationalistic German to see once again the reunification of his country. This neo-Nazi party would fan that small burning ember of discontent into a flaming inferno. The streets of West Germany would be filled with thousands of young people demonstrating and demanding the annexation of East Germany. Soon, the demonstrations would become riots; the riots, as they inevitably do, would get out of hand. Terrorist attacks would spill over to East German cities. Under the pretext of protecting the peoples of East Germany — 'their people' — from the evil revival of Fascism, Soviet tanks would move in to West Berlin, followed by similar action in major Federal cities. Remember, the Russians have violated international treaties before and gotten away with it. None of us here will need reminding of Afghanistan and Poland, and the fact that our predecessors felt powerless to do anything other than make a lot of meaningless noise about it. The Russians could almost justify their actions, and many nations who suffered under the scourge of the swastika might even be supportive.'

The President walked to the chair behind his desk, and, seating himself, leaned back and weighed his words carefully.

'Gentlemen, the Russians would then have achieved what they have lusted after since the end of World War II — total control of Germany.' He picked up a pencil from the desk and casually waved it in the air, indicating that the subject was open for general debate.

There was a moment's silence, then all at once it seemed that everyone wanted to be heard. Possibly because his voice was shriller than the rest, possibly because it was also louder, it was Amos Barnett who ensured that it was he who would command the floor first. He stood up, his eyes blazing.

'Mr President, gentlemen, I've heard some screwball things in my time, but with the utmost respect, sir, this one takes the biscuit.'

The President smiled fleetingly at him, but said nothing. God, how he loathed that man.

There was a chorus of dissent from the others, and Barnett had to pitch his voice even higher to penetrate the noise.

'Listen, listen a moment, gentlemen, please. If — and it's a big 'if' — the Reds are behind such a scheme, as the President fears, then these documents may be nothing more than just clever fakes. Jesus, it wasn't so long ago that so-called learned historians were getting 'hard-ons' over the discovery of the 'Hitler Diaries'. Besides, from what I've heard about Hitler, he was incapable of fathering anyone. Hell, in my opinion, this is all in the realm of UFOs, Big Foot and the Bermuda Triangle!'

'Thank you for your comments, Mr Barnett,' the President acknowledged, in a voice as dry as egg-timer sand. 'I think Mr Wilmot might like to take you up on a point or two here.'

'You're damn right I would, sir,' Wilmot responded angrily. 'I make no claim to being an expert on UFOs and such like, but those documents have been through every test possible in our department, and I can positively say that they are absolutely genuine.'

'Absolutely,' McNabe confirmed.

Barnett sat down and shifted uncomfortably in his chair. He had clashed swords with Wilmot on other occasions and had never got the better of him. He had the feeling that he was going to lose out here as well. But he was determined not to give in without a fight.

'I would not dream of doubting the expert

opinion of Mr Wilmot and his CIA collegues,' he said acidly. 'But even assuming that these documents prove that a Hitler heir exists, surely this man would be er . . . well into his fifties by now. A pretty toothless tiger at that age, don't you think? Hardly an inspiration, I would have thought, to lead a glorious Fourth Reich. Oh, hell, it's too preposterous even to contemplate.'

'Oh, come now,' the President interjected with just a twinkle in his eye. 'Whilst I am well aware that Mr Barnett considers everyone over the age of forty-five to be geriatric, perhaps I could remind him that I will be celebrating my sixty-eighth birthday this year, and not only are most of my teeth still in my head, but many of my political opponents reckon they're rather sharp as well.'

A good deal of hearty laughter greeted this remark. Wilmot even applauded loudly. A sycophantic arsehole was Barnett's silent opinion of him. Nevertheless, he knew that this was not going to be his day. He had never endeared himself to the President — he was too damn honest for his liking — but he felt that, having been shouted down, it would have been unwise to continue to pour scorn on what was clearly a hypothesis that was being taken very seriously.

'Let's have a short recess here, shall we?' the President beamed, as he pressed a button on his intercom. Almost immediately two white-jacketed waiters wheeled in a food trolley. With great expertise one served the gathering with plates of scrambled eggs and smoked salmon, whilst the other dispensed the lemon tea into delicate china cups before departing from the room even speedier than they had entered it.

As they ate, the men talked earnestly and often heatedly. Eventually the President enthusiastically agreed to adopt the proposal initiated by Rabin, seconded by Wilmot and fiercely supported by Payne. This was that the three intelligence networks should pool their resources, each one providing a top specialist agent. The objective of this 'super' trio would be to track down the man named Sokol in Russia, and eliminate him.

'The success of this mission is vital,' the President concurred, 'for without a mystical leader, 'The Chain' will have to remain as they are — a group of fascist cells in countries that pose no real threat to international peace and security. I cannot emphasise how essential it is that we do not fail. I'm sure I can depend on you all.'

'With your approval, Mr President, might I suggest that the mission be known as

'Operation Front Man'?' Wilmot said.

The President nodded thoughtfully. 'Yes, a very appropriate code name.'

Thus at exactly 15.30, some five hours after they had first taken their seats in the Oval Room, the meeting came to an end.

When the door closed gently behind the last visitor, President Jones sat with a fixed expression on his face for some moments. He'd handled that briefing pretty well, he considered — yes, damn well. Then his eyes fell on the bundle of folders in his in-tray. God. All that paper work to plough through, and for each and every one submitted, someone was screaming for a decision or a directive right here and now. Sometimes he felt like he was running a corporation rather than a great nation. He glanced gloomily at his wristwatch, then slowly a defiant smile crept to his lips. He reached over from his chair to depress the intercom button.

'Sir?' a man's voice answered at once.

'Peters,' said the President to his trusted friend and aide, 'if we make it snappy we might just get nine holes in.'

'Yes, sir,' came the enthusiastic response.

14

'You've lost some weight,' McNabe said enviously, as he watched Shears slide into a chair in front of his desk. He patted his own stomach, which bulged over his belt buckle, and grimaced as he felt it.

'Since I gave up smoking, I've put on eleven pounds.' Dan remained silent and crossed his legs, while McNabe continued. 'I told my housekeeper, Mary, to get a lock for the fridge and then hide the key after she's made my dinner, so I can't go raiding it at night. So, do you know what I did? I spent half the night trying to pick it, and finished up going out to 'Creole Sam's All-night Hot Dog Stand'. He's now got himself a regular customer, coz I'm hooked on all that god damned junk food!' He slapped his stomach with the flat of his hand again. 'Now look at the state of me. I'd have been better off smoking, huh Doc?'

Shears eyed him steadily. 'What was the outcome of your meeting with the President, Paul?'

McNabe gave a gravelly chuckle. 'Why don't you learn to ask me direct questions?'

Shears continued to stare grimly at McNabe until he turned his attention to his desk and fiddled with some papers.

'Okay, this is the situation.' McNabe spoke deliberately, as he outlined to Shears exactly what had taken place at the White House, and the course of action that been decided upon. Shears leaned forward attentively as McNabe revealed that the CIA, MI6 and the Mossad would be working in concert on this one. When McNabe finished speaking, Shears only had one question.

'Who's going to be our man, Paul?'

'We haven't decided yet.'

'Really?'

'Well, we've got a few ideas and a couple of guys come to mind . . . '

'What about me?' Shears interrupted.

This was just what McNabe wanted to hear. Of course he had far more experienced operatives than Shears. In fact, almost everyone in the field unit was more experienced — but what they didn't have and this big Texan did, was first-hand knowledge of the men he was most likely to be in conflict with, when they were tracking down that son of a bitch. He was reasonably satisfied that the other two agents should be able to carry him as far as the language aspect was concerned, and the four weeks' intensive training at Langley to which all three of them would be subjected, would give him some grounding on the strategy that would be involved. But it was a dangerous mission, and McNabe felt that, should anything happen to Dan, it would remain on his conscience for the rest of his life — so it had to be Dan's choice, with him seemingly opposed to it.

'Oh, come on, Dan. You're a shrink, not a field man — you told me so yourself.'

'Yeah, and you once told me I was in this up to my neck — remember?'

McNabe sucked his right cheek, and nodded.

'It's going to be no pushover, Dan. And I'll be honest with you. Shirley could wind up a widow. Those Nazi bastards don't give second chances if you screw up!'

'Yeah — I've met a couple,' Shears said solemnly.

'All right Dan, you've asked for it — but it's on your own head, okay?' McNabe said warningly.

'Yep.' Shears grinned. 'Now, who are the other two men I'll be working with?'

McNabe looked at him earnestly, and it seemed to Shears that at that moment he was having second thoughts about accepting him for the mission. Then, with a resigned sigh, McNabe lifted a pink cardboard folder from his desk and withdrew a photograph.

'Right. Let's start with this guy, the Israeli. His name is Avi Solomon.'

15

Avi Solomon was thirty-three years old. He was by profession an actor/director with a renowned Tel Aviv theatre company called the 'Habima'. He was also — to use a word common to theatrical people throughout the world — resting!

Resting to Avi meant working his arse off trying to make an honest shekel to keep the 'goddamn bloody wolf from the door'. Although, as he had so often shouted in one of his more demonstrative and not infrequent outbursts with his live-in girlfriend Shari, he doubted whether he could keep the damned bloody wolf away for much longer anyway. The electricity and telephone had already been cut off, and 'there wasn't a fucking thing to eat in the place'.

He was presently occupied with the latest of his many original, but — as he would be the first to admit — not yet successful schemes that would one day make him a fortune. Though this one, he felt, could be the very one that would take him out of the shadows and place him permanently in the sunshine — horror ware. Surrounding him, as he sat hunched over the table with his brush poised, was a variety of delicately hand-painted crockery bearing sinister messages of doom. 'Have you enjoyed your meal? Good, it will be your last!' 'Too late. You've just been murdered by an untraceable poison.' Others had slugs, spiders, and other creepy-crawly insects all realistically portrayed. Those that he had deemed satisfactory held pride of place on every available shelf and window-sill. The remainder lay smashed at his feet.

Avi waved away, with considerable annoyance, a persistent bee that seemed intent on landing on his still wet handiwork. The bee avoided Avi's hand with metres to spare, and settled on the catch of the half-open balcony window. This time Avi gave chase and, stalking quickly across the small, compact living room of his first floor apartment, situated on the outskirts of the city, he swung the window out on its hinge into the open air, and had the satisfaction of seeing the bee swept away on a light breeze before he closed the window with a mighty tug. The wooden frame, having warped in the blazing sun, always needed 'the damn bloody strength of Samson to shut it.' He slotted the fingers of his hands together and bent them backwards until he heard the joints snap like dry twigs. Then he returned to his cluttered table and sat down. Selecting a fresh brush he soaked it to saturation point in a pot of luminiscent green paint. With his free hand he flicked aside the lank, black hair that totally obscured his forehead and fell across his eyes, giving the casual onlooker the impression that he was forever peering from behind a pair of untidily parted curtains. He chuckled to himself as he put the finishing touches to his latest caption: 'I prefer my stakes more underdone', which encircled a particularly vicious portrait of Count Dracula baring his elongated teeth. The sudden, shrill ring of the telephone startled Avi, and he saw that he had smudged his work. He cursed to himself as he picked up a rag and erased the smear. The peristent ringing irritated him and, without raising his head, he bellowed at the top of his voice.

'Answer the phone, sweetie. I'm up to my neck in it out here.'

A tall, sun-tanned beauty stood silhouetted in the framework of the living room door, her long, raven black hair hanging wet over her shoulders. A skimpy towel covered her breasts and ended just above the top of her thighs. As Avi watched her his anger turned to almost instant arousal. It was, however, a short-lived moment.

'Answer the fucking thing yourself,' she

screamed. 'Can't you see I'm taking a shower? You *Dummkopf!*' Then, turning swiftly, she re-entered the bathroom and slammed the door. The telephone ceased its ringing and Avi, in total frustration, hurled his paint brush, then a pot of paint, against the white wall. The impact made a glorious splash of colour, and Avi gave a cynical smile as he watched the dripping paint create a design that any avant-garde artist would have been proud of. Then suddenly it dawned on him. Surely the telephone had been cut off? He was just about to go after Shari when she reappeared in the doorway fuming.

'You lying bastard. I thought you told me you didn't have any money to have it reconnected?'

'But, sweetie, I didn't . . . I haven't . . . '

'You think I'm so much in love with you I hear bells ringing in my head?'

'But, sweetie, I swear to God . . . '

Before Avi could finish Shari flew at him, her arms punching out in all directions. Avi avoided her blows as best he could without hurting her, but my God, he thought, she could pack a punch. Then Avi started laughing. He always did when she lost her temper like that — he just couldn't help it. He also knew that the more he laughed the madder she became. Holding her tightly in his arms, he started to kiss her neck, while she wriggled and tried desperately to bite him. The towel slipped from her body and Avi eased her as gently as he could to the floor and pinned her like a butterfly beneath him. Shari groaned with pleasure, but before Avi could make his next move the telephone began ringing again. Breathing heavily, their eyes met.

'Let it bloody ring, darling,' she said seductively.

Avi thought about it for a moment.

'No, sweetie. It might be important.'

Shari sighed as she watched him go. It was typical of him to leave her at a moment like this. While she lay there she overheard Avi's whispered conversation. Picking up her towel, Shari quickly draped it around her and crept closer to the door. She heard him more clearly now. The clipped, monosyllabic tone and the intimate way in which he held the telephone made it quite obvious to her that he was talking to a woman. She could not, however, have been further from the truth.

Avi's hushed conversation was due to the fact that he was talking to his Mossad control. Over the years he had become a highly successful member of this organisation. It was the only part of his life that Shari knew nothing about, and, as far as he was concerned, was never going to.

He had first become interested in the Mossad when he had been idly rummaging through some drawers in his grandparents' house and had found some old documents belonging to his late father, Zvi Solomon. These papers clearly established Zvi as one of the founder members of the Lublin group — an organisation dedicated to tracking down ex-Nazis and summarily executing them. They operated under the code name 'Nakam' — a Hebrew word meaning vengeance. Avi had been most impressed at uncovering this hitherto unknown side of his father. He had always remembered him as a gentle, mild-mannered school teacher whom he had been told was tragically killed on the last day of the Suez campaign. Reading these heroic exploits of his father had given Avi a renewed sense of pride, and it was to be the beginning of a new way of thinking for him. His mother had died two years after his father and Avi had been brought up by his paternal Russian grandparents, who smothered him with affection and gave in to his every whim. He had always been full of self-confidence, and was considered amongst his friends to be a real 'show-off'.

For as long as anyone could remember, Avi

had wanted to go on the stage. By the time he was called up to do his National Service, he had already established himself as a most promising actor in the theatre. It was during his service in the army that he acquired his taste for adventure above and beyond the call of duty. On leaving the army, Avi went to see an MP in the Knesset who had fought alongside his father at Suez. He told him how much he would like to follow in his footsteps, and how much of an asset he felt he could be to them. The MP, quickly weighing up the talents and enthusiasm of the young Avi, said he would do the best he could for him.

Weeks later, after a performance at the theatre, Avi was visited backstage by a man who, he later discovered, was a member of the Mossad. In due course Avi was enrolled in the Israeli Secret Service, and was soon put through a most arduous and gruelling training programme, which was finally to result in his qualifying and becoming known inside that elite organisation as Agent 210, attached to Israeli Military Intelligence.

Avi came into his own during the Yom Kippur War; his theatrical training having made him a virtual master of disguise, he was able to penetrate the enemy lines dressed as a bedouin tribesman, and report back on

Egyptian troop movements. His usefulness to the Mossad was manifold and he had, to date, carried out many dangerous and successful missions on their behalf. But, unbeknown to him, he was about to embark on his most important assignment yet.

'Look, it's difficult for me to talk right now,' Avi said, catching a glimpse of Shari at the door. 'Yes, I'll meet you in the usual place at six.'

Replacing the phone, he turned to face Shari.

'Er . . . that was Yuri from the theatre. He told me they had all clubbed together and paid our phone bill. He was just checking the line. Aren't they a great bunch of kids?'

'You must think I was born yesterday, if you expect me to believe that,' Shari said icily. Avi shrugged his shoulders. 'Why don't you be honest and tell me who the little whore is?'

'Huh, look who's talking about whores. The uncrowned queen of the mile high club!'

'I've never been unfaithful to you in my life,' Shari could feel the tears burning in her eyes, 'which is a whole lot more than I can say for you.'

Avi fumed silently.

'So — go on, tell me who you're going to meet at six?'

'Look, sweetie, there are certain things in

my life that are private — and this is very private. Now, if you don't like it you can just fly away, little stewardess.' He flapped his arms like a duck with a fractured wing. 'Just fly away!'

Shari let out a stifled scream and ran into the kitchen. Avi could hear her smashing the crockery and throwing things around. 'The crazy little bitch,' he mumbled to himself.

'For God's sake, sweetie, cut it out. We haven't got much to start with,' he shouted, as he ran in after her. Avi avoided the first two missiles but wasn't quick enough for the third. His head blocked the full impact of a frying pan in mid flight and he dropped to the floor. He could feel the warm trickle of blood ooze through his hands. 'You stupid cow, I think you've killed me.'

'I hope I have, you worthless, womanising shit, you.' Shari was crying bitterly now, so Avi felt that this was the right moment to put his considerable acting talent to use. Letting out a loud groan, he began to die in a fashion that would have got a round of applause from all James Cagney buffs. He grimaced, he gurgled, he clutched his throat, and then, with eyes bulging, he twisted his body in agony before lying as still as a stone. Shari, not quite sure at first, became more alarmed by the minute as she stared at the blood on his white face. She rushed to his side, a mixture of fear and abject apology written all over her lovely features. She placed an ear to Avi's chest, then looked again at his ashen face. His right eyelid closed in a rakish wink, and before she could explode with anger at the way he had tricked her, Avi grabbed her to him and smothered her with kisses until he felt her resistance melt in his arms.

When he was sure she was no longer likely to be violent, he smiled.

'Listen to this idea I got while I was lying on the floor, sweetie. You know Jaffa Oranges are looking for a slogan?'

Shari just stared at him and wondered what the loon was on about now.

'Well, I got a humdinger. Listen to this,' he said excitedly. 'An orange a day keeps the blues away. You get it?'

Shari knew that when Avi was in a creative mood, the last thing in the world she should do was laugh. Perhaps it was all the build-up of tension — she didn't know — but she just burst out laughing.

'What's the goddamned matter with it?' he asked angrily. 'An ORANGE a day keeps the BLUES away. It's brilliant, you stupid cow!'

Still Shari could not stop laughing. That did it. He lost control and struck her hard across the face. Shari retaliated with a vicious swipe at him. Further blows were exchanged until they both lay exahusted on the floor.

It was then that the idea of making love seemed a much better proposition.

16

A fight of a more professional nature was taking place under the glittering light of the huge chandeliers that hung over the ballroom of the Grosvenor House Hotel, London. Two young middle-weight hopefuls were engaged in a bloody battle to decide which one would emerge as the contender for the Southern Area crown — a contest which would be fought in that same ring at the following monthly Anglo Sporting Club's presentation.

Surrounding the sweating, bloodstained boxers outside the raised ring and shouting encouragement or abuse were the evening-suited diners, who, having partaken of a splendid, if hurriedly served meal, had laid their bets across the tables with their fellow members and were now anxiously watching every blow, especially those being thrown by the man they didn't back.

Amongst the most vociferous and caustic of all the male spectators was the sponsor of table number eleven. There, presiding over a gathering of half-a-dozen friends, was the irrepressible antique dealer, Jack Scott. Having reduced his guests to a state of helpless laughter by giving his own commentary on the bout, Scott snapped his fingers at a hovering wine waiter and indicated that the brandy and liqueurs needed replenishing. At that moment another waiter approached the table and whispered something in his ear.

'What's he saying, Jack? That yer can't have no more bleedin' credit?' shouted one of the seated group, still with tears of mirth in his eyes.

'No,' replied Jack, quick as a flash, 'he said that old poof — and he nodded at you — had been trying to flog those crappy silver goblets to every mug down the 'Bello Road, and still drawn a blank.'

'Hey, I've offered you a bleedin' bargain there, mate.'

'I wouldn't have 'em for pouring piss in,' another guest interjected, before having a pretzel stick broken over his head for his trouble.

Jack stood up, still laughing. 'Gotta make a call,' he said, excusing himself. As he walked between the tables the ringside bell rang, and Jack threw a right hook in the air. A diner leaned over to him as he passed.

'If my schmuck had a right like that, I'd have been a ton up by now.'

Jack smiled and nodded his understanding, as he left the boisterous crowd in the ballroom and headed towards the foyer. He picked up the phone on the flower bedecked reception desk.

'Yes?' Jack immediately recognised the voice at the other end, and the humour drained from his face. It was Fraser, Colonel Robert Fraser, his M16 chief. Jack knew that if he'd had to call him there on a fun night — it was trouble.

John Alan Scott, 'Jack' since he could remember, had literally been born with a silver spoon in his mouth. His father, a tough Cockney market stall keeper, and his mother, one of nature's ladies, had graduated from their junk business on sites in Petticoat Lane, Hitchin Market and Romford to an enclosed half shop in the Portobello Road. The shop was so tiny, in fact, that his father was forced to dispense with the larger items of his 'priceless' antique stock — the Victorian urns, pictures, prints, brass fenders and such like — to specialise in smaller articles of interest. It was here that he realised that the bulk of their turnover and profit was in silver. By the time that Jack was old enough to toddle, his parents had established themselves in a highly successful shop in Kensington High Street. 'Scott's Silver Vaults' attracted dealers and buyers from all over the world. A chip off the old block in every way, it would have been unthinkable for young Jack to have contemplated any career other than taking over the family business. Jack left a good private school at the age of seventeen, because he was impatient to learn the game from his father. He soon showed he had a flair for spotting a bargain and loved the wheeling and dealing aspect. He travelled to various auction sales up and down the land, and his father let him learn from his mistakes the hard way. But the static job of serving behind a shop counter was not for him. That was all right for his mother and a couple of assistants maybe, but that life would have driven the restless Jack insane.

When he was twenty-two his father died after a long illness, and although it was a blessing not to see him suffer any more, it nearly broke Jack's heart. While helping his mother get over the loss, Jack spent more time with her and took over his father's London haunts, including regular visits to the big sales at Christies', Sotheby's and Phillips'. It was during a pre-sale viewing at one of these auctions that he became fascinated by a 'lot' of Russian silver. Quite apart from the fact that such pieces were rarely seen or available in the West, the workmanship made his mouth water. He decided he must have the small collection whatever the cost. And cost it did — an arm, a leg, and almost a second mortgage on his house. But it was this first acquisition of Russian silver that was to start him on the road to specialisation. In time, after much research and discussion with museum curators, he became something of an expert himself. He went to evening school to learn the language, so that he could actually trace the history and development of the craft of the Russian silversmiths. By the time he was thirty, he had made several trips to Iron Curtain countries where he had exhibited at antique trade fairs. He had often been to Moscow and had many acquaintances there who respected him as a knowledgeable and reputable dealer.

It was during one such visit to Moscow in 1969 that he had made the mistake of drinking too much in his lonely hotel room. About an hour after he started his solo binge, an attractive chambermaid came to turn down his bed. He half-jokingly suggested that it should be well rumpled up first. Somewhat to his surprise, the girl took up his offer.

When he awoke the next morning around midday, with his brain trying to leave his head via his eyeballs, his memory could only stretch back to one hell of a roly-poly night, and the second glass from the second bottle of vodka. Apart from the boozer's morning-after prayer of 'God, never again,' he thought no more of the incident until the day before he was due to depart. A package was delivered to his room containing several photographs of himself in various animated and acrobatic positions, accompanied by a rather unsubtle blackmail letter which threatened that 'If he didn't want his wife to know, he was to go down to the hotel foyer at once, where a man would introduce himself and have a little chat with him.' He could never recall ever feeling so sick before or since. The KGB had really bricked him up well, he thought. Had the photographs revealing his sexual prowess been that of a typical romp, he could have chatted and joked his way out of it. After all, he had often been called 'Jack the Lad' and was quite flattered by it. But with a man! His frustration and anger over the set-up knew no bounds. He never forgave the bastards who did it, and the burning embers of vengeance smouldered in his breast whenever he had the misfortune to remember the incident.

But the KGB had reckoned without his fighting spirit. Jack pretended that he was terrified his wife would see the photographs if he didn't comply with their wishes, but immediately on his return to the UK he got in touch with his great golfing chum, James Clifton, the Tory MP for Southgate West, who was at one time closely linked with the Ministry of Defence. During their game of golf — both shared a seemingly immovable handicap of twelve — he told Clifton exactly what had happened. Clifton reacted in a very positive way, and asked Jack to join him that evening at his club in Pall Mall. He was dining there with the one person who would be able to help him. That person turned out to be Colonel Fraser, then assistant controller of M16. The Colonel lost no time in telling Jack how useful he could be, if he apparently continued to go along with what the Russians wanted him to do, but in fact reported back to M16 all that took place, and more importantly, with whom he was dealing. They could always supply Jack with 'useful' pieces of information to keep up the Russians' interest. However, it was imperative that he quickly learn a few tricks about the espionage trade.

Over the years in the Service, Jack had become an excellent marksman, and was a second dan at karate. He had been on many undercover assignments in his role as a silver dealer, had had a few close calls, but it had never dimmed his sense of pride and satisfaction in a job well done.

The phone call from Colonel Fraser to the Grosvenor House Hotel was clipped and to the point. He was to be at his office at 09.00 hours the following morning for briefing. Before replacing the receiver, he couldn't resist adding a touch of dry humour. 'Oh, and Jack — pack!'

17

For the next four weeks Dan Shears, Jack Scott and Avi Solomon were put through their paces at Langley in a tough and gruelling training programme. The course was designed not only to bring them to the peak of physical condition, but to test them under combat as a team. As they flopped on to their bunks each night, with their aching muscles a constant reminder of the torture their instructors had inflicted on them, they began to get to know one another. They spoke about their own backgrounds or as much as they wanted to disclose. They argued, they joked, and it was clear that all they had in common, apart from a genuine loathing of totalitarian systems, albeit Fascist or Marxist, was a rather black, even sick, sense of humour.

On the last day of their course, McNabe invited them to his office for drinks.

'I'd like you to go out tonight and enjoy yourselves. Let your hair down,' McNabe said with a grin. 'I fixed up a place for you. My secretary will give you the details on your way out.'

It was an odd place to celebrate the end of their training together, to say the least, Dan thought. But that was typical of McNabe.

'Gloria's Rest Home' was an exclusive down-town massage parlour for tired executives. She had the classiest looking hookers in Washington working for her, and her patrons ranged from priests to politicians, all bound together by the bond of guilt-laden secrecy. Dan was convinced that her establishment was a latter-day version of the notorious World War II SS brothel, 'Salon Kitty's' and had more bugs in it than an entomologist's laboratory. In his mind he had no doubt that everything that took place at Gloria's was duly seen, heard and video-recorded back in that underground cavern of cloak and daggerism, Langley HQ.

'I reckon this place is bugged to the bleedin' eyeballs,' Jack uttered, as though reading Dan's mind as he took his replenished highball glass from the beautiful Chinese waitress. Dan nodded.

Avi smiled as his eyes met those of a stunning redhead seated at the bar. She crossed her legs provocatively, and sipped her martini.

'Well, if they're going to watch me perform tonight with that one,' he drew the attention of Dan and Jack to the girl at the bar, 'I should pick up at least an Emmy!'

The three men shared the joke, as indeed did McNabe, who was watching them on the small black and white TV screen in his office. 'So far they're getting along fine,' he muttered to an aide with a satisfied smirk on his face. 'Let's see how they behave together under fire.' He pressed an intercom on his desk.

'Sir?' came the reply.

'Is everything okay, Murphy?' McNabe spoke quietly into the intercom.

'Just waiting for your 'go ahead', Chief.'

'So go!'

★   ★   ★

There was a stifled scream from one of the girls near the door as it was kicked open. Two balaclavaed men burst in. Both held machine pistols. One sprang athletically to one side of the room while the other remained covering the door.

'Right,' came a muffled negro voice through the woollen helmet, 'we don't want no trouble. All youse guys empty out your pockets — we want money, watches, rings.'

'Yeah,' the other gunman agreed, 'and you, pretty lady,' he nodded to the redhead still seated on the bar stool, 'get that drawer from the till and empty it out in front of me here, so's I can see it.' He chuckled. 'Don't want you rippin' me off, now. Stickin' a few long ones down your tits.'

'Come on, come on,' his partner snapped angrily. 'Empty your fuckin' pockets.'

He moved to Jack who was nearest him and struck him hard on the shoulder with the butt of his pistol.

'Move, move, you mother fucker,' he snarled.

The pain shot through Jack's body like hot needles. I could take the bastard if he were just an inch or so closer, he thought, but he knew the other gunman would have plenty of time to splatter him and the others at his side all over the settee.

The redheaded girl brought the till drawer, which was jammed with dollar bills, to the centre of the room, while all the men slowly started emptying their pockets.

'Don't anyone try and be no heroes,' the gunman near Jack warned menacingly. 'Nice and slow and easy.'

The other gunman cleared the contents of the till, then went around swiftly collecting the money and jewellery that the male customers had placed in front of them, stuffing it into a small canvas holdall. He came close to Dan and picked up his billfold.

Then he spotted the diamond signet ring on Dan's pinkie. His brown eyes blazed hatefully, as he struck Dan hard across the mouth with back of his hand.

'You don't hear too good, do you man? We said take off your rings.'

Dan felt the blood trickling through his teeth.

'It . . . it won't come off,' he stammered.

The gunman produced a flick knife and pushed the button to release the gleaming blade.

'Then your goddamn finger will.' He leaned forward with the knife.

Dan swung his shoe toecap straight into the man's crutch. His gasp could be heard all around the room as he folded over like the lid of a suitcase. As he did so, Jack leapt at the gunman on his right, the force of the impact causing him to fall over the back of a chair. In a flash Jack was on him, cracking him with his tightly clenched fist across his jaw with uncontrolled fury, and he continued to hit him, even though the man had passed out several seconds earlier. The other gunman was still doubled up in pain, and Avi calmly took the gun from his hand as easily as taking coins from a blind beggar's hat.

Gloria, a woman of undetermined years, whose face, it was said, had been lifted more times than Tower Bridge, smiled with great difficulty, since her skin had been so tightly stretched that her mouth seemed to be fixed in a permanent sneer.

'Say, you guys,' the faded southern belle drawled at the trio, 'after the fuzz have taken this scum away' — she pulled the balaclava helmet from the winded negro and spat on his Rastafarian styled hair — 'everything — and I do mean everything, is on the house.'

'I think I'll pass on that, lady,' said Dan, retrieving his billfold.

'Don't be so hasty,' Avi said, smiling broadly at the redhead whose eyes now had admiration as well as invitation in them.

'Yeah, don't be so bloody hasty,' Jack concurred, as he weighed up the delicately lovely Chinese waitress. 'Does that apply to her an' all?' he asked.

'I said everything. Say, you're a Limey, ain't yer?'

'How did you guess?' Jack smiled wryly.

* * *

Jack and Avi went on to spend a happy night at Gloria's, while Dan went home to Shirley. All the while though Dan had had this nagging suspicion that McNabe had set up the raid just to see how they would react together, but he couldn't be sure about it. Anyway, he was very pleased with his two partners, and he hoped they had a similar respect for him. He need not have worried. Both admired his quick-thinking decisiveness, his easy charm and his ready wit.

As for McNabe, he was more than delighted with the way the men had clicked with each other on their first and very unexpected encounter with danger. His only immediate problem was what to tell the two coloured agents who had been ordered to stage a robbery at Gloria's as a security exercise — and had wound up having the shit beaten out of them. Yes — and as one of them was still in hospital with a wired-up broken jaw, that was going to be a problem.

In their final briefing it had been decided that Jack would go to Moscow under his usual cover three days before Avi, and Dan would travel forty-eight hours after the Israeli. They would be met by a CIA contact who would would arrange a secret rendez-vous, and there plans would be made to carry out their mission.

★　★　★

238

The voice on the tannoy in French, Russian, English and German made it clear that Dan should make preparations to board his plane. Adjusting the camera slung over his shoulder, he gathered his two cases, his guide book to the Soviet capital, and tagged on to the end of a queue, looking for all the world just as he was supposed to — a first time American tourist to Russia.

18

On first impression, the capital of a country that could boast of having one hundred different nationalities living therein looked to Dan to be a rather dreary, rather ordinary, grey city.

The taxi came to a halt in the long, semi-circular driveway of the Cosmos Hotel, by Russian standards a high building at twenty-six storeys; by New York standards, where he recalled with affection his young intern days, it was a bungalow! He sorted out his change, handed the driver about a hundred kopeks, and was thanked with a cheery grin.

Dan's room on the tenth floor was clean, bright and small. Gazing out through the picture window he had a good view below of what he knew, through studying the brochures, was the permanent home of the Economic Achievements Exhibition. It was certainly an impressive sight, with its gigantic space monument, tree-lined avenues and sparkling fountains. He stared absent-mindedly for a while at the hundreds of Muscovites weaving their way in and out of the grounds, tiny, soberly dressed citizens, looking like well-drilled woodlice making a track in a rotting piece of bark.

There was a gentle tap at the door, but before he could get there an envelope was slid beneath it. He opened the door quickly and was just in time to see the back of a shapely woman disappearing round a corridor. She wore a neat, plum two-piece suit, a matching hat, and had the best pair of legs he'd seen in months.

The envelope was addressed to Dr Shears. He tore it open and took out a note. It read simply 'Entrance Tolstoi Museum, 14.30 today'. It was unsigned.

★ ★ ★

The long journey was catching up with Dan, and despite the shower he'd had in the hotel, he was feeling jet-lagged and weary. With an expansive yawn he joined a small queue waiting to enter the Tolstoi Museum. He couldn't help but feel that a good night's sleep would have put him in a much more receptive frame of mind for the impending meeting. And why the hell this very public place should be the apparent rendezvous was, in his tired state, an utter mystery to him. A group of excited school children attracted his attention for a moment as they were lined up behind him in an orderly manner by a bespectacled and somewhat harassed teacher doing her best to maintain discipline. Looking down at the children, he saw that two little girls were giggling, and one of them was making gestures with her hand to her smaller companion. He guessed, rightly, that they were rather intrigued by his height. He smiled back at them, and the tinier of the pair, who had her hair tied up in tight bunches, produced a crumpled paper bag of what seemed to contain sticky boiled candy. She shyly offered him one, while her little friend giggled into her cupped hands. He was about to accept the gift, when he felt himself gripped firmly by the elbow and wheeled by a powerful arm to one side.

'Dear me,' a familiar voice tut-tutted, 'Didn't yer mother ever warn you about taking sweets from strangers?'

'Jack!' Dan exclaimed in surprise. 'I didn't expect . . . ' Jack indicated the necessity for silence by shaking his head slightly and furrowing his brow. Dan got into step beside him and they walked in silence into the splendid gardens that surrounded the Museum and up towards Leo Tolstoi Street. Away from the crowd Jack felt it safe to speak.

'We met our man, our CIA contact.'

Dan looked at him, just a shade puzzled.

'He was in his room,' Jack continued with a pause, 'he was dead. The poor sod had been horribly tortured before he snuffed it.'

'So where are we heading now?' Dan asked.

'To a car that's waiting for us in Komsomolski Avenue.' Jack checked his watch. 'Avi's picked up some information. We're going to meet him.'

It took about ten minutes for them to reach the intersection of Leo Tolstoi Street and Komsomolski Avenue.

'That's it!' Jack said, nodding to the blue 'Zhiguli' parked just ahead of them with its engine running. Although Dan could not see the driver's face, he recognised at once the plum coloured suit and hat she was wearing. It was the girl with the lovely legs. She smiled at him as he clambered inside.

'This is Natali,' Jack said with a saucy smile. 'She's been made available to us. Her English ain't bad — her French is something else.' He looked at Dan meaningfully. 'She can also drive a bit.' The car soared away as though Natali were preparing for lift-off. 'As you can see!'

'I sink we're being copied,' Natali said, looking in her rear mirror.

Jack turned and looked through the back window and saw a brown car close on their tail. Natali slowed down slightly before swinging the car sharply around the next corner into a narrow side street. A second or two later the two men staring out of the rear window watched as the brown car came into view.

'You vant me to lose zem?' Natali asked coolly.

'Yeah,' replied Jack.

'Okay. Hold on tight.'

The next ten minutes were the longest that either of them could remember. They were also the most hair-raising. It began by Natali manoeuvering the vehicle into such a tight U-turn that when she mounted the kerb and sped in the opposite direction from the pursuing car, she removed most of the nearside paintwork, the wing mirror and her sidelight. As the car rattled along a row of wall railings, Dan caught the surprised look on the faces of the three men seated in the brown car as they flashed past. Natali had gained an advantage, but it wasn't to last for long. Moments later the other car had turned and was giving full chase. Increasing her speed at an alarming rate, Natali drove towards the embankment of the river Moskva. Soon they were at the river's edge, careering at such a rate past the small ships and boats sailing to and fro on it that they all looked as if they had suddenly dropped anchor. But the more powerful car at their rear was gaining on them rapidly. At Frounzenskaia Quayside, where men were loading and unloading a whole variety of goods in sealed packing cases, Natali really cut loose, weaving in and out of the huge stationary trucks. Still the car behind them was rapidly closing the gap. Natali raced towards a clear section of the quayside, so near to the brink that at any moment Dan felt the wheels would skid on a wet patch, and they would all be plunging down into the river. That fate, however, was to befall their pursuers when, without any warning, Natali did her incredible U-turn trick again and headed, with the speed of an express train, straight towards the oncoming car. A parked articulated truck prevented the driver of the brown car from swerving to his right. At the last moment — almost as a reflex action — he swung the wheel sharply to his left. The car leapt off the quayside into the air, where for a second or so it seemed to defy gravity before it nose-dived into the river. Natali came to a screeching halt and they watched as the car floated momentarily on the surface, then, with a bubbling gurgle, it slowly sank in a great swirling pool of ripples and was gone from sight.

Jack swallowed hard before licking his lips and speaking to Dan.

'You look terrible, mate.'

'I'm not surprised,' Dan quipped. 'It's the sight of your face that's making me feel that way.'

Natali released the handbrake and smoothly eased forward. Jack, still ashen-faced, spoke to Natali.

'How did you know that at the last moment they were going to pull away?'

'I didn't,' Natali replied evenly, 'but von can alvays assume that most men are cowards.'

Jack turned his head towards Dan, and rolled his eyes heavenwards. No one spoke again until they reached their destination.

'This is it — Avi's place,' said Jack, as the car stopped outside a large, red brick apartment block.

'Uh huh,' Dan acknowledged as he got out and stretched himself.

'Shall I call back for you?' Natali smiled prettily.

'No!' The two men spoke in unison.

'We . . . er . . . dunno what time we'll be through,' Jack blustered. 'We'll make contact through the usual channel.'

'Thanks for the ride, honey,' Dan said, then turning to Jack muttered, 'Hell, she's quite a gal.'

'Potty — bloody potty,' Jack replied, shaking his head as they walked through the swing door entrance to the building.

As the rickety elevator took them up to the third floor, Jack, keeping his voice at little more than a whisper, told Dan that Avi was staying with Max Verbolen, a Dutch foreign correspondent employed by Radio Hilversum. He had been living in Moscow for almost a decade, and had been a most useful informant to MI6.

'He's in apartment twenty-two,' Jack said as he stepped out of the elevator.

'Two along, if these are progressing in order,' Dan muttered, glancing at the numbers.

A door opened and Avi poked his head round it.

'I heard the elevator. Come in, come in. And about time, too,' he added impatiently.

The two men slid past him into a small hallway. But Avi did not close the door behind them; instead he peered up the corridor as though expecting the arrival of someone else. After a moment or two he turned to Jack.

'Where are the other guys?'

'What other guys?'

'I asked them to follow you here.' Avi looked a trifle concerned. 'They're our Mossad contacts, and they've got some very strong leads for us.'

'They weren't driving a brown car, were they?' Dan asked, almost dreading the reply.

'Then you did see them,' Avi beamed happily.

Jack cleared his throat. 'I should close the door if I were you, old son. I don't think they're going to be joining us.'

19

'This man's face I've seen somewhere before,' Wolfgang Hollerbach muttered almost inaudibly, as he pointed to a photograph of Dan. 'These other two men — no.' He shook his head vehemently as he studied the photographs of Jack and Avi.

A tall, fair-haired man in his mid thirties, leaning over Hollerbach as he sat in a chair looking for all the world like a bundle of old clothes waiting to be delivered to an Oxfam centre, took the photographs from him.

'The man you recognise attended the same house party as you, which was given by Herr Prama.'

'Of course,' Hollerbach said slowly, as he remembered that dreadful night.

The fair-haired man, known only to Hollerbach by his first name, Horst, spoke in a clipped, military manner.

'His name is Daniel Shears. He is a doctor of psychiatry and works for the CIA. The other two are Jack Scott, British agent, and this one with the swarthy complexion,' he toyed with the photograph of Avi, 'is a man of many faces — an actor who also works for the

Mossad.' He paused momentarily.

'They are here in Moscow to track down the man that we have to determine is the Führer's rightful heir, and to eliminate him.'

Hollerbach sat bolt upright. 'Good Lord! We must prevent that at all costs.'

'Mmm, yes,' Horst said pensively. 'Well, we are going to see that they are kept occupied with other things for the time being, so that we have a clear road to carry out our own plans. But first, we must establish beyond doubt that Vladimir Sokol is our man.'

Hollerbach looked at him attentively.

'Soon you will be given the chance to question and examine him.'

'What — in prison?' Hollerbach said incredulously.

'Er . . . not exactly. We have some friends of the Kameraden in the Lubyanka — wrongly imprisoned for their political views. One of them has been instructed to pick a fight with Sokol and injure him just enough to ensure that he is transferred to the hospital prison wing.'

'And that will be an advantage?'

Horst took a deep breath. This fat little man was beginning to irritate him, but he held his temper in check.

'Very much so. Security is not so tight there and we will, with the help of our friends, be able to get you inside as a male nurse. Your Russian, I am told, is flawless?'

Hollerbach gave an embarrassed cough.

'Well, my interviews with Soviet military historians have been highly commended by my paper, and I have had no trouble in communication.'

'I am very pleased to hear it. For all our sakes it had better continue that way.' The menace in his voice was not lost on Hollerbach. Why the hell hadn't Prama let him be? God — even Hess had been allowed to spend his last days in peace, incarcerated in Spandau though he may have been.

'Now, as soon as we have dealt with these three men,' Horst waved the photographs again, 'we will be able to carry out our objective.'

Hollerbach winced visibly. He had had the misfortune of being present when the CIA agent they had captured had been systematically tortured. Horst and his two henchmen, who now sat quietly in the corner playing chess, had taken great delight in performing their task. Before the poor man had finally expired, he had revealed that the CIA had conclusive evidence that Sokol was still in the Lubyanka. Horst saw the expression on his face and laughed contemptuously.

'Surely you are not concerned by what

happened to that CIA agent, are you? After all, the swine knew the risks involved — all part and parcel of the job, you might say.'

'Oh, yes, quite,' Hollerbach said, lighting up a cigarette with a shaking hand. 'But won't the sudden death of these other men raise a few questions, and might not that make our mission even more precarious?'

Horst laughed again. 'Don't worry. We shall not upset your squeamish stomach again, old man. We shall see to it that the KGB take care of these three agents, at least for the time being. You see, we shall still need them as a decoy later on.'

20

It was in the early hours of the morning, and several glasses of slivovitz later, that Jack Scott had his bright idea.

'I know this geezer,' he said to Dan and Avi, 'he's about as straight and harmless as a coil of barbed wire, but he'll do anything for a bundle of hard currency.' Jack rose wearily from his chair and replenished his glass from what remained of their last bottle of plum brandy. 'Hand him some British pound notes or Yankee dollars and he'd talk the boss of the Politburo into blacking up and singing 'The Old Folks at Home'.'

'I still think we should make contact with HQ and tell them what's happened,' said Avi morosely.

'And I'm inclined to agree with him,' Dan sighed.

'Look, you two, what do you think they'll say? Well done lads, you've knocked off three of our men? They're more likely to say 'Go and see if you can get a job with the KGB — you're more useful to them than to us'.'

'You have a point there,' Dan smiled wryly, 'but do you mean to tell me that those guys at the bottom of the river were the only contacts you have here?'

'Course not,' Jack and Avi said, almost in unison.

'Trouble is,' Jack went on, 'time we make contact and tell 'em what we're up to, that Fascist mob will have got young Adolf out and be measuring up his arm for a swastika band.'

'This is the problem,' Avi flicked back the hair from his eyes, 'we just don't have much time. Tell me, what does this Russian friend of yours do?'

'He's what I'd call a rather successful black marketeer. He's officially a customs officer, but he's one 'ell of a character,' Jack laughed. 'That's how I first met him, about ten years ago it was. I was trying to smuggle out some beautiful antique snuff boxes I'd managed to acquire, when this geezer looks me straight in the eye and gets me to open up my case. He takes one look at the swag, spots a bundle of fivers under me shirts, pockets the money, shuts the suitcase and, with a wink, wishes me *bon voyage*. We've been doing business off and on ever since. If anyone can help us, he can.'

254

'How can you get in touch with him?' Dan asked.

'Easy,' Jack replied, turning the pages of a small black pocket book. 'I got his dog-and-bone number, ain't I?' Jack advanced towards the telephone.

'You going to phone him at this hour of the bloody morning?' Avi frowned.

'You got any better ideas, mate? Anyway, if I know him he won't be asleep. Ten to one he'll still be entertaining a lady.' Jack grinned as he pushed the numbered digits on the instrument.

★　★　★

But it was one of those rare occasions when not only was Prokopy Rastorotsky alone, he was, until the telephone rudely awoke him, in a deep, drunken slumber.

'Oh dear, I haven't woken you, have I, Proky?' Jack said in Russian, without sounding the least bit concerned when he heard the voice of Rastorotsky at the other end.

Rastorotsky, sleepy as he was, recognised the voice of his English friend almost at once.

'Of course not, you capitalist pig. I'm sitting at my desk writing another volume of my great masterpiece on the rise and fall of the Western world.'

'Well, when you've run out of shit paper, I'd like to see you pronto. Me and some friends need your help, comrade.'

★ ★ ★

Rastorotsky arrived at the apartment less than forty minutes after the phone call. The big Russian, who weighed in at close on 210 lbs, beamed from ear to ear as Jack welcomed him at the door. He hugged Jack like a great grizzly bear then, stepping back to take a good look at his old friend, he suddenly became very serious; only the merry twinkle in his eye was an indication to Jack of what might be coming.

'I will have to be very quick — the GRU have followed me here.'

Then he roared with laughter as he watched the colour drain from the faces of Dan and Avi.

'Just look at their faces,' he said to Jack, and the tears ran down his leathery cheeks as he tried to restrain himself from a further outburst of wheezy laughter.

'Oh, just to see the faces of your two friends was almost worth the effort of getting out of bed at this God-forsaken hour.' He ambled over to an armchair and slumped down into it.

'First a glass of vodka — then tell me how I can help.'

While Avi poured the vodka, Jack told him that they were anxious to ascertain whether a man called Vladimir Sokol was a prisoner in Lubyanka Jail.

'That should not be too difficult for me, my friend,' Rastorotsky grunted, 'but of course it will cost money.'

'Of course,' Jack nodded. 'Now, if you do find out that he's inside — we have to get him out.'

Rastorotsky stared at Jack as though he were mad.

'Are you serious?'

'Deadly!'

The big Russian turned to address Dan and Avi.

'Is he really serious, or has he become deranged?'

Dan spoke for the first time.

'I think he means it,' he said pleasantly.

'Oh, you Yankee, eh? Listen — if you have American dollars, I can get you anything your heart desires. I know some . . . '

'All our hearts desire right now,' Jack cut in, 'is the information I just asked for.'

After what seemed an age, Rastorotsky spoke soberly.

'I do not ever recall having heard of anyone escape from the Lubyanka.'

'There's always a first time,' Jack grinned.

'What is so important about this man anyway? Is he a master spy or something?'

'Yes, that's right — something!' Jack said, still grinning. 'Can you help us or not?'

'Well, as I said, I can certainly find out if this man is a prisoner there, but as for getting him out . . . ' Rastorotsky looked at the three men thoughtfully, ' . . . it would take time to organise such a plan of escape — and money, it would take plenty of money.'

'Time is what we haven't got,' Jack said, 'but the money we'll agree to haggle over as usual. Now, can you do it — and fast?'

Rastorotsky slapped the arm of his chair and got up.

'I will begin to make enquiries. With enough money some of the guards might be tempted to look the other way.' He nodded his head and laughed. 'Nothing I like more than a challenge. Now, I shall need some Western currency — an advance to pay the right people, you understand?'

'Sure, sure,' Jack said and, taking out his wallet, he started to remove some notes. Rastorotsky glanced at them briefly.

'Er . . . no offence intended — but if your

friend here has American dollars, I prefer them to sterling.'

Dan shrugged, and took a billfold from his back pocket and handed it to Jack.

'You wouldn't rather have shekels?' Avi smiled, tapping his wallet.

'What — with the Israeli rate of inflation? It's worse than ours.'

Dan had about 2,000 dollars in hundred-dollar and smaller bills. Jack peeled off 500 dollars and handed them to Rastorotsky. He seemed satisfied.

'You, Jack, meet me for tea at the Peking Hotel tomorrow. Four o'clock, yes? Maybe I learn something by then, *tovarisch*.'

'So, what do you think?' Avi eyed Jack keenly when Rastorotsky had taken his leave.

'I think he'll come good,' Jack said, quietly confident.

21

Jack's own words — 'I think he'll come good' — came back to him like a boomerang hitting him in the mouth, as he watched the two powerfully built men bearing down on him. It was already too late to make a run for it. In any case, he ruminated, it served him bloody well right; he should have become suspicious much earlier when, after waiting more than half an hour, there was still no sign of Rastorotsky.

'Mr Scott?' the larger of the two men queried in English.

'That's right,' Jack replied calmly, belying his hammering heart. These were GRU men from the top of their old-fashioned trilby hats to the soles of their big, broad and equally dated shoes.

'We'd like you to accompany us,' the large Russian continued.

Jack's mind worked overtime. Bluff it out all the way, boy, it urged, be co-operative, be cunning and above all, be cool!

'Accompany you where?' he asked, with the wide-eyed innocence of little orphan Annie.

Wordlessly, the slighter built of the Russian

pair gripped him firmly by his arm. His eyes blazed angrily as he almost lifted Jack out of his seat with one hand.

'He doesn't say much, does he?' Jack said with a faint smile to the large Russian, as his companion led him to the door.

★ ★ ★

Back in the apartment Avi was making coffee and Dan was watching a film on Soviet space achievement on TV when there was a tap at the door. Avi crept quietly into the lounge and, switching off the TV set, indicated to Dan to be silent. The tap came again and it was louder this time.

'Who is it?' Avi queried in Russian.

'Parcel post for Max Verbolen' a man's voice replied.

Avi shrugged his shoulders at Dan. It seemed okay, so he opened the door. As he did so he knew instinctively it was an idiotic mistake, but there was not a 'damn bloody thing' he could do about it now. The man on the other side was dressed as a postman right enough. He was carrying a parcel. He was also pointing a revolver straight at Avi's heart. A second man, who had been hiding just out of sight, sprang agilely into view, holding an even more lethal weapon, a machine pistol.

He knocked Avi aside and leapt into the lounge where he levelled the gun with both hands at the seated Dan's head.

'One move, one flicker of an eyelid,' said 'the postman' to Avi, 'and we will take great pleasure in blasting you to pieces.' And both Avi and Dan knew that he meant it.

'You will come with us, please,' said the second gunman.

Avi and Dan reached the street with the gunmen just a pace at their rear. As they did so, a black car swung alongside them and the back door was thrown open.

'Do join me, gentlemen,' Horst greeted them with a triumphant smile from the back seat. With guns poking in their backs, Dan and Avi had little choice but to accept the invitation.

As the car sped away, Horst spoke again.

'Two little spy birds with one stone, eh?' he said. 'Oh, and I am sorry to have to be the bearer of bad news, but Mr Scott will not be making this little journey with us. He had a prior engagement with some officers from Soviet Military Intelligence.'

*　*　*

In the car that took him to the grey stone building, down the steps to the basement, and all along the corridor to the small room that he was now locked in, Jack had protested. He had protested about wrongful arrest, he had protested about infringement of human rights and of his captors being held personally responsible for causing what might be an international incident that could spark off a world war and all the subsequent horrors of that holocaust. All his protests, however, had fallen on completely deaf ears, and as the door was finally closing on him he shouted, in a voice so loud that he was certain it could be heard in the street outside, that he absolutely demanded to see the British Ambassador. 'In person', he screamed for good measure.

That had been more than four hours ago, and he had been shut up in this tiny room ever since. He was beginning to accept that he was in for a very long stay, when he heard footsteps, faint at first, then louder as they echoed down the corridor, and coming nearer and nearer. This is it, he thought, as they stopped outside his room. Dry-mouthed, he heard the key release the lock in the door. He sat bolt upright, mentally bracing himself for what was to come.

22

The door swung open and the tangy smell of oranges permeated the stench of rotting cabbage. This place had at one time, quite recently too, Dan thought, been a fruit and vegetable warehouse. It was also, he surmised, somewhere near the river. All this was pure guesswork on Dan's part, as he had been blindfolded and gagged for most of the journey, an experience he found disorientating and downright frightening. Unseen hands guided him further into the room before pushing him down into a chair. He remained passive while they roughly bound his arms tightly to it before finally removing the gag and blindfold. It took a few seconds for Dan's eyes to grow accustomed to the dimly lit cellar, but as the visual purple took effect, he surveyed his surroundings. Broken pieces of packing-case wood, crumpled old cardboard boxes and bits of decaying vegetable matter lay everywhere. Distant silhouetted figures came through the open door; the last, the fourth of them, closed it noisily behind him. Dan watched and strained his ears to listen as they stood huddled in a group talking earnestly in low voices — but he could grasp very little of the conversation. In a far corner he could just make out another figure, who, like himself, was bound to a chair — it was Avi. His lank, black hair hung over the blindfold and he grunted now and again with frustration as he tried, to no avail, to loosen the ropes and ease his gag. Eventually the whispering stopped. One man turned away from the other three and approached Dan. It was Horst. He smiled pleasantly.

'I apologise, Dr Shears, for the methods we feel compelled to use in order that you should both be our guests here. But you see, we are rather concerned because, not only do we know that you are an agent of the CIA, we also know that you stole some documents that we regard as our property. So now we shall need to ask you some questions.' Horst raised an eyebrow.

Dan remained silent.

'As this is likely to be rather a long discussion,' Horst continued, 'may I offer you some refreshment? Coffee, or something a little stronger perhaps?' Horst saw that Dan was tight-lipped. 'No? Well perhaps later — yes, I am sure you will not decline something later.'

Dan could feel his palms sweating. He remembered McNabe's warning. He knew these Nazi bastards would stop at nothing to get what they wanted, but he would do his damnedest to hold on somehow.

Horst pulled up a chair and sat facing Dan. He clasped his hands together and leaned forward in a confidential manner.

'Now then, would you like to tell us exactly what information you have on the present whereabouts of Vladimir Sokol?'

Dan feigned a look of complete bewilderment.

'Oh, come on now. Don't look so surprised. We already know precisely why you and your colleagues are here. What we are not clear about are your intentions. In other words, Dr Shears, what are your orders from the CIA concerning Sokol?'

Dan felt at this point compelled to speak. He had to try and bluff his way out.

'Look, I don't know what the hell you're talking about. The only thing you've got right so far is my name and profession. Jeeze, I'm just a guy taking a vacation here.'

Horst tutted theatrically.

'Oh dear, and I was hoping that you were not going to be difficult. Wolf, come over here please.'

Hollerbach emerged from the shadows. Dan recognised him instantly, but remained stony-faced.

'Tell me Wolf, do you recall seeing this man at Herr Prama's party?'

'Yes,' Hollerbach replied nervously.

'Thank you, Wolf,' Horst smirked. 'Now let's not have any more silly pretence, mmm? Dr Shears?'

Oh boy. Dan thought, my bluffing sure paid off there. But he remained silent, and just looked past Horst blankly.

Horst sighed deeply. 'Very well, bring over the Jew.'

The two heavies went into the corner and with little effort lifted Avi, still tied to the chair, and placed him down at the side of Horst. Avi no longer struggled. He just sat with his head cocked on one side and waited like a helpless animal, Dan thought, for the next move to be made.

Another man dressed in a white surgical coat wheeled over a trolley. On it Dan saw a variety of medical instruments — a pair of forceps, tweezers, a set of different sized scalpels, a couple of hypodermic needles, a kidney basin, a bottle of what looked like surgical spirit, some other unidentifiable coloured liquids in bottles, cotton wool and other items. An electrical appliance with two leads that looked remarkably like car battery jump leads held a prominent position in the centre of the trolley.

'Some of these instruments you will undoubtedly recognise, Dr Shears. Some have been adapted over the years by our friends in the medical profession. I think you will find that they have been quite ingenious.'

Horst snatched the blindfold from Avi. Dan watched him blink and try to focus, then he saw the fear come into those big, brown eyes as Avi stared at the gadgets on the trolley and quickly assessed the situation.

'Now then,' Horst said brightly to Avi, 'because your friend here is stubbornly refusing to be co-operative, I am reluctantly compelled to see if we can't persuade him to change his mind.'

Horst nodded towards the man in the white coat, who immediately began to uncoil the two wire cables from the electrical apparatus. At the tips of the wires were two terminals. The man took some cotton wool and poured some surgical spirit on two pieces before attaching them to the terminals, and waited.

Avi struggled against his bonds uselessly, whilst Dan fought desperately with his own, with about the same lack of effectiveness.

'Before we resort to becoming uncivilised, Dr Shears,' Horst said reasonably, 'perhaps you would rather answer my questions?'

Dan gritted his teeth and uttered not a sound.

'Very well,' Horst gave a humourless smile and nodded to one of his henchmen, who moved over to Avi. He loosened his belt, unzipped his flies, and deftly yanked his trousers down to his knees. He followed this by pulling away his underpants and exposing his genitalia.

Beads of sweat broke out over Avi's forehead as he held his bare knees together so tightly that even Dan could see that they were white from forcing the blood away from them. God — it was Avi they were going to torture, and he was going to be responsible for it. He felt physically sick. There had been nothing in the crash training programme in Washington to cover this contingency.

'Perhaps now you will reconsider answering my questions?'

Dan looked quickly at Avi, whose eyes said 'no'. Dan turned and glared at Horst.

'I've already told you that I don't know what you're talking about.'

'I see. Then I think that you will find what is about to take place quite fascinating, Dr Shears. You will be able to witness, by observing the needle here,' Horst pointed to the graduated dial under glass on the instrument, 'exactly how many volts the human body can withstand. The amount does of course vary from individual to individual. And naturally it all depends on which part of the anatomy the electrodes are attached to. I am not sure whether it is true, of course, but they do say that those individuals with the mark of Abraham on their penises have a lower pain barrier than those men who have not been mutilated by that barbaric ceremony. However, we shall see.'

★　★　★

'Mr Scott?' said the distinguished looking Englishman as he proffered a hand and smiled amiably.

At least three replies buzzed through Jack's mind as he sat defiantly in the chair.

'No, I'm Mr Mugabe, you berk!' 'Why, who else is in the bleedin' room?' . . . But out of sheer relief to see this man who oozed British Embassy charm, Jack just answered with a meek 'Yes'.

'Seems there's been some frightful blunder. Oh, by the way my name is Harrington — Michael. These security chaps can be rather zealous,' Harrington said earnestly, then added quickly, as though suddenly realising that the room was probably bugged, 'and one can hardly blame them of course.

They have a job to do.'

'So why am I here then?' Jack asked.

'Eh? Oh, but of course you can go — ha, ha.' Harrington laughed nervously. 'That's why I've been sent along — to 'spring' you as it were. Ha, ha!'

'Right,' Jack grunted, 'but why did they take me in?'

As they walked out of the building with the surly approval of the guards at the desk, Harrington, one of the junior vice-consuls at the British Embassy, told him that the KGB had had a tip-off that he, Scott, was in Moscow on behalf of a subversive group, and was about to issue anti-government literature. The KGB had searched his room while he was being held, had found nothing, and decided to contact the British Embassy.

'We were able to assure them that you are a legitimate dealer in antiques, and that you had been here many times over the years with absolutely no problems, and had no political connections whatsoever ... They weren't ... er ... unpleasant to you in any way, were they?' Harrington asked anxiously.

'Oh no, they were delightful — as always.'

Jack's sarcasm was totally lost on Harrington.

'Oh, good, good. Don't want any acrimonious diplomatic incident stuff and all that.

Lots of paperwork, you know. Oh, can I give you a lift anywhere?'

'No thanks,' Jack replied thoughtfully, 'I'd prefer to walk.'

They parted company with firm handshakes, and Jack strolled down Manejnaia Street towards the square, north-west of the Kremlin wall. As he walked on, he heard heavy footsteps and laborious breathing behind him. Immediately alert, he swung round and saw the barrel-like figure of Rastorotsky gasping and waving an arm as he tried to catch up with him.

'My God,' Rastorotsky wheezed and took great gulps of air, 'you could . . . ' he breathed deeply, 'you could walk for Britain in the Olympics!'

Jack grinned and glanced at his watch.

'Bit late for our tea date, *tovarisch*?'

'Listen — you have no time for jokes. When I saw those GRU pigs take you away . . . excuse me,' Rastorotsky was sweating, going purple, and breathing hard all at the same time. It was not a pretty sight, observed Jack. 'I went immediately to tell your friends, and was just in time . . . ' Rastorotsky looked as though he were going to faint from the effort, ' . . . to see them also being taken away. I fear they may be in grave danger.'

'Who took them?'

'None of our lot. I am certain I know most of the KGB and GRU faces in this city.'

'Did you see where they were taken?' Jack asked, greatly concerned.

'Yes, I followed them in a taxi — it cost me almost 100 roubles — I will have to ask you to repay . . . '

'Oh, sod the money for now, mate. We've got to get there, and fast.' Jack slapped him on the back. 'Good on you, you old fart! You did something right for a change.'

* * *

The bulging eyes of Avi and the sudden jumping spasms of his body were truly terrible for Dan to behold. Each time the switch was thrown, the current shot through him from the electrodes attached to his genitals. He could not scream — the gag on his mouth was too tight for that — only those wild eyes, almost threatening to burst out of his skull, mirrored the intense pain he was suffering.

'Leave him alone, for God's sake, you bastards.' Dan screamed at Avi's tormentors. In just this single sampling of their pleasure in carrying out torture, did Dan get a fragmentary glimpse of what it must have been like to be a victim of the Nazis when they were all-powerful. Only Hollerbach turned away, unable to watch the sickening scene. The others just grinned when the voltage was increased and they could observe the convulsions of Avi's pain-racked frame.

'But Dr Shears,' Horst said reasonably, 'you can stop this, you know. All you have to do is tell us what we want to know. It's as easy as that.'

Again Dan struggled to break free of his shackles, but he was bound so tightly that all he succeeded in doing was causing the ropes to cut deeper into his flesh.

'I keep telling you — I don't know what the hell you're on about.'

Horst looked at him and shook his head sadly.

'My only concern is that by the time you do come to your senses, it will be too late to save your Jewish friend here. Not that I would be unsympathetic if you had decided he was not worth saving. We, after all, have a lot of catching up to do. The final solution, alas, was by no means final enough.'

Dan stared at him in utter loathing. He had never had any desire to kill any living creature. The Hippocratic oath that he had taken had been well ingrained in his thinking. But, oh boy, if he could break free right now, he would take the greatest delight in

strangling this monster with his bare hands —
slowly. He knew at that point that the maxim
'Evil spawns greater evil' was undoubtedly
true. But it made no difference to his present
feelings. He would have willingly killed this
man, and gained much satisfaction from the
act.

23

As Rastorotsky drove him in his battered, but just about roadworthy, state-issue Zhiguli through the city, Jack dwelled for a moment on an opinion he had held for many years — that August in Moscow was like April in Paris. The residents were at their most amiable, the shops and street cafés buzzed with business, and there was a general air of harmonious activity throughout the whole metropolis. And there were probably very few sights in all the world, Jack reflected, that, on a day like today, with the sun dancing on its domes and glinting through its spires, could match the breathtaking splendour of the Kremlin.

He was also of the firm belief that a wind of change was in the air. He could see it in the faces of the people, especially the young. They had had more than half a century of tightening their belts under Marxism. He sensed a mood that they wanted to loosen them a little, to get more out of life than just diplomas and medals of achievement for the state. They now openly cast envious glances at their brothers and sisters in the West, and the propaganda that rang out about democracy bringing an inevitable decadence had, he suspected, a very hollow ring to it. All they knew was that those people in the West had houses they owned, cars, colour TV sets, fridges, and lovely clothes to wear, while they still had austerity. He had this intuitive feeling — it was nothing more vaguely discernible — that a potentially violent uprising was bubbling just beneath the surface; a volcano of pent-up subservience to the system about to erupt. Perhaps what had happened to Poland, their closest allies and neighbours in all things, would soon be taking place here. Because it would not be difficult to fall in love with this place, he thought, if only . . . ah, if only . . .

'It's about three kilometres from here,' Rastorotsky said, interrupting his thoughts.

'Good.' Jack tapped his jacket and felt the reassuring bulge of his automatic. His mind now switched to the tactics he would adopt, as he was convinced, by what Rastorotsky had told him, that the men who had kidnapped his two colleagues were not connected with any of the Soviet police agencies. Jack guessed he was about to encounter their rivals in this mission. He had also ascertained from the big Russian that at least four men were involved. So it would seem that the odds were going to be at least four to two against them. He glanced quickly at the sweating, overweight man at his side and decided that the odds had widened to four to one against him. So how was he going to tackle this problem single-handed? An answer had to be quickly forthcoming, as Rastorotsky slowed down the car and proudly announced, 'We are here, *tovarisch.*' He pointed a podgy finger towards an old, red brick building. 'They took them in there.'

Jack weighed up the situation carefully while he studied the building, and as an idea began to form in his brain, he stroked his chin and gave a faint smile.

'Okay chum,' he said, slapping Rastorotsky on the back, 'let's turn this heap around and head for the nearest phone box.' But not for the first time had Jack failed to notice the two men, who wore identical grey, double-breasted suits, and hats that differed only by the merest shades of brown. Here, in an unobtrusive car, they sat in the driving and passenger seats keenly watching his every move, and as Rastorotsky's car clattered noisily away, their car with its almost silent engine followed behind at a discreet distance.

★ ★ ★

The last horrific spasm, following a greater increase in the electric current from that accursed machine, had either caused Avi to pass out completely, Dan thought grimly, or it had — and maybe it was a mercy if it had — killed him.

Horst nodded to the man operating the apparatus and he immediately threw the switch into reverse. Avi's head lolled limply to one side and his body, which a couple of seconds earlier had been ramrod taut with his muscles twitching grotesquely, now suddenly slackened as he lay slumped in the chair looking like a much abused rag doll. The man in the white coat then grabbed Avi by his hair and pulled back his head with one hand, whilst with the other he prised open an eyelid and gazed into it closely. Dan watched him anxiously as the man felt the pulse on Avi's floppy wrist before walking over to Horst. He spoke to him softly in German. Dan just about heard what he said. 'He's all right — but only just.'

Horst lit a cigarette and turned to Dan.

'You could so easily have prevented this. I hope you realise that you are as responsible as we are — perhaps more so.' He shook his head admonishingly. 'Now you force us to concentrate on you — unless of course you have managed to find your tongue?' Dan remained grim-faced. 'No? Very well. We have, however, devised something quite different for you. Kurt, show the doctor what little experiment you have dreamed up for him.'

Kurt grinned spitefully as he rummaged about the instrument trolley, then with a look of real satisfaction he raised aloft what appeared to be a chromium-plated metal headband. There was an adjustable thread and screw fitting attached to it, but that aside it seemed fairly harmless until, that is, Dan was shown the tiny spikes on the inside of the band.

In a stomach-sinking instant he knew exactly how this grisly instrument would be used. It would be clamped over his eyes and the screwing device at the back would be tightened, bit by bit, so that the spikes would at first penetrate the skin, the eyes, and eventually crush his skull. It would be a slow and intensely painful way to die. Could he hold on? But, hell, why should he? Why suddenly become a goddamn hero? He was a doctor, for Christ's sake. It was his duty to save lives — even his own — so that he could do his job. A dead surgeon was of no use to anyone, and in any case there might be another day. What was it his instructor had said at Langley when he was being trained for this task? 'Don't be no hero! The battlefields of Europe and Vietnam are full of guys pushing up poppies who wanted to be heroes; the name of the game is survival.' So maybe this German bastard was right after all. Perhaps he should have called a halt to it when they started torturing Avi. But Avi's eyes had told him to say nothing. Hell, Avi was a pro operative, he was not.

He was no nearer to an answer as to whether he should tell them what they wanted to know or not when Kurt placed the metal band over his forehead. The gloating expression on the face of this animal in the white coat made the final decision for him. He was damned if he would give them the satisfaction of seeing him crack. If Avi could take it — so would he. He would summon up every shred of strength he had and pray to God that if his interrogators believed that he knew something, it would be in their own interest to keep him alive. It was all he had to hang on to.

* * *

The wail of the siren in the distance brought with it a look of alarm to Horst's face. He swung round and shouted to his henchmen, 'Quickly, we must leave at once.' Regaining his composure almost immediately, he spoke quietly into Dan's ear, 'We shall have to part company for the moment, Dr Shears, but I promise you we will certainly meet again.' His eyes were as cold as steel, and he almost spat out the words as he said them.

God, I hope so, Dan thought, and all I want is to have both hands free when we do.

The vehicle's siren was becoming louder by the second, and without pausing further Horst, followed by Hollerbach and the two heavies, rushed through a small wooden exit door at the rear of the building. Kurt, disappointed at being deprived of his entertainment, looked at Dan regretfully then, taking off his white coat, he hastily headed after the others. As he reached the door, Jack, holding his automatic, clambered through a broken half-open window less than a couple of yards away from him. They saw each other at the same moment. Kurt's hand went inside his jacket as though to reach for a gun. At that instant Jack fired once. The bullet went through Kurt's breast-pocket, his hand, the skin on his chest, two ribs, his lung, came out of his back and lodged in the exit door behind him.

Jack crouched to the ground, his eyes darting around the gloomy warehouse, his gun cocked for further action. When he was sure it was safe, he called out softly, 'Dan? Avi? Where are you? It's me, Jack.'

'Over here,' Dan shouted.

With giant steps Jack sprinted towards the voice. He'd had no preconceived idea of what he might find, but the sight, and the state of his two collegues, especially Avi, was more horrific than he could possibly have imagined. He quickly began to remove the metal band from around Dan's forehead, pricking his finger on one of the spikes as he did so.

'Ouch!' he yelled, and sucked the blood that beaded on his finger. 'Can't leave you blokes alone for a moment, can I?'

Avi groaned quietly in the chair, and Jack looked at him more closely.

'Is Avi all right?' he asked anxiously.

'If you untie me, I'll let you know,' Dan muttered impatiently.

'Oh, sure, sure,' said Jack, as he set about the task. 'I must say he looks in a bad way.'

'So would you be if they had done the same to you,' Dan snapped.

Suddenly the big warehouse doors burst open and in rushed the chief fire officer followed by four firemen bearing a giant hosepipe. The chief looked nonplussed.

'Where's the fire?' he barked.

It was essential for Jack to ensure that the fire chief and his quartet of bewildered firemen advanced no further than they already had. It would have been difficult enough for him to explain the state of the two men in there amid all the pseudo-medical paraphernalia — but as for the dead body at the exit door — well, silver-tongued he might be, but there would have been no way he could have talked his way out of that. So he did what he had found always worked for him in the past in this country — he resorted to unabashed bribery. Producing a wad of British banknotes, he handed the fire chief several twenty-pound notes and, with a friendly arm around his shoulder, he wheeled him amiably but firmly out again through the big doors.

'There is no fire. You see,' Jack said in conspiratorial tones, 'there are certain people in this venture who would stop at nothing to spoil our chances.'

'No fire?' The fire chief frowned as he pocketed the money and waved to the driver to turn off the flashing revolving light on the fire engine.

'This old warehouse would be the absolutely perfect venue for our plans,' Jack continued, 'and it would have been a real example of East-West co-operation — détente at its finest level.'

'Venue, venture, chances? I'm sorry, but I

don't understand what you are talking about,' the fire chief said, unable to contain himself any further.

'Oh, I'm so sorry, comrade,' Jack said, feigning a look of dismay. 'I thought you knew. Didn't you read about the scheme for the new stadium in *Pravda*?'

The fire chief looked a little worried as he indicated to his men to wind up the hose. For, like so many other citizens, he found the Government newspaper incredibly boring to read, but wouldn't dare admit it.

'Er . . . well, I must have missed the item you refer to,' he said.

'The basketball stadium,' Jack said, trying to be helpful, 'is to be a centre for the World Championships. Can't you see what a perfect site it is? Thousands of people would gather here annually to see this great international event. It would bring in huge sums of revenue . . . and that's why they want to sabotage our plans, of course.'

'Of course,' the fire chief said, looking at Jack even more curiously, 'but . . . er . . . who?'

'Them,' said Jack, tapping his nose. 'They would do anything to discredit us. This fire call hoax is just one in a catalogue of really appalling dirty tricks they have perpetrated to try to get our plans scrapped. And that would be tragic. So I hope you won't find it necessary to pursue this matter any further. Oh, and just a little something for your men as well, chief.'

Jack took out some more notes and pressed them into his hand.

'Er . . . well, I will have to make a report, though,' the fire chief said in a businesslike manner, hardly able to conceal his pleasure at holding so much money.

'Of course, I realise that. But if your report just stated that it was a hoax call, it would be true, and it wouldn't ruin our wonderful scheme, eh?' Jack tapped the end of his nose again.

'I'll do my best,' the fire chief smiled reassuringly at Jack as he climbed into his cab.

As the fire engine drove slowly away, the fire chief unwound the window and shouted back.

'You know, I can't see that a basketball stadium would prosper here, comrade. It's too far from the town centre.'

Jack nodded and gave a broad smile as he waved them off.

'Bloody marvellous, isn't it?' he muttered under his breath. 'Now he's suddenly become an expert on where a basketball stadium should be.' He didn't know why he should feel just a little hurt about it — but he did. After all, it wasn't such a bad idea.

24

They knew at once, by the open door, that the apartment had been broken into. It had been a thorough and expert job — drawers emptied on to the floor, pictures smashed and torn from their frames, carpets lifted, and furniture overturned. In a word, and the word came first from Jack, 'Shambles — it's a fucking shambles!'

A few hours later the scene was slightly improved with some kind of order restored. It was also, Dan silently observed, faintly amusing, although perhaps only an outsider would have been able to appreciate the absurdity of the strange sight that they presented.

There was Avi, trouserless, with his legs splayed open and two crushed ice-packs around his testicles, wincing painfully every time he moved, and bellowing, when he did that his balls felt like 'bloody over-ripe melons.' Rastorotsky was pacing up and down, holding a bottle of vodka from which, every now and again, he would take a long gulp, and muttering darkly to Jack that he didn't know how his old and trusted friend could have got him into such a position. Whilst Jack, who completely ignored him, stood bare-chested at the sink washing his blood-stained shirt and humming a little ditty like a busy little housewife as he did so. And as for himself, Dan conceded, he must have looked a bit odd too, with a white tennis sock — all that he could find as a bandage — soaked in a solution of honey and water, and wrapped around his forehead where the spikes had scratched his skin.

'It'll only be a matter of time before the KGB catch up with me,' Rastorotsky continued mournfully. He had only just avoided getting snared by the GRU when they picked up Jack at the hotel. He had also been sniffing around the Lubyanka asking some of the off-duty guards about security there. Oh, they'd been happy to take the bribes all right, but if the KGB pounced they'd turn on him like a pack of starving wolves.

'I'll be lucky if I get twenty years in Siberia.' He took another long gulp of vodka, and shuddered at the thought.

Jack smoothed out the collar and cuffs of his shirt with his forefinger, as it dripped from the hanger he had attached to the window fastener. Seeming happy with his handiwork, he turned his attention to Rastorotsky.

'Look — sit down and shut up! You've been well paid for what you've done so far — you've got no cause to complain.'

Rastorotsky stopped dead in his tracks. 'No cause to complain?' he said, wild-eyed. 'Do you have any conception of what can happen . . . ?'

'I want you to find out where those German bastards are staying,' Jack interrupted him impatiently.

Rastorotsky picked his nose with his free hand and looked decidedly shifty-eyed.

'Er . . . well, now that is going to take some time . . . as you know,' he blustered. 'I have been concentrating on finding out about the security at the Lubyanka. Believe me it's not easy. You do realise, of course, that the Lubyanka Jail is also the headquarters of the KGB.'

Jack had spotted Rastorotsky's uneasiness, and a thought flashed through his mind. It was not a pleasant one. Suddenly, and to the surprise of Avi and Dan, he grabbed the big Russian by the scruff of the neck and pushed him roughly against the wall. Then, through gritted teeth, he snarled quietly but very menacingly in his ear.

'You've been doing business with those Krauts, haven't you?'

'No, of course not,' Rastorotsky spluttered.

'Stop it, please. You're choking me.'

'Haven't you?' Jack shouted furiously whilst increasing his grip on the Russian's collar. Rastorotsky was now going a bright shade of purple and his eyes were bulging out like a pair of white billiard balls.

'They were the ones who came up here and turned us over, weren't they?' Jack grunted in his ear, 'Weren't they?'

'Uh huh!' Rastorotsky nodded, as he tried to free himself from Jack's iron grip.

'Now listen, you fat swine, and listen well. I want to know where they hang out, and fast. Clear?'

Rastorotsky nodded again, all sounds from his throat having been stifled at source. Eventually, and with a look of sheer contempt, Jack released him. Rastorotsky, panting like a huge dog, rubbed his neck with an acutely pained expression.

'You didn't have to do that to me, Jack. I was only trying to get information from them so that I could pass it on to you.'

'Oh yeah.' Jack sneered. 'Start talking.'

'They are staying in an apartment above a baker's shop in the district of Babuskin,' Rastorotsky mumbled. 'The baker was a German soldier, captured by us when we were advancing towards Berlin in 1945. He gave his name as Keisel. When he was finally freed, he met and married a Russian girl called Tamara, and was given state permission to continue his pre-war trade as a master baker.'

'You're telling me about this Keisel for a reason?' Jack asked brusquely.

'Yes,' Rastorotsky replied, still rubbing his neck. 'I believe he was really a high-ranking SS officer, wanted for war crimes.'

'Oh,' said Jack sceptically, 'and do you mean that the GRU haven't tumbled him — but you have?'

'No. I believe the GRU know all about him, but sometimes it suits their purpose to leave the odd bit of bait free in the hope of catching bigger fish.'

Jack understood that kind of Russian logic fairly well, and what Rastorotsky said made sense.

'Now, how did those Krauts know you were connected with us?'

'I think I must have been observed talking to some of the off-duty guards in this drinking place they go to near the Lubyanka.'

'Go on.'

'Well, one evening, when I was sitting alone in this bar, a man who had been with a group of others came over to my table. He introduced himself as Horst — a German, but he spoke good Russian. He asked me why

I was interested in the prisoner Sokol. Of course I denied all knowledge of such things, but he was very insistent.'

'You mean he bunged you a hefty bundle of marks.' Rastorotsky gulped visibly, but made no direct reply.

' . . . Then he asked me who I was working for.'

'And you sang like a bleedin' skylark, didn't you, you turd.'

'Ah, but you see, *tovarisch*, I only told him a little, but said I could probably get him more information. When he left with the others I followed them back to this baker's shop, and kept their place under observation — in your interest, of course.'

'Of course,' Jack said drily. 'Now I know how you could be so certain that the geezers who snatched my two friends here weren't your KGB louts. You knew they were this Nazi mob all along.'

Rastorotsky licked the sweat from his lips and nodded.

'The important thing is, surely, that I know where they are staying, yes?' Rastorotsky obviously believed that this statement was of great value and allowed himself a brief smile.

Jack wiped the smile off his face with a swift slap from the back of his hand.

'You also told them where we lived, and now just look at the state of us — you bloated bastard!'

Dan, who had kept silent while all this was going on, felt that in their own interests it was time to intervene.

'Er ... Jack, under the circumstances, might it not be a good idea if you got him to take you to this baker's shop. You could do a little recce on the place, while I give Avi a shot and get him to bed.'

Jack, still looking as if he wanted to commit murder, sighed reluctantly. 'Yeah, I suppose you're right. Yeah, okay.'

Jack, turning his attention to Avi, smiled sympathetically.

'How are you feeling now, my old cock?'

'I find your choice of words in rather poor taste,' said Avi, wincing, 'but the thought that I might be able to get my hands on the pigs that did this to me, makes me feel better by the minute.'

Jack nodded. He had really grown to like this Israeli. He was a man fashioned in the same mould as himself.

'Proky, get off your big arse — we're going to hunt the Hun, my son.'

★   ★   ★

Jack, accompanied by a decidedly nervy Rastorotsky who was trying to conceal himself behind a tree that was only half his girth, kept the busy baker's shop under surveillance for almost four hours. He had already recognised one of the heavies coming out of the building through a side door adjacent to the shop. As Rastorotsky was unwilling to leave his position behind the tree, Jack had joined the customary Russian bread queue in order to case the place at closer quarters. When he finally got to the counter to purchase a large loaf of black bread, in addition to observing the two internal doors, one of which he guessed led to the apartment above, he'd been quick to appreciate the striking good looks of one of the three female shop assistants. He'd given her a friendly smile and, to his pleasant surprise, she'd returned it with an even warmer one. After exiting from the shop clutching his bread, he decided that he'd accomplished all that he could at this stage, and there was little point in remaining there. He would now return to his colleagues and report on his findings.

25

Although Dan had been optimistic about Avi being able to go on duty in a couple of days, it was a full five days before he felt fit enough to walk and move about without pain. In that period they had laughed little, but quarrelled frequently. What had added to the strain was the claustrophobic smallness of the apartment, and the fact that they had to share it, not only with Rastorotsky who, they all agreed despite his constant protests must not be let out of their sight, but also with Max Verbolen who had now returned after a trip to his native Amsterdam. Even the normally amiable Dutchman found it hard to keep his temper under control on occasion, especially as he was now acting as errand boy, buying the necessary shopping and supplies.

Jack, now having established to his own satisfaction that Rastorotsky had indeed discovered the hide-out of the Nazi gang, intended to return to the place next time in strength. The memory of their last, less than successful encounter with disaster was still fresh in their minds. They had decided to keep around-the-clock watch on the premises, until such time as they could be reasonably assured that the apartment was either unoccupied or manned by so few of their opponents that overpowering them would be a relatively easy task. Then they would turn the tables and ransack their abode in the hope of finding out how near they were to achieving their goal.

⋆ ⋆ ⋆

At 05.30, with a dense dawn mist just rising, they drove off in Max's lovingly cared for old Mercedes 330, which he had special permission to import, provided of course that he did not sell it in Russia.

'Sell it in Russia for their worthless roubles,' he exclaimed, when telling his guests how he had managed to bring it in, 'I would rather crash it into the Kremlin wall.' Then, realising what he had said as he handed Jack the car keys, he added quickly, 'That was only a joke. This car is more precious to me than my dear wife, Roxanne.'

'I'll bear that in mind,' Jack had retorted with a wink.

With Rastorotsky in the passenger seat directing Jack once again to the district of Babuskin, Dan and Avi sat in the rear and gazed with interest at the sights in the early morning streets. Queues were already beginning to form outside some of the food shops. At the bus stops people waited to be taken to work. Others were walking briskly towards the pride of Moscow's transport — the Metro's spotless underground palaces of glittering chandeliers. Few cars were to be seen at that hour, but bicycles were plentiful. As they stopped at some traffic lights, one of the rare cars on the road pulled up alongside them. The driver, a Russian orthodox priest, looked at their car admiringly, and gave them a cheery smile as the lights changed and they drove away. This started an animated conversation about the Church's role in Soviet politics, until Jack, who had contributed nothing to the discussion, with the stark realism that they all recognised as being so characteristic of him, cut in with a cryptic, 'Unless you're praying for some bleedin' miracle, what the fuck has the Church got to do with what we're about now? Don't you think we should be talking about that?'

'The man's got a point,' Dan agreed meekly.

Avi folded his arms and sulked a little. He had been very impressed with his own eruditeness. He felt offended that he should be shot down like that when in full loquacious flight. The mood did not last long, however.

'There is nothing in the bloody world I want to do more right now than get my hands on that bastard who ordered the electrocution of my balls!'

'That's more like it, my son,' Jack turned to him briefly with a cheery grin, 'so cut all that bloody rabbit and let's get on with the job in hand.'

'Take a lef . . . , no a right up there,' Rastorotsky pointed hastily.

'Make up your bloody mind,' Jack snapped as he swerved from left to right and back on to the crown of the road.

'Sorry — I still get confused in this area,' Rastorotsky muttered apologetically.

'Now he tells us,' Avi shrugged.

★　★　★

When they at last reached their destination, Jack pulled up and parked between two stationary cars, about eighty yards away from the baker's shop. From this position they could keep the shop under surveillance without themselves being observed from any of the windows in the apartment above it. The baker's shop was already a hive of activity, and people passed the four men in the car holding loaves of all shapes and sizes.

Avi wound down his window, and an aroma of freshly baked bread came wafting in. This prompted him to break the silence that had descended on the conversation in the car to remark, 'Boy, what I'd give for some of that hot bread right now.' And for Jack to reply, 'You get caught by those Nazis in there, mate, and next time they'll bake your arse.'

The side door of the baker's shop opened and four pairs of eyes at once saw the man, whom they all knew now was named Horst, step out on to the pavement. He appeared slightly agitated as he looked up and down the street. He began tapping his foot and must have glanced at his wrist-watch at least three or four times before a black car came into view and swung in alongside him.

'So that's what he was waiting for,' Jack said, as they watched Horst remonstrate angrily with the driver, before he furiously tugged open the passenger door, got inside and slammed it.

'How many other guys are in the car?' Jack said quietly, 'I can't quite see from here.'

'There's four, including the driver,' came Dan's speedy reply.

'How many are in their bloody outfit?' Avi chipped in, a little incredulously.

Jack glared at Rastorotsky, 'Answer the man.'

'I don't know exactly, Jack. But perhaps half a dozen in all, I should think.'

'Well, you'd better be right, my friend, coz you're going to be with us when we do their gaff, and if we get any aggro, you're going to be right in the front line — savvy?'

Rastorotsky began to sweat again. 'Look Jack, I can't be sure. How can I be?'

Avi leaned over to Jack. 'This girl working in the shop you said was . . . er . . . 'a tasty bit'? Do you think she might be there today?'

'Why? You couldn't do much good with your soggy dumplin's, mate,' Jack said with a laugh.

'She doesn't know that, though,' Avi responded shirtily. 'I still have my charm. I think I'll take a wander.'

'Gawd help us,' Jack growled, raising his eyes heavenwards.

'You can't start asking her questions in the shop,' said Dan warily.

'Exactly,' Jack concurred. 'It's a pity you couldn't have treated his brains as well as his bollocks, Doc.'

'Look,' said Avi, opening the car door, 'I know what I'm doing — just you leave this to me. Okay?'

Before another word of protest could be

uttered, he had clambered out of the car and was heading towards the bakery.

'You wanna know what I think?' Dan said, after they had watched him disappear into the shop.

'What?'

'I think we could have learnt more if we had tailed those Krauts.'

'Yeah, I was just thinking that myself,' agreed Jack, drumming his fingers on the steering wheel with an exasperated sigh.

It was almost twenty minutes before they saw Avi emerge from the baker's shop. Considering what he had been through in the last couple of days, he had quite an energetic spring to his walk, Dan observed.

As he approached them, he turned and saw that two of the baker's customers were only a few feet behind him, so he strolled on past the car, waited until the shoppers had overtaken him, and then, ensuring no one was watching, he doubled back and quickly got into the car.

'I'm seeing her this evening when the shop closes, at about six o'clock,' he said, a little breathlessly.

'Oh, delightful.' Jack scowled, 'So we've only got to hang around here . . . er . . . ' he looked at his wrist-watch, 'for seven and a half hours.'

'Look, I think it will be worth it,' Avi snapped. 'I'm sure Lydia is going to be very co-operative.'

'Oh, it's Lydia now, is it?' Jack said, and Dan noted that there was a positively jealous cutting edge to his remark.

'She's not all that special,' Avi snorted. 'From the way you described her to me, she sounded like a cross between Bo Derek and Meryl Streep!'

'By Soviet Union standards, she's a hot little number,' Jack said defensively. 'Perhaps you just don't fancy blondes!'

'Blondes?' Avi countered. 'Lydia is a brunette.'

'Tall and slim?'

'No — small, plump and a little spotty.'

'It's the wrong bird, you arsehole,' Jack grinned, and this time Dan noted the sigh of relief in his voice.

'So what. I've got a date with Lydia instead. But I swear to you I'll learn something — that I promise.'

'Well, in that case it doesn't seem that we can do a lot more here,' Dan commented. 'I reckon we should all go and grab a bite to eat.'

'That's a great idea, my old son,' Jack said, brightening up. 'Then after we've had a nosh, action man here can go off and see his Russky tart. And when he's made his excuses and left her, we'll all meet up back here.'

'Listen, I won't have to make any excuses. If I have to perform tonight, don't you worry — I can do that standing on my head,' Avi flashed.

'You may have to.' Jack said with a broad grin.

'They say there's a good place to eat not too far from here,' Rastorotsky said eagerly.

'Then what are we waiting for?' Jack started up the motor, 'Lead on McDuff.'

★   ★   ★

After a hearty meal Avi left, having arranged to rejoin them again between ten and eleven o'clock that evening.

Dan, Jack, and a morose Rastorotsky spent a boring couple of hours in a cinema watching a Polish film that was totally incomprehensible to all of them. Then, later, they cheered themselves up by visiting a couple of good bars recommended by Rastorotsky, who by now had become a little more amiable and not a little drunk. Dan and Jack had carefully watched their own alcohol intake, knowing that tonight they could well need all their wits about them.

At the appointed hour for their rendezvous

with Avi, Jack drove the car down the street and past the bakery. To Jack's annoyance, he saw there were no parking spaces in that proximity at all, and he had to drive to the furthermost section of the street before he could find a place he could comfortably pull into. And there they sat, listening to Rastorotsky snoring like an ancient lion. Jack smoked two good Coronas, Dan made a few attempts at conversation, mainly about his boyhood in Texas, whilst Jack tried to make comparisons by recounting some memories of his own young years spent in the East End of London. Anything to pass the waiting hours.

At twenty to one, a solitary figure of a man came walking hurriedly from the direction of the baker's shop. As he came closer, Dan and Jack saw to their unuttered relief that it was Avi.

Getting into the car, Avi wasted no time. He began:

'The daily routine is this. The good baker, Keisel, closes his shop at around six o'clock. He then goes upstairs to his living quarters for an early supper. It seems he commences work at 03.30, when he prepares the ovens and dough with his wife, Tamara, and his daughter, Valentina. So that by 10.30 at night, at the latest, they are in the 'Land of

Nod'. Now Lydia and Valentina share a room on the same floor as the baker and his wife. And this is the bit I think you will find interesting.' Avi took a deep breath before continuing, 'the floor above them has another three rooms, and Lydia says that they are occupied at the moment by some of the baker's relatives who are over here on holiday from East Germany. This is where I think you will find our friends.'

Avi folded his arms and sank back into his seat with a satisfied smirk on his face.

'Did you find out how many there were?' Jack asked.

'Do me a favour — what do you want — blood?' Avi bellowed.

'Okay, okay!' Jack held up his hands in mock surrender. 'I think the Kosher Kid has done pretty well, don't you, Dan?'

'Uh, huh,' Dan nodded slowly, 'Pretty well.'

'And that's not quite all,' Avi continued smugly, 'I've just left Lydia's room. The baker's daughter, whom she shares with, was also very friendly. I think they must share everything.'

'You mean you've had . . . the both of them?' Jack said, open-mouthed.

'Ssh! Ssh!' Avi said, putting a finger to his lips. 'A gentleman never talks of such things. Anyway, when I left their room, the baker and his family were snoring like this slob here,' he poked a finger at the dead-to-the-world Rastorotsky, before going on gleefully, 'I've left the main door on the latch. So just wake me up when you've finished your part in all this — as I'd like to have all the details while they are still fresh in your mind.' And Avi closed his eyes, and began breathing deeply.

'You gotta be joking, mate! I go, we all bleedin' go,' Jack said tersely.

Avi chuckled mischievously and opened one eye, and Jack realised at once that Avi had been 'taking the piss' out of him.

He gave a quirky grin. 'All right, you cocky sod — let's go.'

'What do we do about this one?' Avi asked, nodding towards Rastorotsky.

'Nothing. That's him till the morning, mate.'

The three men climbed quietly out of the car, and, with the stealth of alley cats in the still, moonless night, they walked towards the baker's shop.

26

Hollerbach sat staring blankly at the half-written page in his typewriter. He had felt this desperate need to work, and whilst his companions were asleep he considered that tonight would be an ideal opportunity to complete his article. But the ideas were just not flowing. That, in fact, was a great understatement — the ideas weren't even trickling. His mind was occupied instead by an overwhelming sense of foreboding. This necessity to write something really worthwhile, something memorable, was as though he were being driven by a force outside himself — urging him to do it now, while there was still time. He had this feeling that tomorrow would be too late. And it was this very powerful premonition that was acting as a barrier and damming up his thoughts. He was sure that his involvement with this fanatical bunch, whom Prama had virtually blackmailed him into co-operating with, had not helped his present state of mind. But that was his own fault, he should have refused Prama, whatever the cost. Oh, God, he was such a weak-willed bastard! He lit up his umpteenth 'Lord' of the evening and tried to concentrate on his article again. Then, tentatively at first, he recommenced typing.

His efforts to define the complexities of character of the World War II Russian commanding general, Marshal Zhukov, would have been dealt a final blow had he even the remotest idea of the drama that was, at that moment, being enacted just a few feet below him.

★　★　★

The baker, Keisel, heard just a metallic click as the safety catch of the revolver was released for firing. He sat up with a start, still bleary-eyed from such a rude awakening, only to feel the cold steel tip of the revolver's barrel pressed firmly against the side of his head. Simultaneously a hand came tightly over the mouth of his wife to stifle the scream that she was about to emit, as she too stirred to consciousness. The hand that smothered her mouth belonged to Jack, who sat calmly on her side of the bed, whilst Avi, who held the gun at Keisel's head, bent over him and spoke in a voice that was barely above a whisper. Dan leaned nonchalantly by the door, watching with admiration the icy coolness of his two highly professional colleagues.

'One tiny sound,' hissed Avi, 'and I'll put the first bullet through your head and the second through hers. Understand?'

Keisel, his eyes widening with fear, nodded.

'Right, get up very quietly, both of you now,' Avi continued. The couple climbed out of their respective sides of the bed, he dressed only in his pyjama bottoms, she in a black, silky nighty, intended for a woman at least twenty years her junior.

'We're going first to the girls' room,' Avi said, prodding the gun into Keisel's back. He turned to address the baker's wife. 'You stay glued to his side — move.'

As they all walked softly towards a room at the end of a small passage, Dan saw Jack remove an automatic from his hip pocket and deftly attach to it a silencer almost as long as the barrel itself. He held the weapon at his side, and crept just a pace or two behind Avi. Recognising the door to the room he had only recently left, Avi turned to whisper in Keisel's ear, 'Is anyone else staying on this floor?'

Keisel's wife overheard the question and answered hastily, 'No, no — only my daughter . . . and . . . an . . . another girl who works here. No one else . . . no one.'

'Mama, is that you?' A girl's voice asked drowsily from the other side of the door. Avi put his fingers to his lips demanding silence, then, throwing a meaningful glance in Jack's direction, he gently turned the handle on the door, opened it and tiptoed inside the room. Keisel swung round as though to make a bolt for it and found himself looking into Jack's poised gun. Jack smiled at him pleasantly.

From behind the half-open door they heard the sound of two female voices giggling, as though sharing a schoolgirl joke, then some whispering, then a stifled scream. Avi called out softly for the others to come in. When they entered the room, they were greeted by the bizarre sight of two scantily clad women huddled in a corner shivering with fright, while Avi sat on a corner of one of the twin beds toying with his revolver. What made it an even more unusual spectacle was the contrasting physique of the women; one was very tall and had the build of an Olympic shot-putter, and, Dan guessed, was the baker's daughter, Valentina; while the other girl, who was considerably younger, was just as Avi had described her — short, dumpy and spotty — this was clearly Lydia.

'You, woman,' Avi pointed the gun at the baker's wife, 'will stay here with these two — while my friend here,' he looked towards

310

Dan, 'who is a merciless assassin, will ensure that you stay silent until we have finished what we have to do.'

Observing Jack's gun at the ready, he got off the bed and with a faint smile at Dan, which only he could see, handed him his revolver.

'Keep an eye on them. I've told them that you will not hesitate to use it if necessary,' he said softly to Dan. 'We will be as quick as we can. Will you be okay?'

Dan nodded, grim-faced. So when it came right down to it, he thought, this is how useful he was in the mission — keeping guard over a bunch of women. Still, he was philosophical about it. His experience was virtually nil, so what did he expect. 'Hey, before you go — tell them to sit down, and stay quiet, will you?'

Jack rattled out his order, then gave him an encouraging wink, as though to say — you're learning fast, my son.

'All right, let's go!' Avi commanded the baker.

'W ... where to?' asked the surprised Keisel.

'Upstairs to visit your friends,' snapped Avi, 'and for the sake of your family, I suggest that you don't make one single wrong move — got it?'

Dry-mouthed, the baker, looking now all of his seventy-three years, nodded in the affirmative.

Outside the door, Avi had tried to grill Keisel into telling them how many there were in the rooms above. At first Keisel had stubbornly refused, and it was not until Avi had threatened to go back inside and shoot the women in front of his eyes, that he reluctantly blurted out that there were only three occupants at the moment. Two young men, who were relatives of his wife's sister, and a journalist in his late sixties, who was over here on an assignment for the newspaper *Deutsche Nationale Zeitung*.

As they climbed the last creaky, short flight of stairs, they heard the clackety-clack of a typewriter in use.

'Knock and say that you want to talk to them,' Avi murmured to Keisel.

The old man clenched his fist and was about to speak, when Jack shot out a hand, caught him by his bony arm and restrained him.

'Wait a minute,' he whispered to Avi. 'Do you speak to them in German?' Jack asked the baker menacingly. Keisel's eyes confirmed that this was so.

'Just as I thought. Right, my friend and I both speak fluent German,' Jack continued to

312

speak softly in that language to emphasise his point, 'so don't try to warn them, okay?'

Keisel trembled visibly, and nodded his understanding, before tapping gently at the door. There was no response, so he tapped again, louder and crisper this time. The sound of the typewriter ceased abruptly, and they heard heavy footsteps coming to the door.

'Who's there?'

'Wolf — it's me, Johann. I must see you.'

'Can't it wait till morning? I'm right in the middle of ... Oh, all right.' They heard Hollerbach sigh impatiently, as he unfastened the latch chain, threw back the bolt and opened the door.

Jack leapt into the room and pressed the cold steel silencer tip so firmly against Hollerbach's temple that when he finally withdrew it, a circle of about the size of a British pound coin appeared on his skin. Avi pushed Keisel forcibly past the shocked Hollerbach, and the four men stood in a group.

In a low, controlled voice Jack spoke to Hollerbach. 'Where are the other two?' he demanded.

Hollerbach nervously pointed to the door just behind him.

Jack levelled his gun at Hollerbach and Keisel warningly, as he backed away from them towards the bedroom door. Then, with a speed that surprised even Avi, he booted open the door, and with two hands round his gun took aim.

One man stirred murmuring, and was about to raise himself from the pillow when there was a swish and a dull plop as Jack fired. The man crashed back on to the pillow, eyes staring blankly. The man in the adjacent bed went from an undisturbed sleep into an eternal one without even being aware of it, as Jack fired another lethal shot through the bedcovers.

'Now I hope we will not be interrupted,' Jack grunted, as he walked back to the others. 'We have a lot of questions to ask you both.'

'Let's go into that room there,' Avi said, pointing through a wide open door to a sitting room. On a small table they saw a typewriter and the sheets of typescripts on which Hollerbach had been working.

'All right, sit down,' Jack said, gesturing with his gun to Hollerbach and Keisel when they had all entered the room. Avi strolled over to the typewriter and glanced casually over the typescript. Considering that it was of no consequence, he returned to the others.

The two old men sat side by side on a sofa that had seen better days. When they were settled, Jack began to question them.

'Now then, you can start by telling us about your set-up here. I'm giving marks out of ten for answers, and let me warn you both now, anything less than ten out of ten, and I'll have no hesitation in dealing with you in exactly the same way as them.' Jack inclined his head towards the bedroom.

'Oh, and believe me, he means it,' Avi affirmed.

There was little doubt in the minds of either of the elderly men that Jack might be bluffing. Hollerbach spoke freely, aware that the ex-SS man at his side was bristling with mounting rage as he began to reveal so much information, but Hollerbach could not care less now, because at last he could unburden his soul and he was damned if he would die for a cause he hadn't believed in for nigh on half a century. As Hollerbach answered question after question, Jack would occasionally stop him and ask him to repeat some detail in order to scribble it down accurately. Then, almost casually, Hollerbach dropped his bombshell.

'Vladimir Sokol was transferred from Lubyanka Jail to the Mordovia Corrective Camp Colony.'

'When?' Jack gasped.

'Er . . . yesterday, I believe. He was flown there in a Russian Red Cross aircraft.'

'Bloody hell!' Avi said, scratching his head. 'That's about 500 miles from here.'

'To be precise,' Hollerbach said, almost warming to the subject like the practised journalist that he was, 'the Mordovia Corrective Labour Camp complex is in Barashevo, on the borders of the Mordovian Autonomous Soviet Socialist Republic — some 450 miles south of Moscow.'

'Wait a minute,' Jack said, 'why did they move him so suddenly?'

'It appears that the authorities feared that next time the prisoners might not just beat him up — but kill him. So it would seem he was moved for his own protection.'

'I see . . . ' Jack's mind was working overtime, 'and your leader here, Horst . . . er . . . ?'

Hollerbach opened his mouth to speak, but this time it was too much for Keisel to take. Up until now he had felt that these Zionist agents had little chance of achieving their aim. After all, Barashevo was a long journey from Moscow, and by now their own men were probably halfway there. But with this snivelling turncoat telling all, it could really jeopardise their slim advantage. He turned angrily towards Hollerbach, and almost spat out his words.

'Shut up, you treacherous pig!'

Without a second's hesitation, Avi struck Keisel hard across the face with his tightly clenched fist. The blow knocked Keisel's frail frame over the side of the sofa and on to the floor. Blood trickled from the corner of his mouth. He sat up slowly, thoroughly dazed, holding his chin and working his jaw gently back and forth to feel if it had been broken.

'You open your mouth again and next time it will be a bullet through your head — understand?' Avi snarled. The baker sat still, making no reply.

'Go on,' Jack prompted Hollerbach, 'Horst who . . . ?'

Hollerbach gulped, and ran his finger around the collar of his shirt as though to loosen it. He was beginning to feel very unwell.

'Er . . . Horst Schreiber . . . but he left this morning with the others.'

Jack swung round to Avi, who was glaring hatefully at Keisel on the floor.

'So that's where he must have been heading when we saw him leave in that car this morning — Barashevo.' He turned to face Hollerbach again. 'Is that right? Is that where they were going?'

Hollerbach nodded — he could no longer speak. He felt a sharp, shooting pain stab across his back and down his left arm. The

317

arm went numb. At almost the same instant he felt a knife-like pain in his chest. It was as though his left and right breasts were being crushed together. He could no longer breathe. As he gasped to take air into his lungs, the pain became excrutiating, and all he could manage to do was open and close his mouth like an enormous fish that had just been landed.

Jack realised at once that Hollerbach was having a coronary. By the time he got to him, Hollerbach had already slumped sideways on to the sofa. Jack quickly lifted his feet, dragged him on to the floor, and hastily loosened his clothing. He then administered the 'kiss of life' for a few seconds, before placing his right hand over his left and pumping him weightily on the ribcage. So forcibly did Jack carry out this emergency drill that he was fearful that he might have cracked a few ribs. At intervals he placed his ear to the man's chest to listen for a heartbeat — there was none. After two or three minutes of this procedure, he turned slowly to Avi.

'He's a gonna.'

'Shall I get the Doc up?' Avi said, staring at the prostrate man.

'No — waste of time, mate. He's well gone,' Jack replied.

It was as though, on the departure of

Hollerbach's spirit, an evil one took possession of Avi, for all at once he seemed to go berserk. He lunged himself at Hollerbach and began kicking the lifeless, pallid body with a viciousness that Jack found truly frightening to witness.

'You fucking, fucking bastard, bastard!' Avi screamed as he kicked him with all of his might. 'Speak, speak, you Nazi filth.'

Jack watched this for only as long as it took him to get over the initial shock, then he rushed forward and held a restraining arm round Avi.

'Cool it, mate, for Christ's sake. You won't bring him back now.'

Jack stared at Avi's face — his nostrils were flared and his eyes wild. It reminded him of a crazed Arabian horse he had once seen at some obscure rodeo.

Almost as quickly as it had begun, Avi's uncontrollable fury seemed to fade. He came closer to Jack, grinned and murmured in a very low voice, 'I did it to scare the shit out of this Kraut. He's all we've got now.'

Jack knew that Avi was a professional actor, but if that terrifying exhibition had been just a performance, the man was quite brilliant. But to his dying day Jack would never be sure how much of that was purely acting.

★ ★ ★

After the startling information that Hollerbach had given before departing this life, both
Avi and Jack realised that they would need
many more details about Sokol's precise
whereabouts. Although neither of them had
ever been to the Mordovian Autonomous
Soviet Socialist Republic, they had heard
many harrowing stories of the grim camp
colony that was situated on its vast, sprawling
plains.

It was essential that Keisel should talk, and
quickly. Avi commenced the interrogation by
walking over to the baker, who was still seated
on the floor, and kicking him heftily near his
left buttock. The baker's face contorted in
pain, and he held his hands in front of him as
though to protect himself from further
violence.

'Get up,' Avi commanded.

Keisel rose slowly to his feet, rubbing the
bruise he felt forming on his leg, and
cowering away from Avi as he did so.

'Sit down.' Avi pointed to the sofa. Keisel
sat down warily, his eyes watering like a sick
dog's.

'We need to know which colony Sokol has
been taken to at Mordovia,' Avi's eyes burned
into Keisel's like laser beams, as though they

were searching out the innermost thoughts that were locked in his brain.

'I . . . I don't have that information,' Keisel said after a moment's pause. Jack and Avi threw each other an anxious glance before Avi, with his jaw set determinedly, went on, 'Oh, yes you do, you bastard. You are the head of this little Nazi rat pack here, and I know that your Kamaraden could not have left for Mordovia without that specific information. I know the way you pigs work — so you will tell us everything now.'

'I really don't know . . . anything.' Keisel shook his head protestingly.

'If you continue to refuse to talk,' Avi went on casually, 'I'm going to take you downstairs where you will witness the shooting of your wife and daughter. Then you will help us to take their bodies down into the basement where the ovens are. We shall light the ovens, then place their bodies inside. Then you will have the privilege of joining them — but alive, like so many of the six million of my people you murdered in this way. Our Hebrew law demands an eye for an eye. Three for six million is not much in terms of revenge, but it is a beginning. So you see, in a way I hope you do choose to remain silent, because it will give me great pleasure to see you and your family go up in smoke.'

Jack looked over to Avi, and he was aware that this was no idle threat. More importantly, Keisel knew it too. He had already seen enough of this man's brutality to convince him that he meant every word. Brutality was something he admired, provided that he was on the side that was inflicting it. Being a victim was a situation he had no stomach for. He decided to co-operate. He licked his lips nervously and hung his head almost in shame.

'I . . . er . . . believe the Führer's son, er . . . Sokol is in Colony Three. He is . . . er . . . still not well, and there is a large hospital in this section. He will be receiving medical treatment there, until he is fit enough to be put into the labour force.'

'You will give us the layout and plans of the camp, the hospital wing, and everything else that you know about it, and you will tell us how you intended to organise Sokol's escape.'

There was just the tiniest flash of defiance in Keisel's eyes as he raised his head, but one look at Avi's stony face soon dispelled all remnants of this.

'There are some sketches in my bureau downstairs,' Keisel murmured.

'Let's go,' Avi said harshly.

★ ★ ★

With the sketches held tightly in Avi's hand, they returned once more to the bedroom where the women were being held.

Jack and Avi noted the relief on Dan's face when he saw them.

'Everything all right?' Jack asked him.

'Yeah, I guess so, but the old woman here indicated that she wanted to go to the john, and I saw no way of keeping an eye on her and these other two, so I refused,' said Dan.

'You did the right thing, mate. But there was nothing stopping you from opening the window, 'cos it don't arf bloody pong in here!'

Avi spread out three sheets of paper on to one of the beds and saw that they were detailed photostatted sketches of part of the Mordovian Camp complex. On one of the sketches was a ground plan of Zone No. 1 (Special Regime) in Corrective Labour Complex Zhkh 385. On the next was a section of the hospital wing and a sketch of a hospital detention cell, presumably where Sokol was now incarcerated, as the letters 'VS' were arrowed to it. Whilst on the third sheet was a scale drawing of the high, barbed wire fences surrounding the camp, the guard posts, gun turret tower, and searchlight positions. Avi and Jack looked at the drawings for some moments, assessing the tight security arrangements. The sketches and written observations made depressing reading. Getting in and out of the Mordovian Corrective Camp was going to need meticulous planning and a lot of luck.

Avi continued with his tough line of interrogating Keisel, until he was entirely satisfied that the elderly baker had told him all that he knew. It had become obvious to Jack and Avi, from Keisel's answers, that his German colleagues had no pre-set plan to extricate Sokol from the camp. Apart from the sketches the Germans had obtained of the Mordovian Colony, copies of which they themselves now possessed, and some dark hints from Keisel that Horst Schreiber had some contacts on the prison staff in the camp, it appeared that the Germans would have to wait until they had arrived in Barashevo, and only then would they be in a position to consider the tactics they would adopt. This gave Avi and Jack their first glimmer of hope, for it might buy them that most valuable of all commodities — time. But it was precious time, and they could not afford to waste a second of it. Jack knew that Rastorotsky was going to be a most useful ally in their own scheme of things, and he now began to worry that perhaps he might have awakened and fled.

'Listen, I'm going back to the car,' he said to Avi. 'I think we are going to need a lot more help from Rastorotsky, and I don't want to let the bugger out of my sight — okay?' Avi nodded.

'What are you going to do about this lot?' Jack whispered to him.

Avi looked into Jack's eyes. 'It's a pity about the women, but what the hell can we do? We just can't risk them talking — it would be too dangerous.'

Jack's eyes acknowledged his agreement. Unobserved by Keisel and the women, he handed Avi his gun. Dan suddenly realised that he was about to witness cold-blooded murder, and opened his mouth to protest, but it would have served no useful purpose — if the mission was to succeed they really had no other choice.

With deadly accuracy Avi fired four shots in rapid succession, and following four dull thuds, four more deaths were added to the toll.

* * *

When they stepped out into the street, Dan felt a distinct chill in the night air. He took great gulps of the air to stem the nausea that he felt rising from the very pit of his stomach after seeing such carnage.

Avi was also in a contemplative mood as they walked briskly to catch up with Jack, who was just a few metres ahead of them. Although Dan could see no apparent emotion on Avi's face, he was aware, as a practising psychiatrist, that it did not mean that Avi was not feeling as sick as he himself was over the killing of those innocent women. It was only that Avi had been trained to keep a tight rein over all his responsive feelings.

As Jack reached the car, he could see that his sudden hunch had proved to be correct — Rastorotsky had gone. He quickly opened the passenger door and felt around the comfortable, well-worn leather seat where Rastorotsky had been sleeping. It was still faintly warm. Avi, seeing no sign of Rastorotsky, turned angrily to Jack.

'That's him for the night,' you said. Now what the hell do we do?'

'Get in,' Jack said gruffly, 'he could only have left a few moments ago.' Jack got in behind the wheel and turned on the ignition. It was a hell of a long shot to find him, he knew, but unless Rastorotsky had hailed a taxi — a most improbable possibility at that time of night — then it was likely that the fat slob was hoofing it; in which case, carrying all his bulk, Jack considered that he could not have walked too far.

Although Jack did not know this area of Moscow, he decided to use the back streets, keeping as closely parallel as possible to the main road that led to the city centre, but Rastorotsky was nowhere to be seen. Jack was about to tell the others that, under the circumstances, they would be better off going straight to Rastorotsky's home and waiting for him there, when Dan, suddenly seeing the largish figure of a man walking ponderously in a side street, illuminated briefly by one of the few street lamps in operation, shouted, 'Hold it!' Instinctively Jack slammed on the brakes.

'Pull back about twenty yards,' Dan continued excitedly.

When Jack had reversed the car, they all stared hard through the car windows down the narrow street — but there was no one, not even a solitary cat.

'I could have sworn I saw someone of his build down there,' Dan said.

'Okay, I'll cruise down it, just in case,' Jack said, manouvering the car round in the direction of the street. A 'no entry' sign greeted them.

'It's a one-way street,' observed Avi.

'That's okay,' Jack replied drily, 'I'm only going one way!'

Jack drove at a snail's pace for about thirty

yards before they saw him.

'I'd know that fat arse anywhere,' Jack said happily as he speeded up the vehicle and decelerated as he pulled in alongside the panting Rastorotsky. Jack wound down his window, and called out cheerfully,

'Hello, Proky, looking for a lift?'

Rastorotsky thought momentarily of making a run for it then, thinking better of it, he resignedly walked to the waiting car. Jack opened the passenger door, and Rastorotsky heaved his huge frame into the seat. Without saying a word, he folded his arms and sat back sullenly as Jack drove off.

27

The ingenuity and resourcefulness of man under pressure had never ceased to amaze Dan. Back at Max Verbolen's apartment he had watched while Jack and Avi worked, plotted and schemed like a pair of indestructible demons. They had run through every permutation of possible means of entry and exit to the heavily guarded hospital wing at the Mordovian Camp complex in Barashevo. Finally, when they had all agreed that they at last had a viable plan, Jack had left the apartment with Rastorotsky to try and obtain the vital travel visas, permits and letters of authority that were going to be absolutely essential if that plan were to succeed.

The big Russian, as though inspired by the other two, had wheeled and dealed with corruptible officials in high places like a stock exchange wizard, to acquire genuine and forged documents, as well as other essential items they would need; whilst Jack had stood by and supplied the most persuasive aid any Iron Curtain operator can possess — US dollars.

The germ of their idea had come from

Hollerbach's statement, which Jack had been quick to note, that Sokol had been transferred to the Mordovian ASSR Camp Hospital by means of a Red Cross aircraft. Working on the assumption, which was confirmed by Rastorotsky, that many prisoners who were invalids or seriously ill were taken to the more remote labour camps and detention centres of the Soviet Union's known 330 prisons by means of that transport, they had decided to travel as a medical unit.

Like all good plans, the premise of this one was simple. Avi was to pose as a chronically sick, important political prisoner being transferred from that most infamous and feared of all Moscow's prisons, Lefortovo. Countless unfortunate men had passed through that oppressive fortress, including the American pilot, Gary Powers, and internationally respected dissidents, such as Solzhenitsyn. It was logical, therefore, that Avi would be well guarded and, in addition, would be accompanied by a doctor, and possibly a *feldsher* — a medical orderly, recruited from the ranks of minor prisoners, and given a very limited training in medical procedure. Dan, of course, would be the doctor, Rastorotsky a uniformed armed sergeant of the GRU, and Jack the *feldsher*.

In the late afternoon of the following day Jack and Rastorotsky returned to the apartment, Jack looking tired and travel-stained. But Rastorotsky was beaming like a benevolent uncle, and after going to the drinks cabinet and helping himself to half a tumbler of vodka, he unzipped a canvas Aeroflot travel bag, cleared a space on the small dining table and, as though he were a master magician performing in front of an enthralled and mystified audience, he proudly produced the results of their hard bargaining. With a flourish he placed the contents of the bag, one by one, on the table.

When the holdall was at last empty, and the table cluttered with a variety of items ranging from medical apparel to official-looking documents, he stepped back, swept out his arms graciously, took a mock bow, then gestured to Jack.

'Thank you, Proky, beautifully presented. Now, this lot, gentlemen,' Jack went on, inclining his head to the table, 'is our way in and, with a lot of luck, our way out of the Mordovian camp.'

Avi walked over to the table to pick up what looked like an identity card. Jack's hand shot out and slapped Avi's wrist.

'Don't touch,' he reprimanded with a faint smile. 'You'll get to see the goodies all in

331

good time.' He beckoned to Dan who was lolling in an armchair, his long legs stretched out before him, looking on at the proceedings with bemused interest. 'Come on over, Dan, and I'll explain what all this stuff is for.'

Some two hours later not only were they all thoroughly familiar with Rastorotsky's and Jack's prized acquisitions, they had also been briefed in their use by Jack. Each man was aware that the odds of success were weighted heavily against them. The idea of penetrating a tightly guarded Russian prison camp, liquidating a major captive, getting out alive and leaving the Soviet Union in one piece was, as Jack succinctly put it, going to be as difficult as trying to out-fart an elephant in a tunnel! But whenever such doubts arose, they were pushed far away into the recesses of their minds. They had a job to do and were about to get on with it.

A detailed map of Moscow was spread out on the floor. Jack had ringed the key positions on the map in red pencil.

'All right,' he said, clearing his throat, 'let's go over the first stage once more. Avi, why don't you take us through it, my voice is getting a bit croaky.'

'Okay — we are here,' Avi said, pointing to their present position, as three necks craned over the map.

'Now, as you all know, our small ambulance car, with its Red Cross emblems temporarily concealed by two posters advertising this week's performance by the Bolshoi Ballet Company, is safely locked away in Max's garage, just behind this apartment block. By 20.00 hours we shall all be dressed as planned — me in my denim prison garb, Jack and Dan in their white medical jackets, and Proky in his KGB uniform.'

'GRU.' Rastorotsky interjected.

'Okay, GRU — so sue me! Anyway, wearing our plain civilian topcoats over our respective outfits, we make our way in the ambulance to Aerodinamicheska Street and park near the administration section of Lefortovo Prison here,' Avi indicated the location on the map, 'which, as you can see, is situated next to the Central Aerodynamics and Hydrodynamics Institute. We must be in our position no later than 20.30 hours. At roughly 20.45 the administrative gates open to allow in the Voronok with its fresh intake of prisoners.'

'The what?' Dan interrupted.

'The paddy-wagon to you, mate.' Jack smiled.

Avi, when assured of their undivided attention, continued.

'At the same time an outgoing Voronok,

with prisoners who have been processed for detention centres in Mordovia and Perm, heads for this military despatch airport here.' Avi's finger jabbed forcibly on to a red circle. 'We follow the Voronok at a discreet distance until just before it reaches the security gates at the airfield, then we dispense with our topcoats and the posters, and we proceed as planned. Jack will be driving and Rastorotsky, as our GRU custodian, will be in the front with all the necessary papers. Dan will be in the back looking after me. Now it is vital that we reach these gates just as the Voronok goes through, because it must appear that we are part of that consignment. That, I believe, is the plan — yes?' Avi looked towards Jack for confirmation.

'Yes, that's about it in a nutshell,' Jack said, then turned his attention to Dan.

'Dan, what is the name of our important political prisoner?'

'Boris Chernyshov,' Dan rattled out his reply.

'And who is he?'

'He's an astrophysicist who was formerly head of his department at the Space Technology Laboratory of DOSAAF.'

'What crimes against the state has been convicted of?'

'Anti-Soviet agitation.'

'Be more specific,' Jack demanded.

'He wrote an essay which expressed his concern over the gathering arms race between the Soviet Union and the United States. He'd sent it anonymously to the magazine *A Chronicle of Current Events* — but he had also let his views be known to some of his fellow workers. One of them passed on this information to the GRU and it eventually led to his arrest.'

'What is his sentence?'

'Five years' forced labour and psychiatric rehabilitation.'

'Where?'

'At Colony One Special Regime Mordovian Camp Complex.'

'All right, Doc. Now, what about yourself?'

'I'm Dr Andre Lubik, a Pole, who speaks virtually no Russian. Because I studied at medical school in Warsaw, my qualifications are considered vastly inferior to those awarded in the Soviet Union, therefore I am not allowed to practise outside the prison service. I am attached to Lefortovo prison and sometimes I assist at the Kashenko Psychiatric Hospital Special Section for political prisoners. I have applied to go back to Poland on several occasions, but all my applications have been rejected.'

'What were you doing in the Soviet Union in the first place?'

'I had a sweetheart here whom I met when she came to Gdansk for a holiday. I came into the country to try to see her when she stopped corresponding with me. My papers were not in order, and I was charged with false entry and possible subversive activities. After two months in custody, I was informed that I could only avoid a stiff sentence if I were to remain in Russia and work for the prison service. I have been here ever since.'

'Good — well done, Dr Lubik. Now then, Proky knows who he is supposed to be — I bloody well hope so, anyway, and yours truly is ex-dissident tractor driver Comrade Mikhail Tabakov, serving out the last three months of his sentence on special parole as a *feldsher*. So I think we're in fairly good shape. What I suggest we do now is synchronise our watches,' he glanced at his watch and grinned, 'I've always wanted to say that. I make it 18.33 precisely. We've got less than two hours to freshen up, gather all this stuff together, get dressed, and be on our way.'

Jack looked around him at the others who were in various poses of relaxation, and after a minute's pause he barked at them like a sergeant major,

'So, what the hell are you waiting for? Move!'

28

On a night that matched the gloominess of the building that cast its giant shadow over them, the four men sat waiting in the ambulance car, silently occupied with their own thoughts. They had arrived on schedule and parked just a few yards north of the Central Aerodynamics and Hydrodynamics Institute, a splendid structure that stood out in marked contrast to the stark and sombre monument to the misery of man, known as Lefortovo Prison.

As the three agents had learned from Rastorotsky, and as they could now observe partially for themselves, Lefortovo Prison is a series of seven four-storey blocks which, if viewed from the air, would have the appearance of being fan-shaped. These blocks are linked by an inter-communicating corridor and are surrounded by a high stone wall. All four corners of the wall have watch-towers manned by machine gun posts.

At 20.42 hours a shiny black Voronok drove noisily past them and pulled up sharply at the administrative block gates. The huge gates parted and two armed guards, accompanied by two uniformed officials, formed a semi-circle around the driver's cabin. They watched as one of the officials leaned over to the half open window and referring to a sheet of paper in his hand, spoke to the driver. There was a brief exchange of documents before the official finally stepped aside and allowed the vehicle to pass into the compound. At almost the same moment an identical Voronok came from within the confines of the prison and waited while the official carried out a similar process of checking. Satisfied, he waved the vehicle out on to the highway.

'That's it,' Jack said under his breath and was about to turn on the ignition when they all saw that following the Voronok was a police car. As the big van began its journey towards the airfield, the police car tagged on closely behind it.

'Shit, that's all we need,' Jack turned accusingly to Rastorotsky. 'You didn't tell us there'd be a police tail.'

'I didn't expect it myself,' blustered Rastorotsky. 'There's enough armed warders inside the Voronok as it is. All I can suggest is that there must be someone very special in that wagon.'

'Well, that's bloody charming, that is,' Jack said exasperatedly.

'Look on the bright side. It could be to our advantage,' Rastorotsky said encouragingly.

'How come?'

'Well, to my knowledge, the only time those Voronoks get a police escort is either when there are dangerous criminals to be transported, and it is very unlikely to be the case here.'

'Why?' enquired Avi.

'My dear friend, they know how to deal with such men in Lefortovo — and the only way that they leave that place is in a wooden box.'

Watching the police car reach the brow of a hill and vanish below it, Jack switched on the engine and cautiously started to follow.

'So what's the other alternative?' Jack asked, when he saw the crimson rear lights of the police car.

'Have you heard of Professor Georgy Bukovsky?' Rastorotsky answered his question with another.

'Vaguely,' replied Jack. 'Isn't he that dissident forensic psychiatrist?'

'Yeah, I've heard of him,' said Dan.

Rastorotsky half-turned round to face Dan.

'You probably also know that he totally renounced the experiments that were carried out on 'patients' in the Serbsky Institute where he worked, was arrested and thrown into Lefortovo. His views have recently attracted a lot of world attention. And, as you all know, the Soviet authorities are very sensitive about that kind of publicity. So it's my guess that he's in that van on the way to Mordovia or Perm. You see, representatives from Amnesty International and similar organisations are not allowed to visit prisoners there as they do here in Moscow.'

Jack now had a glimpse of the Voronok as it turned a corner at the bottom of the hill. The police car was hanging on to it like a terrier with a bone.

'Look, I'm sorry if I seem a bit dim, Proky, old son, but how can a notable prisoner in that paddy-wagon with that bloody police escort on its arse help our cause?'

'I said it could, *tovarisch*. You see, all eyes will probably be focussed on the luckless Professor Bukovsky, so the guards at the airfield may be a bit too jumpy to check our documents thoroughly.'

'Listen, you told me that our papers were so good that even the head of the KGB would have trouble spotting them as fakes.'

'That is true, but unfortunately he will not be at the airfield to examine them,' Rastorotsky laughed uproariously at his own joke.

The other three men stayed grimly silent,

ever watchful of the two vehicles ahead. Eventually Jack spoke.

'Well, my only consolation, Proky, is this. If they do tumble us, it's going to be you they shoot first.'

The smile that was still on the big Russian's face froze and faded.

The drive to the airfield was uneventful. It was only when they came on to the roughly surfaced, narrow approach road and could actually see the twinkling landing lights in the distance that their troubles began. For although Jack had been positive that he had not been spotted by the police car in front — he was wrong. All at once the police car made a screeching three-point turn and doubled back towards them. It was too late for Jack to take any evasive action, and all he could do was to alert the others in the back to be prepared for anything. In a few moments, seconds only it seemed, the police car had borne down on them and had swung right across their path, forcing Jack to slam the brakes on hard. With a scream of tyres and a cloud of dust they came to a juddering halt. The Voronok a few hundred yards ahead also came to a stop, its engine ticking over loudly. The doors of the police car were flung wide open and the driver and his partner stepped out. Both withdrew pistols from their holsters, held them at the ready, and approached the vehicle warily.

It seemed that the moment of truth had arrived much sooner than anyone could have expected. Dan saw Avi's hand slide smoothly to the gun in his pocket, as he laid back on to the stretcher, and out of the corner of his eye, through the open glass panel, he watched Jack, who was already holding a gun in his hand, place a clipboard over it and rest it on his knees.

The driver of the police car indicated with his side-arm that they should all get outside. Rastorotsky made the first move. He clambered out of the ambulance awkwardly, his face bright red with anger. He confronted the slightly older of the two policemen.

'What the hell do you think you are up to?' he roared about an inch from his face.

'Good on you, mate — that's the way,' Jack hissed through gritted teeth, as he saw the policeman clearly taken aback.

'W . . . why are you following us?'

'I beg your pardon?' Rastorotsky almost exploded.

'You've been trailing us for miles. Now, tell your companions to get out . . . I . . . '

'Do you know whom you are addressing, my young comrade?' Rastorotsky was really laying it on thick now. 'Do you?' he bawled.

'Not yet I don't, but I soon will,' the policeman replied, his confidence returning a little as he remembered that he had been given explicit orders by his commander to stop and investigate anything that might be regarded as suspicious, or could pose a threat to them while they were escorting their prisoners.

While these thoughts were whizzing through his mind, Rastorotsky was removing his grubby raincoat and revealing the GRU uniform beneath, showing he had the rank of sergeant. Everyone in Russia, including the police, had reason to fear this lot. The GRU — *Glavnoe Razvedyvatelnoe Upravlenie* — had terrifying powers.

But a Russian is not like a German, who generally tends to jump to attention and follow the orders of a superior — especially shouted orders, without question. A Russian is a mixture of many nationalities and his richness of blood builds a strong character and gives him a natural assertiveness. This policeman was not going to be put off so easily.

'I would like all the others to get out, please,' he said firmly. Rastorotsky was a Russian too, through and through. He would try a different approach.

'It is good that you are so conscientious,

comrade, but your own head will be on the block if you endanger our mission. I will make sure of that.'

He went to the ambulance and tore off the Bolshoi posters from the sides to show the Red Cross emblems beneath.

'You will see that this vehicle is an ambulance. Inside we have an even more political hot potato than you have in that Voronok.'

The policeman gave a worried look towards his partner, who merely responded with a slight shrug of his shoulders.

Rastorotsky's eyes lit up. He'd got him — yes he saw the capitulation in his face. Now he would press home his advantage.

'Look, trying to do your duty is one thing, and very commendable, of course, but you have already delayed us considerably. We must catch that Red Cross plane to Barashevo and get the scum we have in here ... ' he banged the side of the ambulance with his clenched fist, ' . . . locked up where he belongs. Now, do you want to see our papers?' He impatiently clicked his thumb and finger at Jack, who was slightly surprised by this sudden demand. With his free hand Jack withdrew a slim document case and passed it through the window to Rastorotsky, still keeping the trigger finger on his gun. Rastorotsky unzipped the case and leafed through some papers until he found what he was looking for. It was a letter written on authentic headed notepaper from the Soviet Department of Justice, and had cost them a bundle. The fictitious letter made reference to the sick, discredited astrophysicist, Chernyshov, and underlined that his transfer to Barashevo from Lefortovo was to be conducted in as unobtrusive a manner as possible.

'I see,' the policeman said as he handed the letter of authorisation to his partner. 'Is he very sick?' He walked over to the ambulance and peered through the window.

'Very. But I wish he were dead,' Rastorotsky said as he spat a slug of phlegm on the ground contemptuously. 'It would save us all a lot of trouble. Would you like to examine the rest of our papers as well?' He glanced at his watch impatiently.

'No, it's all right. The Red Cross plane leaves shortly. I'm sorry you have been delayed, but we cannot be too careful, you understand.' He handed back the letter to Rastorotsky. 'Look, follow us and I'll see that you get through and on to the plane with the minimum of formality and fuss.'

★   ★   ★

The policeman was as good as his word. As though expecting that the wrath of Stalin's ghost might be visited on him if this lot missed that flight, he did his utmost to ease all of them through the two airport checkpoints, where, after his assurances, the guards gave only cursory glances at their travel permits, whilst Avi was carried by two burly soldiers on a stretcher all the way on to the plane.

Only when in the air and on their way to the Mordovian ASSR Camp did Jack allow himself the luxury of a fleeting smile. He turned to Dan and Avi and whispered, 'In this life you need a little bit of luck.'

Rastorotsky overheard him. 'Luck had nothing to do with it,' he said a little churlishly. 'It was my brilliant and quick-witted thinking.'

'Yeah, I've noticed that your brilliant quick-witted brain functions at its best when your pants are filling with shit.' He winked heavily at the others.

29

In terms of air travel time, it was little more than a hop. Just ninety minutes after take-off they were preparing to land outside the capital of Barashevo in Mordovia. It had been anything but a joy ride. Prisoners, many of whom were desperately ill, were lying on makeshift stretchers, some of these no more than planks of wood covered by moth-eaten blankets. Because of the space that these prostrate men and women occupied, and the fact that their numbers were great, actual seats were at a premium. The few that had been available were already taken by armed guards when the four men got on board. So whilst Avi was taken forward with the other stretcher cases, Dan, Jack and Rastorotsky were forced to sit on the bare metal floor with the majority of prisoners and medical staff, looking like paratroopers awaiting a jump.

Accompanying them, throughout the journey, had been the stench that came from severely ulcerated sores, bowel and other intestinal disorders, and the groans and cries of prisoners in terrible pain. Occasionally a *feldsher* or even more rarely a doctor, would tend the patients in their charge, but this was only done under extreme duress, usually egged on by other prisoners who would shout at the 'medics' to do something to shut up their bloody row. The agonised moans increased as the plane made the final descent before landing. Stretchers slid this way and that. To prevent themselves being tossed about like peanuts in a can, Dan gripped a metal section that was part of the framework, while Jack and Rastorotsky positioned their feet in a strut on the floor and braced themselves against the superstructure at their back. Some violent bumping as the wheels made contact with the tarmac, and it was all over. The flight had felt like an eternity to all of them. The plane slowly taxied to the processing station. Their welcoming committee was a group of armed soldiers with automatic rifles at the ready, as surly-faced officials stood at the plane's doors and checked the papers of all who were able to disembark on their own two feet. Rastorotsky took a leading role again, and explained to the man in charge that their prisoner needed to be taken to hospital as quickly as possible. Jack overheard his reply to Rastorotsky.

'Doesn't it make you sick, comrade?' he said sourly, 'we give men like this . . . ' he read the authorisation of transfer letter

Rastorotsky had handed him, ' . . . Cherny-shov the finest free education in the world, he becomes a man in an exalted position, a respected scientist, and then how does the ungrateful bastard, and all the others like him, repay the debt he owes to his mother country? He denounces it.'

'This is so true,' Rastorotsky nodded gravely.

'And that's not all. When they get ill, what do we do? We namby-pamby them, put them into hospitals and take care of them like little children. We should put the bastards up against a wall and shoot them, that's what we should do.'

'Yes, you are so right. We are too damn soft in this country,' Rastorotsky shook his head sadly and giving his chest three thumps, he continued, 'we have too much heart, comrade.'

'All right, get your prisoner and your medical unit over to that transport section there,' the official said, happy to have had a sympathetic ear listening to him. Rastorotsky followed the man's gaze over to where a line of stationary trucks was parked beneath a blaze of tall, overhead lights. 'An ambulance leaves for Colony Three Hospital in about twenty minutes. Ever been there, comrade?'

'Where?' asked Rastorotsky.

'Colony Three.'

'No, I've never been to Barashevo before.'

Watching to see that Dan and Jack, who now carried Avi on the stretcher, were out of earshot, he beckoned Rastorotsky closer to him and, with a sly grin on his face, whispered softly, 'The hospital is slap bang in the middle of the women's camp. I tell you, my friend, some of those females have not had a good man for years. There's a few rosy apples in that orchard that are always ready for plucking. A gift of soap or some cigarettes, and you have a choice that would make a sultan of a hareem envious. My wife keeps nagging me to return to our home in Leningrad, but I tell her that all my requests for a transfer are refused.' He chuckled. 'Make the best of your stay while you are here, eh!'

★   ★   ★

If the conditions in the plane had been bad, the two hour journey from the airfield to the hospital was appalling. In an ambulance designed, Dan reckoned, to take four, maybe at a pinch six, stretcher cases, and perhaps two to three orderlies, twenty-three human beings were jammed in that tin sweatbox on wheels, which traversed roads in such a poor state that donkeys would have had difficulty trekking over them. But, after what Dan felt was the longest day in his entire life, certainly the longest he'd ever gone without sleep, they finally arrived at their destination. As the rear doors of the ambulance were opened and the people literally fell out, Dan could see that they were inside the prison hospital compound. He looked around for the others who, having got in first, were well up in the front. A woman administrator, clutching a clipboard tightly in front of her, spoke to him in Russian. Oh, God, he thought, don't say I'm going to blow it now — not after all this. He smiled at her and nodded politely. But her expression remained immobile, as though her face were carved in granite. She asked him the same question — if question it was — again.

'He doesn't speak Russian — he's a Pole,' Rastorotsky said as he tumbled out of the vehicle, followed by Jack.

The woman gave Jack a sideways glance, the look promising more than just a passing interest, which he was happy to note. She was no beauty, but just how useful she might be to them they were very soon to discover.

Waving her clipboard like a flag, she informed them that she was the intake clerk. All patients, she said, referring to a typed list of names secured to the board, had to be checked in by her before they could be admitted to the diagnostic ward. The good news, Jack thought quickly, was that this woman must know where in that bleak, dimly-lit building with bars on all its windows Vladimir Sokol was confined. The bad news was that nowhere on her list would she find the name of Boris Chernyshov.

Several orderlies helped to unload the stretcher cases and placed them in a line on the ground, immediately in front of the hospital entrance. Avi was approximately in the middle of the line. The other prisoners, some of whom were on crutches, were made to stand in rows behind the stretchers. The woman, having received all the papers from the guards assigned to the prisoners, began her roll call. As each patient responded to his or her name being shouted out, the woman clerk checked their particulars to see that they corresponded with the information on her own intake sheet. When she was satisfied with this she would then strut over to the patient concerned and study their features carefully, comparing them with the ID card photo pinned to their lapel or blankets. Only then would she tick off the name on her list, after which she would give a curt nod to the orderlies to conduct the patient into the hospital. It was a slow process, but she remained throughout completely impervious to the obvious discomfort and distress of the patients. As the intake began to thin out, four minds thought as one. It was Rastorotsky who quietly echoed those thoughts to Jack.

'It is time to put your plan into operation. She's a stickler for detail, that cow, but you have a good chance. I think she has taken a bit of a shine to you.'

Jack gave him a look which read 'thanks for nothing', but decided that the big Russian was right. He must act now. This was a situation they had discussed at length and had made provisions for should it occur, and occur it had. Wrapped up in a roll of bandage and concealed in Jack's white jacket pocket was a stick of dynamite — an adapted military thunderflash. But it was only when he tried to work the bandage loose with one hand that he realised that, in an effort to disguise the explosive from any sudden examination, he had bound the gauze around it too tightly. As drops of sweat started to fall from his armpits and roll down his body, his fingers moved at a feverish pace. But the bandage would not shift. If only he could get to the wick, he could ignite it with his cigarette lighter as it was, he thought, but which bloody end of the dynamite should he be attempting to untwine? As his hand ferreted about in his pocket, he gazed at the scene around him with a calmness that belied the panic that was building up in his mind. Added to which he was conscious of the anxious glances being cast in his direction by the other three — and all the while the woman was getting closer to Avi.

Then his fingers found it. Never had a piece of greasy thread felt so good to the touch. He smoothed the wick out between forefinger and thumb, with a hand that was trembling a good deal more than it should, until he had about an inch clear of the stick to light. Standing it upright in his pocket so that the wick was as accessible as possible, without being visible, he withdrew his lighter from another pocket and swiftly passed it from one hand to the other behind his back. Then he hastily took stock of the position. As the woman came towards Avi, he held the lighter tightly in his grip and clicked it. He glanced down into his pocket and saw the thin flame shoot upwards. It was just sufficiently bright for him to see the bandage-covered dynamite and the thin, yellowish, protruding wick. He put the flame to it and, in a second, heard a faint sizzle as the wick ignited.

A prisoner, shabbily dressed in torn denims

at least two sizes too large for him, stood in agony not far from Avi. He had a thick untidy growth of beard and a complexion that was pasty grey and pockmarked. It was he, whoever he was, who was to be the unfortunate victim. But, Jack thought, the poor sod looked half dead anyway.

Jack, still making sure that he was unobserved, quickly took the dynamite from his pocket and, turning sideways on to the chosen victim, he bent his knees slightly and rolled the stick smoothly along the ground. It came to a spitting stop just a few centimetres from the man's feet. At the same time he pointed a finger at the bearded prisoner and yelled at the top of his voice, 'He's got a bomb! Quick — take cover.'

Then Jack hurled himself at the startled woman and, with an expert rugger tackle, brought her crashing to the ground, while others did their best to get out of the way. There followed an ear-splitting explosion and, after a few seconds, a couple of bursts from an automatic rifle as one of the bewildered guards considered that he ought to make a gesture and fire at something — even thin air.

In that chaotic instant two things had occurred. Avi, as planned, had sprinted into the hospital building and was searching for a temporary hiding place, and Jack had managed to get a hand to the woman's clipboard and had wrenched the tell-tale admission sheet from it, crunched it into a ball and slipped it into his trouser pocket. As some sort of order was being restored, and medical staff and guards alike, who had followed Jack's warning, were picking themselves up from the dusty ground, Jack helped the dishevelled and badly shaken woman to her feet. Rastorotsky, now taking over and exercising his GRU authority, was staring down at the luckless bearded prisoner, who had been flung a good three metres by the blast, and was lying sprawled out, unconscious, injured and bleeding, but miraculously not dead.

'Is this the swine who had the bomb?' Rastorotsky pointed downwards at the man and looked at Jack for confirmation.

'That's him,' Jack said.

'Well done, comrade. It is due to your quick thinking that no one was killed.' This was said mainly for the benefit of the woman. It was intended to spark off some kind of admiration for him, and it did the trick.

'I can't thank you enough,' she said, all the officiousness now gone from her voice. In the background they heard Rastorotsky giving orders for the 'anarchistic pig' to be carried into the treatment room and to be heavily guarded.

'Then we shall see who else is behind all this — there must be others involved,' Rastorotsky went on ominously. 'And when the pig comes round we shall find out — we shall most certainly find out'.

'Glad to be of assistance,' Jack flashed his best smile at her, the one he was once told made him look like that famous movie star, whose name had temporarily slipped his mind. 'My name is Mikhail Tabakov,' he gazed into her blue eyes.

'Katya Slepyan,' she smiled. Her teeth were good too, very white and definitely her own. She offered him her hand. Although it was a small hand, her skin was rough like a labourer's. It was a bit off-putting to Jack — oh, he did like his women to be feminine. But he had to admit to himself that in the line of duty he'd had worse — much worse.

Suddenly he remembered Dan. He looked around for him but he was nowhere in sight. What Jack had missed seeing in all that confusion was an orderly, who had rushed out of the hospital looking for a doctor. Spotting the lapel badge on Dan that stated he was a Dr Lubik, he had grabbed him by the arm and tugged him towards the hospital. The orderly was jabbering away in a state of panic, and Dan was in two minds whether to go with him or not, but he'd seen Avi hare into the hospital and thought he might be of more use to him on the inside. In any case there was no time to catch the attention of Jack or Rastorotsky, who were both clearly otherwise engaged. Within the space of less than five minutes after the explosion, Dan was scrubbing up to assist in an open heart operation on the deputy head of the prison hospital, after the original assistant doctor had suddenly been taken ill. Now, complete in green gown and a mask, which he had hastily tied around his face, he was ushered into the theatre and took up his place alongside the surgeon, who stared over the top of his mask at him for an instant before giving him a brief and friendly nod, an acknowledgement of Dan as a fellow physician, then he recommenced his work.

Dan's brain was racing. It had been years since he had been involved in surgery of any kind, but major surgery like this — never! He cast his eyes around the theatre, fascinated by the apparatus. It was ancient. It looked as though it had been hired from a Hollywood studio that had made a Doctor Kildare film in the 1950's. The surgeon, observing Dan's wandering gaze, nudged him gently, muttered some muffled words in Russian and drew his attention to the patient on the table. The chest cavity was wide open and muscle tissue clamped back, displaying the pumping heart. A male nurse swabbed away some oozing blood and the surgeon, using his scalpel as a pointer, showed Dan where he would make his incision in the aorta — the great arterial trunk that carries blood from the heart — remove the infected area and insert a small segment of plastic tubing. This complaint induces symptoms of breathlessness and fatigue, and is known as aortitis. The 'assisted passage technique' was a fairly routine operation in most countries today, although Dan figured that never would surgery on this scale be attempted in such primitive conditions anywhere else but here. He bent over the patient, with a mixture of feigned and genuine interest. And then the unimaginable happened. Not even in a nightmare could he have dreamed of anything so horrific. His mask, which was tenuously secured, slipped its fastenings and fell with a faint splodge right into the patient's chest cavity. He felt half a dozen dumbfounded eyes turn on him. The surgeon's hand froze in mid movement. The breathing apparatus was eerily noisy — there being a total absence of sound from every other source. If ever there was a time to remain calm it was now. He quickly selected a set of forceps from the instrument trolley, gripped the mask, which had soaked up blood like blotting paper, adroitly lifted it out, and walked to a pedal bin. As the lid yawned open he dropped the soggy mask in. Then, fully in command, he clicked his fingers to a nearby orderly and indicated that he required an immediate replacement. The surprised orderly did as he was bid, and Dan walked back to the operating table. If only Dan could have seen the surgeon's face under his mask he would have noticed that his jaw had remained steadfastly open in sheer astonishment. But the expression in the surgeon's eyes was enough — it was a look which said 'My God, what kind of doctors are they sending me these days?' A moment or two later the operation recommenced, and Dan was assisting with the ligaturing of the artery, and not making too bad a job of it either, everything considered.

★　★　★

While this black comedy was being played out, Avi, who had managed to find an unlocked cleaning equipment cupboard, had donned a pair of hospital overalls, and taken a bucket and mop into the main corridor, where he was proceeding very slowly to clean the floor with a highly pungent disinfectant which nearly made him throw up. When hospital staff and army personnel appeared, he would turn his head away and mop the floor for dear life. But he never took his eyes off the main entrance for more than a second. At last he saw Rastorotsky walk through with some armed guards accompanying a man being carried on a stretcher by orderlies. The problem was that Rastorotsky was heading in the opposite direction. How was he going to attract the big Russian's attention without drawing any to himself? Looking up and down the corridor to ensure that he was not being observed, he picked up his bucket and mop and ran on tiptoe, like the cartoon character Sylvester the Cat, until he was only a metre or so behind them. A bit breathless, he let out a throaty cough. But no one took the slightest notice of him. Everyone in that place had bad coughs — bad everything — he had to think of something else, and fast. Just before they disappeared through a door marked 'Casualty', he forcibly kicked the bucket over. It made a loud, hollow clanging noise, and was followed by the clatter of the mop handle hitting the tiled floor and resounding down the corridor. This made Rastorotsky turn round all right, and the guards, ever alert, did likewise, their guns ready to fire. Avi shrugged his shoulders apologetically.

'Leave this clumsy idiot to me,' Rastorotsky snapped at the guards when he saw that it was Avi. He walked briskly up to him.

'Do you know what time it is? This is a hospital,' he snarled, 'not a bloody circus, you clown.' Then, softly, he said, 'Watch out for Jack. He's with the woman administrator. He is the one you must look out for now.'

'But where the hell is he?' Avi queried under his breath.

'Somewhere in the grounds. Don't take your eyes off the entrance.' Then loudly Rastorotsky reprimanded him, 'Any more of that stupidity at this hour of the morning and you'll be laying sewers in Siberia.'

The guards smiled at Rastorotsky's threat and had a little joke about it when he rejoined them, and Avi watched them as they walked into the casualty room.

Picking up his 'props', Avi impatiently began mopping up the water, and wondered how long he would have to wait for Jack. This role of hospital cleaner was not only boring, but bloody hard work.

★　★　★

Katya's commanding officer, a man of advancing years, had lusted after her from the moment he had first set eyes on her, but had been scared stiff to turn his fantasies into reality. Seeing her now, white-faced and quaking still, he relieved her of her duties and sent her to her quarters to rest. Playing on his sympathy, she asked if Jack, as a *feldsher*, could accompany her. The commanding officer was not too happy with this request, but as she was clearly distressed he reluctantly complied.

Her quarters, Jack was to discover, were about the same size as his late father used to call 'the box room' in their semi-detached in Hackney.

He sat on the edge of the bed, and she took a chair from beneath a castorless surgical trolley, which now served as a dressing-table and was positioned under a wall mirror. She sat in the chair facing him, their knees touched but she did not immediately withdraw them, enjoying for a moment the feel of him. Jack's eyes swept round the tiny room. It was most enlightening. He could never have guessed that this typically emancipated Russian woman would have surrounded herself with so many girly knick-knacks. Soft toys and traditional cos-tumed dolls were all over the place, and jammed so tightly together on the window ledge that they concealed the lower half of the bars outside, while the top half were hidden by crossover blue gingham curtains bordered by pretty ruffled frills. The makeshift dressing-table held bottles of perfume in all shapes and sizes. A couple even bore a Paris tag on the labels. A variety of make-up completed the picture. She seemed to read his thoughts.

'Are you surprised that I should collect such things, Mikhail?'

'Er . . . no, no,' Jack smiled. Surprised? He was bloody amazed.

'It's just that the life here makes you so hard — you have to be like a rock to survive. I need these,' she swept an arm to encompass the room, 'to remind me that I am still a woman.'

'I knew you were a real woman the minute I set eyes on you,' Jack lied.

'Did you?' she asked, childlike, wanting him to tell her more.

It was true that he must try to extract that vital information about Sokol from her, but there was nothing in the rule book that said he shouldn't enjoy his work. He wasted no more words. He grabbed her and pressed his mouth hard against hers. The kiss took her breath away and she responded at once.

'Oh, take me to bed, Mikhail. Make me feel alive — hurt me,' she gasped.

If this lady was a masochist, he'd willingly oblige her. He snatched her up from the chair and into his arms, real cave man stuff this, he thought, as he tossed her on to the bed. Leaning over her he tore at her clothes, almost ripping them from her. She helped him, pulling and tugging at the buttons on the severe grey hospital tunic, then slightly more gently he eased her out of it. She bundled it up and hurled it, with the sudden contempt she now felt for it, into the corner of the room. Her underwear was another revelation for Jack, for the obligatory black nursing stockings were hooked on by a crimson red suspender belt showing an expanse of porcelain white thighs, and the flimsiest bra and panties he'd seen in a long time. He had no idea that such items were available in the USSR.

'Oh, please hurry,' she breathed urgently, and reached out a hand to his crotch to feel the powerful manhood she just knew was there — a curled-up snake, but rising now as she fondled him, like a cobra about to strike. She moistened her lips in anticipation.

He needed no more encouragement — he'd been aroused enough. In seconds he had undressed and, as he did so, she had removed the last scanty remnants that separated her from complete nakedness. They gazed at each other's bodies for a moment, desire burning in their eyes, Jack delighting in the sheer loveliness of her. Everything about her was in perfect proportion, from the full, firm breasts, topped with their pink upright nipples, down to her slender waist, the tight, rounded buttocks, and the slim, shapely legs that stemmed from them. It was difficult for him to believe that only moments ago she had been no more than a dowdy caterpillar cocooned in drab hospital garments, but now, having shed them, she had burst forth transformed into a beautiful butterfly. She had eyes only for his tight, firmly muscled body, and the proud erection that jutted from it, almost commanding her to take it to her hungry mouth. She gave a whimper like a puppy and her tongue darted all over it. She held its throbbing fullness in both her hands and, gazing at it in wonder for just a moment, she plunged it deep into her mouth, so deep the tip almost touched the back of her throat. Feverishly, almost violently, she brought her head to and fro on it, increasing her movements all the time, while her hands now squeezed his buttocks so hard that Jack could stand it no more;

fearing he would reach his climax, he pulled away from her and she let out a disappointed sigh. In an instant he was on top of her and she spread herself to meet him, to take him into her. He bayoneted the moist, warm well of pleasure she offered him, and as their bodies twisted and writhed together, she panted and pleaded for him to beat her, hurt her, make her obey him, emitting animal cries as he complied with her wishes. At last they felt an orgasm commence like the grumbling of a volcano about to erupt, and with a scream she could not control they came together.

Jack gently kissed her neck and face before easing himself on to his back. He lay there utterly spent, with that unique smell of sweat and sex permeating the small room. He felt he could have slept for a month, but this was where he had to be sharper than ever.

Eventually she broke the silence and, gazing admiringly at his face, she propped herself on an elbow.

'Was I what you expected, Mikhail?'

'You were better than any man could ever hope to expect,' he replied — and he meant it.

She blushed slightly. 'Would you like a cigarette?' she asked, tracing a finger over his mouth.

'Mmm, I'd love one.' Jack watched her bottom dispassionately as she searched in a drawer. This was to be the time to probe — in this aftermath of mutual passion, when lovers have given themselves totally to each other and when their innermost thoughts and feelings are most likely to be shared. With two lighted cigarettes in her hand, one of which she placed tenderly in his mouth, kissing his forehead as she did so, she climbed back into bed beside him.

'It must be hell for a girl like you — working here,' he said.

She puffed out a cloud of smoke. 'I must go where I am ordered, Mikhail. But at least it's only for a year, then I get transferred back to the city and a normal life, I hope.'

'But how do you cope with so many types of prisoners? I mean in here you have everything from political dissidents to out-and-out rogues. However do you differentiate between them?'

'We don't. A sick person is a sick person, whatever his crime. Do you know, Mikhail, whatever your first impressions may have been, our problem here is not a lack of concern for the patients, it's a lack of qualified medical staff. That is why we have to be so vigilant to spot the malingerers, healthy people who are just trying to avoid work in the camps. This hospital only has 120 beds.'

'Well, that's not bad.'

'No, I agree — but do you know how many medical staff we have to attend them?'

'No.'

'One surgeon, one visiting doctor, three therapeutists, one dental technician — no dentist, mark you — three full-time trained nurses and ten *feldshers* like yourself,' she sighed. 'It is then you realise what an impossible situation this puts us in.'

Jack nodded sympathetically. 'Can't you ask for more help?'

'Doctors do not readily volunteer to come to Barashevo. They say we are lucky to have those we do have.'

'It's a fair argument, I suppose,' he said nonchalantly, but his heart was beginning to pound. The question he was about to ask her would have to seem so offhand that it would not arouse the slightest suspicion.

'But I bet you there's still a few who shouldn't be in here!'

She looked surprised. 'Pardon?'

'I mean, like this character ... er ... what's his name — Sakov?'

'Sakov?'

'Er ... no, Sokol,' he corrected himself. 'Vladimir Sokol.'

'How did you know about him?' She threw

back her head and laughed.

Thank the Lord she'd taken the bait. Please don't let me screw it up now, he thought. 'Oh, rumour travels fast, you know. He's somebody important, I gather.'

'Important? Do you know what I heard?'

'What?'

She leaned into him and gave him an affectionate peck on his nose. 'Well, it is said that he claims to be the son of Adolf Hitler!'

Jack laughed. He knew it was a hollow one, but what the hell — it was the best he could muster.

'You're joking,' he said disbelievingly.

'No, seriously, that's what they say.'

Jack grinned. 'Where do you have him locked up? In a padded cell?'

This was it. If she didn't tell him now, it would be almost impossible for him to broach the subject again.

'No, he's in cell sixteen. It's just an ordinary guarded cell at the end of the security wing.

'That's on the first floor, isn't it?'

'Ground floor,' she said quickly, 'Why — do you want to go and stare at him?' She giggled.

'Of course not,' Jack scoffed. 'But purely out of interest, have you seen him?'

'No, I was off duty when he came in — and I've got better things to do than gawp at madmen.' She sidled into him seductively.

Oh, Christ, she was ready for it again, he thought. Now that he had cracked Sokol's whereabouts, he couldn't wait to get his butt out of there — but he had to be a bit subtle about it.

'Listen, darling, I fancy you like mad, but I'll have to let my custodian know that I haven't gone over the wall. He'll probably clap me in irons as it is. He's a hell of a disciplinarian.'

All the time Jack was talking, he was putting his clothes back on.

'Yes, I saw him,' she said sadly. 'He's the fat one isn't he?'

'That's him, a sergeant in the GRU, and he's got a temper that matches his size.'

Dressed again, he leaned over her and kissed her firmly on the mouth. 'Don't go away,' he said softly, 'I'll do my damndest to come back soon. Try to get some sleep, eh?'

'I will,' she murmured, and with a yawn she pulled some bedcovers over her and closed her eyes.

When he left the room, he felt a growing sense of anticipation as the adrenalin flowed through him, giving him renewed energy, a second wind. The sense of purpose that had begun to languish, mainly through sheer mental and physical fatigue, now returned in full.

30

While waiting, Avi had nearly cleaned the entire length of the corridor. If his girlfriend, Shari, who had often called him 'the laziest bastard on God's earth, who would never so much as pick up a cloth to dry a goddamn cup' could have witnessed for herself the wonderful job he was doing now — she would never have believed it. You could actually see your reflection so clearly on the polished surface that you could look up your nostrils and count the hairs! He smiled to himself at this irrelevant thought. But why he should find it so amusing he had no idea. Maybe the fatigue and strain of waiting to see Jack, or even one of the others, was getting to him and he was quietly going gaga — who knows!

His smile disappeared in a flash when he thought he saw, dressed in a Russian soldier's uniform, the unforgettable face of his torturer, Horst Shreiber.

Working methodically with the mop where he stood, he lifted his eyes to take another look. It was no mistake, it was that Nazi sadist Horst, and he was chatting to one of his henchmen who was similarly attired. They had just come out of a room marked storage and were walking slowly in his direction. Avi turned away and carried on mopping. Then the thought came to him — a compelling one. With the element of surprise on his side, and the gun with the long silencer tucked in his trouser belt, he could blow them both away with ease. Oh, how he would love to do that. But it would probably blow their mission as well, and he was too much of a pro to let his feelings get the better of him. Nevertheless, he slid his hand swiftly on to the handle of his weapon — just in case. Then, almost as suddenly as they had appeared, Horst and the other man turned on their heels and marched straight out of the main entrance.

Avi found himself shaking. Perhaps the memory of the torture they had put him through, and the chance he'd had of taking his sweet revenge which had now been missed, had given his nervous system an emotional jolt. Whatever it was, his hands were trembling like leaves on a tree. He gripped the mop handle to steady them — and himself. A man in a white coat turned the corner and walked hurriedly towards him. Avi quickly dropped his head and dipped the mop into the bucket. The footsteps stopped right next to him and a voice said:

'Do you want to do this corridor again, or would you prefer to know where Sokol is?' The voice was Jack's.

Avi looked up instantly, relief etched all over his face.

'Put that bloody mop and bucket down and come with me,' Jack ordered. Avi fell into step behind him as Jack led the way, moving now like a man possessed.

'Where the hell have you been all this time?' Avi inquired, trying like a small boy to keep pace with his father.

'Never mind that now, I'll tell you later.'

'But Horst and some of his men are here, dressed as Russian soldiers,' said Avi. He looked very worried.

'Yes, I know. I've seen them. We've got to move fast now — very fast.'

'Have you seen Dan?' Avi asked.

'No, have you?'

Avi shook his head. 'I've seen Rastorotsky though. He told me to keep a look-out for you.'

'Smart bloke, is old Proky,' Jack said under his breath.

They did not speak of their concern for Dan. Their mission must come above everything else. Friendship — however close — counted for nothing in this profession when the chips were down.

As they walked, Jack quietly outlined to Avi what he had learned. The more Jack told him, the more Avi became exhilarated. At last they arrived at the far end of the security wing and stood talking casually to each other, showing no apparent interest at all in the two guards who were there, but observing their every move like a duo of kestrels waiting to swoop on their prey. Jack glanced at his wristwatch. It was 04.11 hours.

'Those buggers have been on picket duty since midnight,' he whispered softly to Avi. They both looked at the guards briefly again. They appeared anything but vigilant. One was smoking a cigarette, whilst the other was reading a magazine. Both, however, held automatic rifles.

'We should be able to take them,' Jack muttered, 'but first we've got to get to them.'

'You should have let me bring my bucket and mop along. I could have worked my way down there without causing too much of a stir,' Avi said pensively.

Jack stared at Avi for a moment, and Avi could see that he'd given him an idea.

'All right, just argue with me when I start bawling you out — okay?' Jack said.

Avi seemed puzzled, but caught on quickly when he realized what Jack was trying to do.

'What do you call this?' Jack said, pointing to the floor. 'It's filthy,' he shouted.

'You think so? Well see if you can do better,' Avi snapped.

'Don't you dare be impertinent to me; you damn well do it again,' Jack bellowed.

'You go to hell,' Avi responded fiercely, getting quite carried away with the situation.

'Say that again,' Jack challenged.

'Go to hell, you arsehole!'

Both the guards looked up at the commotion. It made a change from their monotonous routine to watch a couple of idiots having a ruckus, as long as it didn't get out of hand.

'What did you call me, you piss ball?' Jack screamed, beside himself with rage.

'Shut up, you two,' one of the guards called out, 'we've enough trouble without you waking up the scum in here.'

Avi completely ignored him. 'I said you were an arsehole — an arsehole!' he goaded Jack, so close to his face that their foreheads nearly met. Jack went mad and grabbed him by the throat, and started to throttle him. Falling to the ground, they began wrestling and throwing punches, which they pulled by the dozen. In seconds the guards came thundering towards them. One, in his haste, left his rifle propped against the wall. As they bent over the rolling turmoil of flying fists and angrily tried to separate them, Avi and Jack suddenly stopped fighting and pointed their guns straight at the startled guards. Then, springing agilely to their feet, they forcibly pushed the guards ahead, whilst snatching furtive glances around to ensure that they were not being observed. Step by cautious step they proceeded along the corridor, looking at the numbers over the cell doors. And then, in a moment of jubilant expectation, they both saw number sixteen. They looked at each other, their thoughts unuttered, but they read: Was he here? Was he really here? The man they had come all this way to track down, put their lives in constant jeopardy for? Was the son of Adolf Hitler really on the other side of that door?

Jack looked behind him again. The harshly lit corridor was still deserted. Then, beckoning Avi to follow suit, he pistol whipped the guard in front of him on the back of his skull. There was a faint gasp from the man as his legs folded beneath him and he concertinaed to the ground. Only in the time difference it took for Avi to raise the butt of his gun, was the second guard falling like a pole-axed ox to join his comrade.

Jack wrenched the bunch of keys from the guard's belt. As he did so, Avi noticed that his hands were shaking as his own had done earlier. Strangely, seeing Jack in this tense state seemed to calm his own fears, and gave him the strength that he needed to take control and skipper the final stage of their long journey. As Jack scanned the numbered keys, Avi kept an ever watchful eye on the corridor. At last, with his heart missing a couple of beats, Jack slotted the key into the cell door and turned it. There was a satisfying metallic clunk as the tongue of the lock snapped back into the steel door. Avi gripped Jack's arm firmly and looked grimly into his face.

'Me, Jack — you must let me do it.'

Jack nodded. There could be no dispute between them over that. The Israeli was like the providential messenger of death, sent to reap revenge for six million souls deprived so hideously of their lifespan by the most evil tyrant in history. Hitler may have cheated them once by putting an end to himself, but his only son, his true heir, would not be able to rob them again in this day of reckoning.

Jack gave Avi a faint smile, a mixture of encouragement and acknowledgement of the confidence he had in him to complete their mission successfully.

Checking that the silencer on his gun was screwed on tightly, Avi threw Jack a last poignant glance before he tentatively entered the cell. Coming so suddenly from the clinical brightness of the corridor outside into this dimly lit, dank place he found eerily unnerving. His eyes darted everywhere, rapidly getting accustomed to the change in light. He stared at the bunk. It was as though he had been dealt a sickening blow, for the bunk was unoccupied. Then he heard a sound, just a faint creaking. He swung his gaze to a corner and there, just discernible in the shadows of a barred window, was the outline of a man sitting in a wooden chair, rocking himself gently back and forth.

The seated figure, who had his back to Avi, seemed totally oblivious of his presence. He just stared fixedly at the peeling, grey painted wall. Avi raised his gun and took steady aim. But then, without appearing to move the rest of his body, the figure slowly turned his head in Avi's direction. Avi froze, almost paralysed, not with fear, but with a skin-pricking sensation that he had witnessed all this before — *déjà vu*. It was not just the face that now confronted him — although even in the poor light and minus that idiosyncratic moustache, Avi could still see that the man bore a chilling resemblance to Adolf Hitler — it was the same straight brown hair and the way a lank quiff fell at an angle across his forehead, the same deep-set blue eyes and sharp features. The similarity between the photographs and films he had studied of Hitler and this man bore a striking, and weirdly uncanny, resemblance. But there was something else about him. It rekindled a memory of a scene he had often played in the theatre — the final act of Ibsen's *Ghosts*. For the man in this chair, who had now started to make strained grunting noises at this unannounced intruder, was quite clearly an imbecile. Saliva dribbled down his chin as he mouthed an unintelligible stream of protest at Avi. He lifted a bony, clenched fist at him, as if to emphasise his displeasure. Avi lowered his gun and smiled bitterly to himself. God — what an ironic twist, he thought. Was there any point, any satisfaction to be gained from killing this pathetic, drooling creature? None whatsoever, he decided. But he had to make one final check, one unmistakable piece of evidence had to be sought. He strode over to the man, who cowered back from him in the chair protecting his face by holding his arms in front of him, a movement he made so rapidly that it seemed as though it were second nature. Avi struggled with him for a few moments then, grabbing at the man's shirt sleeve, he violently ripped it back so that it hung in tatters all the way to his collar. With further mouthings of disapproval, but only token resistance from the man, Avi lifted his spindly arm. And there, under his armpit, tattooed in his chalk white flesh were the faded blue initials AGU, the mark that confirmed beyond doubt that this man, and this man alone, could lay claim to being the son of Adolf Hitler. For those initials pricked into an infant's skin over half a century ago stood for *Adolf, Geli, Unehelich'* — lovechild.

Avi paused for a moment, staring at him. The moral was in that Ibsen play, which was a reiteration of the Biblical prophecy that the sins of the father shall be visited upon the children. It was *Nakam* — vengeance. But a greater vengeance than the old Lublin group could ever have extracted. This was surely divine justice.

31

McNabe sucked at his pipe. He had taken up smoking again and seemed much happier for it. His debriefing of Dan in his office at Langley had commenced at 08.30 hours, just one hour after Dan's plane had touched down in Washington DC. Now, some three hours later, they were presented with welcome coffee by McNabe's attractive secretary, who made just a fleeting appearance in order to serve the first cups. When she had closed the door behind her, McNabe looked at Dan thoughtfully, but with a twinkle in his eye.

'Listen, if ever I have to have a by-pass on the old ticker here,' he pointed with the stem of his pipe to his chest, 'just promise me you won't be there to assist, huh.'

'Oh, we had a few more incidents on the way back that nearly topped that,' said Dan, and he went on to recount how Rastorotsky had met him as he had finally emerged from the operating theatre, and without even giving him time to shed his gown, had hurried him to an army truck where Jack and Avi, dressed as Russian soldiers, had been impatiently waiting for him. He told McNabe how Jack, driving as if he was on a Grand Prix track, had almost collided with a wagon transporting sheep, and how, when the other driver swerved to avoid the crash, his wagon turned over, scattering the animals all over the place and completely blocking their path. Jack had then made the decision to ditch the truck. Being close to the Vindrey River, they had walked along its banks until they spotted an unattended row boat, and had made their way in it as far as Sel'khoz.

'Believe you me,' Dan grinned, 'the Volga boatmen had nothing on us.' After catching the slowest train on wheels in the world, Dan went on, they finally arrived at Potma, and then caught a further series of trains to Moscow. There they said their farewells to Rastorotsky, giving him, by way of thanks, the last of their spare Western currency. He, full of gratitude, ensured that they had safe conduct out of the USSR.

Completing the account of their return to the West, Dan dropped the light-heartedness from his voice and became serious. At the back of his mind had been a constantly nagging suspicion, and one that was shared by Jack and Avi, but, since the mission was over, there would have been little that they could have done about it anyway. All of them were just too damn thankful to get the hell out of Russia unscathed. But now, back here at Langley, he knew he must give vent to his own feelings.

'You know, Paul,' he said at last, 'something's been worrying me.'

'Yeah?' McNabe cocked his head to one side with interest.

'Yep — it all went just a bit too goddamn smoothly. Sure we had problems, lots of them, but it's all wrapped up just a little too tidy for my liking.'

'Explain yourself.'

'Well, we got away with murder there — literally. So did the neo-Nazi group, and yet we were never taken to task over it. Sure, Jack was pulled in for questioning briefly, but he was released a few hours later. And listen, do you mean to say that Prama had no idea either that Hitler's son was mentally handicapped? I dunno, Paul, there's too many loose ends.'

McNabe looked at the bulb of his pipe, poked round the tobacco in it and seemed a bit peeved that it had gone out.

'Let me come to your last point first,' he said, staring steadily at Dan. 'I don't think that Prama's neo-Nazi gang had any more information about his mental state than we did. Hitler's own fears were well founded

384

though. He guessed what might have happened if he made his niece Geli pregnant. Closeness of their blood and all that. But the Russians weren't going to let any of us know that. You see, I believe they set us up.'

'How come?' Dan peered at him curiously.

'Well, between you and me, we think the KGB were behind it,' said McNabe, leaning back in his chair. 'They used Hitler's son as bait. He had to be the genuine article, of course, and they leaked through just enough information to get the neo-Nazis on the hook. Then they let us know that the Prama group were hot on his trail, hoping to free Hitler's rightful heir from their country and bring him to West Germany, where they would have caused all kinds of problems for us — electing him as their new Führer, sparking off riots and all that kind of thing. Well, they knew that we would never allow that to happen. The Russians played on our fears that if there was a neo-Nazi uprising, particularly in West Berlin, their tanks would be in there to put an end to it before you could say 'Tchaikovsky'. They figured, and rightly so, that we would have to nip it in the bud. So we had to enlist a lot of our top undercover agents to help us get the 'Front Man' mission underway. You and your two colleagues had help from our guys all along, whether you realised it or not. The KGB must have monitored everything.' McNabe sighed deeply. 'It's my guess that some of our best men over there have already been arrested. It's a process known in our trade as 'flushing out'.'

★　★　★

McNabe's theory made a lot of sense to Dan, and he hoped that Avi's and Jack's respective controls would be equally frank with them.

In fact, neither of them had the opportunity of meeting their departmental chiefs. They'd been asked to submit a confidential written report, as they were both engaged, on their return, in other activities that took priority. Jack was briefed on an assignment that would take him to Libya, whilst Avi was ecstatic to learn that his 'horror ware' range of crockery was to be mass-produced by a major manufacturer. The cheque he received for his designs and the rights was far more than he had earned in a lifetime in the theatre.

As for Dan, he'd had enough of the 'spy game' for ever. The ruthlessness, the brutality, the intrigue was not for him. He couldn't wait to get back to his family, and the problems of his patients, because these, he felt, he was well equipped to deal with.

McNabe had made a full report on the mission which was handed to the President by a special CIA courier. It was in a government sealed package and marked 'Most Secret — for your eyes only'. At the end of a lucid summary of the operation, McNabe had added a few deliberations of his own.

A few days after it had been received at the White House, President Jones called McNabe on the scrambler.

'I've read your report,' he said. 'Interesting — very interesting. Nevertheless, close the 'Front Man' file for now, but keep it nearby. Remember, 'The opera ain't over till the fat lady sings'!'

'Yes, sir, I'll certainly remember that,' he answered just before the President replaced his receiver. The obscure message, however, was somewhat lost on McNabe. Perhaps it would have had more meaning, considerably more, had he been present in a tastefully furnished apartment in south-west Munich in the Federal Republic of Germany.

★ ★ ★

Three men sat in leather chesterfields, sipping cognac. One of the men, Wilhelm Prama, was in an expansive mood, seeming most pleased with himself. He turned to the elder of the two others in the room.

'I think we've overcome the last hurdle. I have received information that the CIA have now completely accepted that the 'madman' in the prison hospital was the man they had come to liquidate, and that they left him unharmed believing, in their stupidity, that if we rescued him and elected him as our leader, it would make us a laughing stock.' Prama threw back his head and laughed. 'Anyway, the CIA have now closed their file on Vladimir Sokol. As far as they are concerned, the matter is at an end.'

The man Prama had addressed put his brandy glass down on the table in front of him, locked his fingers together and sat back with a satisfied smirk on his face.

'Tell me, Willi, how did you persuade the actor to play the 'madman'? After all, he must have realised that his life was very much at risk in all this.'

Horst Schreiber, the third man, joined in the conversation.

'There were two factors involved here, sir. The first was that our actor is a most loyal member of our party and was, if necessary, prepared to risk his life for the cause; secondly, should everything go as planned,

Herr Prama's bank is providing the funds to finance a feature film. We promised our character actor a leading role in this film if he proved that he was capable of playing the most dangerous and important role of his life. That is the sort of challenge this actor could not refuse.'

'But the Israeli agent — is he not also an actor?' the man queried.

'Indeed he is,' said Prama, 'and we banked on the fact that he would be chosen to make the hit. You see, being a Jew he would have insisted upon it, feeling that it was his right. And working on the principle that no one is easier sold than a salesman, then no one was more likely to be taken in by the performance than another actor.' Prama smiled and added, 'In that profession, it's all a question of ego. Of course he was well made-up for the part, right down to the tattoo under his arm.'

Horst chuckled. 'Unfortunately, we doubt whether the Russians will be sporting enough to release the actor in time for him to be able to play the part in Herr Prama's film.' They all shared the joke.

'Yes, well in this life we all have to make sacrifices,' said the man. He was about to pick up his brandy glass, when there was an electronic buzz from a device attached to the frame on the intercommunicating door. The three men responded by immediately sitting up straight.

'I'll go,' said the man. He stood up, his military bearing prominent despite his age, and marched briskly to the door. He knocked, but without waiting for a summons he entered the room. This room, a wood-panelled study with shelves of finely bound volumes, had as its focal point a magnificent desk with handsomely carved legs and ormolu fitments.

A man stood up behind it and offered a congratulatory hand. In his other hand he held a thick document. He held the document aloft.

'I have read this fully now. My father would have approved of every word. He would also have been proud of the way you have organised everything, Herr General.'

'Thank you. But it was, and is, the duty of our new order not to fail,' the general replied. 'Will there be anything more, mein Führer?'

Alois Hitler, alias Vladimir Sokol, shook his head and sat down again, watching the elderly general depart from the room. He absent-mindedly fingered the short bristling hair of his newly growing moustache. He glanced briefly at the document's cardboard cover. Under a symbol not entirely unlike a swastika were the words: 'The Manifesto of the Fourth Reich'. He looked up; his eyes fixed on a silver framed photograph of Adolf Hitler in uniform that was perched on the edge of his desk. 'This time, Father, we shall succeed, I promise,' he said softly.

THE END

We do hope that you have enjoyed reading this large print book.

Did you know that all of our titles are available for purchase?

We publish a wide range of high quality large print books including:
Romances, Mysteries, Classics
General Fiction
Non Fiction and Westerns

Special interest titles available in large print are:
The Little Oxford Dictionary
Music Book
Song Book
Hymn Book
Service Book

Also available from us courtesy of Oxford University Press:
Young Readers' Dictionary
(large print edition)
Young Readers' Thesaurus
(large print edition)

For further information or a free brochure, please contact us at:
Ulverscroft Large Print Books Ltd.,
The Green, Bradgate Road, Anstey,
Leicester, LE7 7FU, England.
Tel: (00 44) 0116 236 4325
Fax: (00 44) 0116 234 0205

Other titles in the
Ulverscroft Large Print Series:

STRANGER IN THE PLACE

Anne Doughty

Elizabeth Stewart, a Belfast student and only daughter of hardline Protestant parents, sets out on a study visit to the remote west coast of Ireland. Delighted as she is by the beauty of her new surroundings and the small community which welcomes her, she soon discovers she has more to learn than the details of the old country way of life. She comes to reappraise so much that is slighted and dismissed by her family — not least in regard to herself. But it is her relationship with a much older, Catholic man, Patrick Delargy, which compels her to decide what kind of life she really wants.

PAINTED LADY

Delia Ellis

Miss Eleanor Needwood was about to be married to a most unsuitable suitor when Philip Markham came to her rescue. He arranged for Eleanor to be in London for the Season, a guest of his sister, who decided that everyone would benefit if Markham married Eleanor. And thus the rumour started. The surprised couple decided to play along with the mistaken impression until a scandal-free way to end the betrothal could be found. But when Eleanor agreed to pose for a daring artist, the result was far more scandalous than any broken engagement.

IF HE LIVED

Jon Stephen Fink

Lillian is a woman who feels too much. As a psychiatric nurse, she empathizes with her patients; as a mother, she mourns for her lost, runaway daughter. Now suddenly she has a new feeling, that her house, one of the oldest in the small Massachusetts town where she lives with her husband Freddy, has been invaded, violated by some past evil. And then Lillian sees the boy . . .

SLAUGHTER HORSE

Michael Maguire

The Turf Security Division is surprised and suspicious when playboy Wesley Falloway's second-rate horses develop overnight into winners. Simon Drake investigates, but suddenly there is a new twist — someone is out to steal General O'Hara, the star of British bloodstock, owned by Wesley Falloway's mother. With a few million pounds at stake, lives are cheap; Drake finds himself both hunter and quarry in a murderous chase where even his closest associates may be playing a double game.

MERMAID'S GROUND

Alice Marlow

It's been five years since Kate Williams' beloved husband died, leaving her with two young children to raise. Now she's built a good life in one of Wiltshire's prettiest villages, and she has her dream job, as gardener at Moxham Court. For the last year, Kate has had a lover, roguishly attractive Justin Spencer, but he won't commit to more than a night here and there. When she takes in a male lodger, Jem, Kate's secretly hoping his presence will provoke a jealous reaction in Justin. What she hasn't reckoned on is exactly how attractive Jem will turn out to be.

HOT POPPIES

Reggie Nadelson

A murder in New York's diamond district. A dead Chinese girl with a photograph in her pocket. A plastic bag of irradiated heroin in an empty apartment. A fire in a Chinatown sweatshop. The worst blizzard in New York's history. These events conspire to bring ex-cop Artie Cohen out of retirement and back into the obsessive world of murder and politics that nearly killed him. The terrifying plot uncoils first in New York — in Artie's own back yard — then in Hong Kong, where everything — and everyone — is for sale.